Readers love the Carlisle Troopers series by ANDREW GREY

Fire and Sand

"Fans of found families, second chances, and guys with hearts of gold will love this contemporary romance."

—Fresh Fiction

"Another amazing book by one of my favorite authors and of course I read it in one sitting like every other book Mr. Grey has written."

—Paranormal Romance Guild

Fire and Glass

"Andrew Grey delivers with another touching second chance story with great, easy to love characters."

—The Geekery

Fire and Ermine

"The two are definitely from two different worlds, but they can't let each other go."

—Sparkling Book Reviews

By Andrew Grey

Published by DREAMSPINNER PRESS
www.dreamspinnerpress.com

Published by DREAMSPINNER PRESS
www.dreamspinnerpress.com

Published by DREAMSPINNER PRESS
www.dreamspinnerpress.com

FIRE AND IRON
ANDREW GREY

DREAMSPINNER PRESS

Published by
DREAMSPINNER PRESS

8219 Woodville Hwy #1245
Woodville, FL 32362 USA
www.dreamspinnerpress.com

Fire and Iron
© 2025 Andrew Grey

Cover Art
© 2025 L.C. Chase
http://www.lcchase.com
Cover content is for illustrative purposes only and any person depicted on the cover is a model.

Mass Market Paperback ISBN: 978-1-64108-693-6
Trade Paperback ISBN: 978-1-64108-692-9
Digital ISBN: 978-1-64108-691-2
Trade Paperback published January 2025
v. 1.0

To Dean A. and Sue O. for all their help. This book would not have happened without you.

CHAPTER 1

BEING A state trooper was a lot like being a lone wolf. Fillian O'Connell's days were often spent on traffic duty or patrolling the backroad areas of Pennsylvania, and this day was no exception.

"I'm sorry to have bothered you, Mrs. Greene, but your neighbors hadn't seen you in a few days, and they were worried."

Mrs. Greene leaned on her cane and kept adjusting her head like she was trying to see him. Those big clouded eyes told Fillian just about all he needed to know. "I forgot to plug in my phone, and now I can't find it." She sounded lost.

"Would you like me to help you?"

She stepped back to let him inside the house, which was fairly clean, if a little dusty, and he began looking around. "Do you remember when you had it last?" He checked around the living room and then went to the small dining room. The old table and chairs were neat and set in place, if extra dusty. She probably didn't use that room very often any longer. The thought only reinforced his impression of Mrs. Greene's loneliness.

Fillian continued looking in the pin-neat kitchen, where he found the phone on the floor. "I found it, Mrs. Greene." He reached around the trash can at the end of the counter, picked up the phone, and set it on the counter, plugging it into the cord that lay there. Then he returned to where she stood in the living room. "I plugged it in for you, and it's on the kitchen counter."

"Thank you, young man."

"It will take a few minutes for the phone to come up, but you should be good now." He smiled, not knowing if she could see it or not. "You have a good day."

"Would you like some coffee?" Mrs. Greene asked.

"No, thank you." One of the rules was that you never accepted food or drink, even from a harmless elderly lady—no matter how good a cup of coffee sounded at that moment.

"Well, I won't keep you," she said.

Fillian left the house, pulling the door closed behind him with a sigh before returning to his cruiser and reporting in that he was done with the wellness check and that everything was okay. Those were the best kind of calls.

Too bad he didn't get them very often.

"Roger," Dispatch responded. "We have a domestic disturbance call at 1897 Wilson. It's about twenty minutes from your present location, but you're the closest officer."

"Roger." Fillian pulled out of the drive. He waited until he was away from Mrs. Greene's so he didn't startle her before flipping on his lights and siren and taking off over the country road, heading west to the edge of his territory out toward Newville.

"Details have been sent to you," Dispatch said. The screen in his car showed the address as well as the information gathered from the call. "It's a small grouping of three houses, and one of the neighbors heard breaking glass through an open window, as well as yelling."

"I'm en route," Fillian acknowledged and stepped on it.

"Backup has been requested," Dispatch informed him. Fillian went as fast as he dared, his siren wailing as he concentrated on getting there in one piece. His heart pounded, senses heightening along the drive.

Fillian had been a state trooper for about eighteen months. He'd cut his teeth out in Beaver County, but when an opening was posted for the Carlisle area, he'd applied to be closer to his family. There had apparently been quite a bit of interest, and Fillian was a little surprised that he got the posting. Granted, while he worked out of the Carlisle State Police post, he was hardly ever there and spent much of his time in the rural areas of Cumberland and Perry counties. Still, at night he went home, and he spent one evening a week with his mom and dad—when they were in town, anyway.

He pulled up to the address in question with full lights and sirens, turning into the drive as the front door to the house opened and a man ran outside in a pair of jeans and little else. He jumped off the steps and dove between the house and the bushes as a shot rang out from inside the house.

Fillian braked to a stop.

"Shot fired," Fillian reported. "ETA on backup?" He kept low and watched the bushes where the man had gone. There was no movement, and Fillian hoped to hell the man was down on the ground and out of the line of sight and fire.

"Come out of the house with your hands on your head," Fillian said through the car's loudspeaker. He cracked open the far door and got out, using it as a shield. "This is the state police." His radio beeped, and Dispatch informed him his backup was minutes away. Fillian's best course of action was to stay where he was, but damn it all, he didn't know where the other man was or what he'd do next.

The shot had come from inside the house, which meant that the shooter wasn't the bush guy. But was the man in the bush the victim, or another assailant trying to make a run for it? Fillian figured it was likely the guy hiding in the bushes was a victim, but he wasn't sure. Fortunately, a second and then a third unit arrived. They pulled in next to him, making a wall of cars.

"What's the situation?" Wyatt Nelson asked. A fellow trooper, he had been the first one to welcome Fillian.

"Possible victim hiding around the house and at least one shooter inside. Single shot fired," Fillian reported just as another shot pinged off the front of Fillian's patrol car.

Fillian flipped the microphone back on. "Think about what you're doing. Take a breath and calm down. All you need to do is put your gun down and come out with your hands on your head. None of us wants to hurt you." He kept his voice calm and spoke as clearly and gently as possible. "The back door is covered as well as the front. There is nowhere to go, so come out, hands on your head, and let us try to help you." He waited for a response.

"Just get the bastard to show himself," Williams, the third trooper to arrive, said. "I can get a shot at him and this will be over."

"Calm down and be quiet," Wyatt hissed. "No one is shooting anyone if we can help it." He shook his head. Williams had a reputation for aggression that was going to get him in trouble. Fillian was glad that Wyatt handled him.

"You won't shoot?" a man called from inside the house. He sounded shaky and scared all to hell.

"Put the gun down and come out with your hands on your head. We won't shoot as long as you aren't a threat." Fillian watched the front door as it opened and a single man came outside. He had on a pair of jeans, a flannel shirt, and a loose pair of old boots. He had his hands on his head as instructed. "Lie down on the ground, slowly, hands where they are." Fillian swallowed hard, hoping this incident was going to end the way it looked. Once the suspect was on the ground, Fillian sighed. "Stay where you are. The man in the bushes, stand slowly, hands on your head."

A man about Fillian's age with messy brown hair and pale skin emerged from the shrubbery near the corner of the ranch-style house. He was shaking. Williams hurried over to him while Wyatt approached the man on the ground, cuffed him, and then searched him before getting the suspect to his feet and moving toward the patrol car.

"What's your name? Is there anyone else inside?" Fillian asked the shaking man as Williams approached with him.

He shook his head. "I'm Gregory Montrose." He seemed to get control of himself and shook less now that he knew he was safe. "It was just Lawrence Little and me. I was doing some work for the guy, repairing some of the outlets that were faulty. He decided he was interested in something other than my electrical work, and when I refused, he went crazy. Lawrence ripped off my shirt and pinned me to the floor. I managed to get away and threw a vase at him. The asshole was strong and probably on something, because he just kept coming and I couldn't get away. I finally made it to the front door as—"

An explosion ripped through the afternoon. Fillian crouched low, and Gregory went right down to the ground. What had been the house was now a fireball, sending debris everywhere. Fillian's ears rang as he looked up from where he'd crouched behind the car door.

"We need fire assistance, *now*," he told Dispatch. "The house has exploded. Nearby structures are in jeopardy."

"Get that suspect out of here," Wyatt called.

Williams pulled the suspect up from the ground again and got him into the back of the car before backing away. The heat from the fire was intense as Fillian got Gregory off the grass and into his car. He closed the doors and reversed out of the drive and onto the road, getting the car away from the extreme heat.

"Are you all right?" He parked behind a truck along the side of the road near the end of the drive.

"Yes. Thank you. My ears are ringing." Gregory crossed his arms over his chest. "Can I ask, aren't you Fillian O'Connell, and didn't you grow up on Baltimore Street?" Fillian nodded, trying to place the other man. "I grew up next door."

Flashes of memory settled into place. "Yes.... Gregory." They had never been close, even though they'd lived next door for years. He and Gregory had gone to the same school, and their properties might have been next to each other, but they could have been worlds apart. An eight-foot-tall fence had separated the properties, and it might as well have been the border to a hostile country. Their parents hadn't gotten along and rarely spoke. Fillian remembered the view from his bedroom window, overlooking Gregory's backyard with his sparkling swimming pool and a lawn filled with games, toys, and bicycles—things Fillian could only dream of.

Growing up, he had resented Gregory and his family so damned much. They seemed to have everything, and Fillian and his family barely made ends meet. He remembered Gregory getting a bike when he was six and another when he was eight or nine. They were always brand new. Fillian's first bike came from a church rummage sale, and he knew his mother had scrimped to be able to afford that.

He cleared his throat to try to wipe away the trip down old resentment road. He had a job to do, and he needed to stay on task. "Is this your vehicle just ahead of us?"

"Yes. Would it be okay if I got another shirt? I know you need a statement and stuff from me, but...."

"Of course," Fillian said as sirens sounded. Gregory got out of the vehicle and hurried to the truck. Fillian watched him, noticing for the first time how slender and handsome Gregory was, not that he was supposed to look at things like that while he was on duty. Still, he was trained to be observant, and it was difficult to put those skills on hold, especially when there was something so enticing to look at.

By the time the fire trucks arrived, the fire had spread to the two nearby homes, which were quickly evacuated before they became fully engulfed. Fillian helped direct traffic while the fire department extinguished what was left of the three homes. Additional police units arrived, with one escorting the suspect back to the station while Fillian and the others did their best to control the flow of traffic while he kept an eye on Gregory, who sat in his truck.

After an hour, the fires had either been put out or had burned themselves to nothing. Water sprayed from the various trucks, dousing the last of the flames. Fire crews made sure the fires were out, and Fillian got a chance to talk with Gregory to get his statement.

"I'm an electrician, and the house had a number of electrical issues that I was hired to fix by the property owner. The guy who attacked me is apparently a renter, and he seemed squirrelly at first, moving with me from room to room, watching what I did like I was going to steal something from the shit piles he had filled the house with."

"Was he a hoarder?" Fillian asked, writing down his answers.

"Oh yes. And the longer I was there, the more tense and creepy he became. I had just a few more outlets to fix when he attacked me. I was almost done and would have been gone and—" Gregory's voice broke. "He seemed to go crazy, and all I could do was try to get around all the crap in the house. When I fell over some of it, that's when he grabbed my shirt. The buttons popped as I tried to get away—" He began to shake.

"It's okay. You're safe now. We're here, and he's in custody." Fillian continued making notes. "Tell me about the crazy or obsessive behavior. Give me as much detail as you can." He continued taking notes as Gregory told him about the condition of the place and how angry the suspect got when Gregory moved things to get to the outlets.

"The guy was off his rocker. He yelled at me for moving an empty box from the area I needed to work in. There was another box of what looked like restaurant ketchup packets in the living room that I asked him to move. And there were tons of boxes of just weird stuff." Gregory seemed a little breathless.

"Why didn't you just leave when you saw how bad the place was?" Fillian asked. It might have seemed like a callous question, but it was one he needed to ask. And he needed to ensure Gregory wasn't involved.

"Because I needed the job. It was a full day's work, and I was being paid full scale. I have two kids at home, and my parents had agreed to watch them for the day, so I figured I could really make some bank with this. Then I turn up in a rat's nest overseen by a crazy person… but I still needed the money."

"I'm sorry," Fillian said. "At the very least, you were able to get out of the house. Did you have any indication that he seemed to be a danger to himself or intended to blow up the property?"

Gregory shook his head. "I wouldn't think so. He seemed intent on holding on to everything inside, including his box of ketchup packets. I would think that the house burning would send him over the edge because he lost everything inside. So if you want my opinion, I don't think the fire was something he set. The house was in bad shape, and it's possible there were gas issues. I didn't smell anything when I was inside, but I was intent on my work and just getting out of there."

"Thank you. I appreciate your help." Fillian spent a few moments reviewing his notes, making sure he had a record of everything Gregory had said.

Gregory nodded. "Is there anything more that you need from me? I need to get home soon. I have to pick up my niece and nephew from my mom's and get them home and fed."

"Are they Arthur's kids?" Fillian asked. He remembered Gregory having a brother a few years older than them. He used to have parties around the pool, and Fillian would watch them from his bedroom window. He never got an invitation to come over, but that didn't mean that he didn't long to be included.

"Yes." Gregory seemed a little more relaxed. "He and his wife were on a business trip to Europe two years ago. Arthur was the director of product development for an AI-based gaming company. They were over in Germany working with some of the development staff. He took Stephanie with him, and they spent some time in Italy after he finished the business. Arthur was driving one evening, and the roads in that part of the country are very steep. He was going too fast and didn't make a curve." Gregory lowered his gaze. "Both he and Stephanie were killed."

"I'm so sorry," Fillian said. "I really am." He cleared his throat. "I have your address and telephone number. If we need additional information, I'll call." He kept hoping he'd think of more questions to ask just so he'd have a little more time with Gregory, but he was done, and Lord knows there was going to be a ton of paperwork for him to fill out.

"Okay." Gregory turned back toward his truck. "Oh, I had a toolbox inside the house. I had to leave it behind. Is it possible to have that added to the report so I can make a claim with the insurance company? There were some pretty expensive pieces of equipment in it that I'm going to have to replace."

"Sure," Fillian said, adding a note. Then he watched as Gregory turned and walked to his truck.

"Nice-looking guy," Wyatt said from next to him, and Fillian found himself nodding before he could think about it.

"Not that it matters," he said softly, thinking it was unlikely their paths would cross again, and what a shame that was.

CHAPTER 2

GREGORY WAS ready for some action on the field. He didn't go in for many sports, mainly because of having the kids, but he wasn't about to give up rugby if he could help it. He had discovered a love of the game just after high school, when he met a group of guys who played at the gym he went to. They'd talked him into giving rugby a try, and Gregory had never looked back. There was something raw and powerful about the game that really spoke to him.

"Stevie!" Gregory called, giving his teammate a near bone-breaking hug and getting one in return—one of the cool things about being part of a rugby team that formed super close bonds. These guys were his mates, and he knew he could rely on all of them.

"Gregory, what's up?" Stevie smiled. "How's fatherhood?" He grinned because he had just gotten married, and Stevie's wife was already on him about having kids.

"How's trying for fatherhood?" Gregory asked.

"Better than actually having one. I don't know what the all-fired hurry is. Cherie and I got married a year ago, and she's all about jumping my bones every night." That infectious grin told Gregory that Stevie was more than happy about that part of the arrangement. Stevie was their outside center, while Gregory played inside center, at least most of the time. "Did you hear? Gillespie got transferred to New York, so we need to find us another hooker."

Gregory felt himself deflating. "Jesus. We finally got the team up to full strength too." He sure as hell hoped that Coach had some ideas or a ringer in his back pocket. He turned as a number of the other guys began arriving. They all greeted each other and began getting in gear. Well, that and gossiping like old ladies. Get fifteen guys together to play rugby, and half the time was spent catching up and sharing secrets. "What are we going to do for a hooker?"

Coach Rayston strode across the field with another man behind him. "I'm sure you all know about Gillespie. Hell, if I know this team, that information got around faster than the clap in a whorehouse. Now, it just so happens that a friend recommended someone who can fill in as our hooker. So, guys, this is Fillian O'Connell. He's a member of the police force here in town, and he's our new hooker. Say hello and get ready, because we've got to get ourselves in shape, and fast."

The guys all shook hands with Fillian, but Gregory held back, unable to take his eyes off him. Fillian in uniform had been handsome, but in his rugby kit, he was stunning, especially the way his legs filled out his shorts and that chest of his stretched his T-shirt, exuding power. Gregory turned away to suppress the inclination to lick his lips.

"Gregory," Fillian said when he approached after letting the other guys introduce themselves. "How are you doing? Did you get what you needed?"

"Thanks, yeah."

"You know each other?" Coach asked.

"Fillian helped me the other day when I was on a job with a lunatic. He and his partners came in and saved the day." Gregory hadn't told the group about his ordeal. It wasn't something he wanted talked about, and Lord knows with a story like that, they'd yammer like hens.

"Gregory and I grew up next door to each other," Fillian added.

"Good. Because teamwork requires trust, and we need to build that, and fast." Coach knew how to get them all to work, and he went right at it. Drills, tackling equipment—all of it was put to good use. Gregory kept himself in shape, but damn, after half an hour, he realized just how much he'd slacked off since last season. Fillian, on the other hand, seemed to have boundless energy and a talent for sidestepping other players.

"Take five and we'll go back at it," Coach called. He'd been standing with his notepad, writing constantly. Everyone headed for the cooler to chug down some cold water.

"You must have one hell of a workout routine," Gregory told Fillian.

"The department has regular fitness tests." He finished his water and tossed the bottle in the recycling. "I also believe that staying fit keeps me sharp, and if something does happen, it improves my chances of coming out the other side in one piece."

"Why did you become a cop?" Gregory asked. He was curious about Fillian and wanted to know more, but he was hesitant. Gregory didn't talk about himself a great deal, so it didn't seem right to ask about others. At least that was how he usually felt. With Fillian, his curiosity was definitely getting the best of him.

"My granddad. He was sheriff here for a number of years in the seventies. He was a great man, at least that's what I thought of him, and after he died, I decided to try to become the kind of officer that he was. My father wanted me to be a lawyer or a doctor. His dream for me was to be more than what he or Granddad had been."

"Does he support your decision?" Gregory asked, and Fillian nodded. That must be a nice feeling, and definitely something Gregory wished had occurred in his family. Sometimes he wondered what family he really had.

"Break's over," Coach called. "Let's get back to work. Those Red and Blues aren't going to take it easy on us because we decided to slack off."

Fillian rolled his eyes. "What the hell?"

"He is the coach," Gregory said. And he certainly had a way about him. Coach was good, and he had a real instinct for this game. "And he's got the gift." Coach loved rugby with everything he had, but an accident had left him with a left arm that shook and occasional spots in his vision, so he couldn't play any longer. "Before his accident, he lived and breathed rugby." They jogged out toward the field, where the other guys were gathering. "How did he find you, anyway?"

Fillian smiled. "I used to play trucks with him when we were kids. He's my cousin. I guess it's hard to think of someone you used to call Ray-Ray as having authority." Fillian winked and joined the others as Gregory wondered if he had just passed some kind of test.

THE REST of practice was grueling and incredible. The team was really coming together, even after such a short amount of time. The amazing thing was how Fillian fit right in, as though they were a puzzle and he was the missing piece. Their play was better, and Fillian seemed to have a gift for timing that made everything better.

"Beers at Molly's!" one of the guys called. Hands went up as they all headed for the cars.

Gregory stayed back, watching Fillian.

"You know, if you keep doing that, everyone is going to know you have the hots for him," Stevie said.

Gregory rolled his eyes and shook his head. "I have the kids, and they take everything I've got." He wasn't willing to admit was that Fillian was one hell of a sight, but... damn.

"Don't try to play that bullshit with me. I may not understand this whole gay thing you got going on or why you can't see the hotness in women, even after they spend half the night throwing themselves at you all the damned time. But I do know that look."

Gregory groaned. "Yeah? How? It's not like Cherie followed you around panting."

"I wooed her. How else was a guy with a mug like this going to ever catch a lady with as much grace and beauty as my wife?" He straightened up and grinned. Stevie was living proof that anything was possible. He and Cherie truly loved each other. Cherie was gorgeous and could have had any guy she wanted. Stevie was unremarkable in the looks department, but he went after Cherie in the most amazing way, showing her exactly how he felt with flowers and thoughtful attention. He truly wooed his way into her heart. "And it doesn't hurt that I have hidden talents." He grinned and turned away, heading for his car, as though he'd just had a mic-drop moment. And since Gregory wasn't going to touch that comment with a ten-foot pole, he headed for his truck.

GREGORY COULDN'T help whistling as the new guy on the team pulled up next to his truck in a deep red Mustang GT convertible. "That's some car." It was a few years old but in sparkling condition, the saddle leather seats setting off the otherwise black interior.

"I love it." Fillian got out and closed the door, leaving the top down. "It's a great ride, and when the top's down, it feels like I'm in California, ready to head to the beach to catch some waves, even if I'm in landlocked PA. I'll take you for a ride sometime."

"That would be sweet," Gregory said as they went inside. The guys had already arrived, and the beer was flowing. Coach didn't attend these sorts of things, even though he was always invited. Gregory had never asked why.

"We're going to kick those Red and Blue Carpet bastards' asses next week," one of the guys said, which sent up a cheer.

"What will you have?" Gregory asked once he and Fillian said down near the group. "I like the Red Coat."

"Sounds good," Fillian agreed, and Gregory ordered the beers and some food, because after all that exercise, he needed something more than beer or else the alcohol would go right to his head, and he was well aware that he was drinking with a cop.

"So...," Gregory began, unsure of how to start a conversation around the minefield of things he didn't want to talk about.

"Yeah...," Fillian said as he got the server's attention. "Seems strange after all this time, and then to meet again the way we did."

That was an understatement. "There are stranger ways, I suppose, but I can't really think of any." Gregory wasn't interested in going over the details of how they met either time—in the house of horrors he grew up in or the one he'd been in the day before. Just the thought made him shiver. If he hadn't needed the job so badly, he would never have set foot in the place at all. The condition of the house should have been a clue that the guy was off his rocker, but Gregory had hoped to just get in and get out again. Really, he hadn't thought the guy would attack him or anything. He just wanted to get away from the mess and the cluttered chaos.

"Are you doing okay?" Fillian asked gently and, to Gregory's relief, quietly.

The last thing Gregory wanted to do was recount the entire story to the rest of the team. He shrugged. "It is what it is, I guess." He was grateful when the server brought their beer. It gave him something to look at rather than those intense blue eyes that seemed to see past his defenses. "I can't change it, so...."

"Yeah, I get that. But you need to talk about it with someone."

Gregory stopped himself from rolling his eyes. Yeah, Fillian had been one of the officers there to help him and had looked after him once he got away from that weird monster who now seemed to inhabit his dreams. *Nightmares* was a better word. He shivered, and Fillian leaned a little closer, concern in his eyes. At least Gregory hoped it was concern, because he couldn't take pity.

"I suppose, but...." He wondered if Fillian meant he should talk to him. Gregory shook his head, having no intention of opening up to Fillian. He barely knew the guy. "I'll figure it out." He had the kids to take care of, and just paying the bills kept him busy enough. There was some money from Arthur's insurance, but not a lot, and Gregory wanted that to stay intact so the kids could have a chance at college. He was determined to do his best for them.

"I'm here for you. And I know the two of us have a weird sort of history, but I'm here if you want to talk. We aren't kids any longer."

Gregory had to agree about their history. "I guess I have a hard time letting things go."

"I suppose I can agree with that. We lived next to each other all that time, and yet…." They had nothing in common. Sure, they had been neighbors, but it wasn't like they had been real friends. Gregory had always been so busy with piano lessons, sports, tennis, and soccer, as well as summer camp, that he'd never really had a lot of time with the neighborhood kids. When he was at home, everyone else already had their groups of friends, and he'd never felt like he could just join in, so he'd stayed home with his brother, who was kept equally busy. Dad worked all the time, and Mom was always consumed with her part-time jobs at the organizations she belonged to. At the time he hadn't given it much thought, because things were the way they were, but now he realized he'd had a lonely time growing up.

"Yeah. You always kept to yourself," Fillian said and then drank some beer. "You had all those toys, the pool, your clubs and everything, so I guess you didn't need to be part of the neighborhood pack of kids."

Gregory leaned over the table. "You all never asked me to join in." That was the thing that still stung after all that time. Yeah, he was busy, but there had been times when he had wanted nothing more than to just be like the other kids—to have happy families the way they all seemed to, to get away from the simmering tension that seemed to permeate his family.

"You could have come out any time," Fillian said. They blinked at each other, and Gregory was the first to roll his eyes. It had never occurred to him that the other kids thought he wasn't interested in playing with them. He had thought they didn't like him, so he'd stayed away. He tried not to think about how many times he'd been up in his room watching the other kids play chase, tag, and even baseball in the street and wished he could join in… when all he'd needed to do was go on out. "There wasn't much organization to it. All of us had parents who were busy, so we just got games together and started playing. You were the one with the pool and all the toys who never invited any of us over."

Gregory shrugged. "I guess I thought you didn't like me, so...."
God, it seemed they had all misread the situation.

Fillian shook his head. "None of us really knew you. I guess we all
thought you had everything and you didn't need any of us." He finished
his beer and drank from the glass of water the server had also brought.

Gregory swallowed hard. "Had everything? If you mean parents
who fought all the time and to this day can barely stand to be in the same
room with one another, then maybe. My mom always kept me busy so I
wasn't hanging around the house or so she didn't have to be there. That
way she could do whatever she wanted. My father worked all the time
so he could make the money that my mother spent and so he didn't have
to be around her any more than necessary." Gregory drank his beer and
ordered another one.

"I didn't know," Fillian said. "I don't think anyone on the block
knew. Everyone thought you and your family had everything."

"Dad made a lot of money. He still does. But he and my mother
were miserable together. Looking back, I think they stayed together for
me and my brother. It certainly wasn't because of each other. All they
did was fight. Mom and Dad divorced when I was seventeen." He paused
because there was no need to go into his family drama. God, no one
needed to get dragged into that. "You and the rest of the kids always
looked like you were having a fun time."

"I was pretty good at making up games for us to play. We used to play
hockey with yardsticks and an old softball. Other times we played chase and
tag or hide and seek. I was always a good hider, and no one ever found me."
Fillian grinned. "I guess most of us made do with what we had."

Gregory sighed. "And I had everything, but rarely had anyone to
play with unless some of my cousins came over. And even then, they came
over in the summer and swam in the pool while the mothers sat under
the umbrella with a pitcher of frozen margaritas. My brother, Arthur, was
always the one who watched over us those days. He was a good swimmer
and worked as a lifeguard through college. So Mom and her friends did
what they wanted while Arthur sort of stood guard as we played."

"Still, that must have been a lot of fun. I mean, a pool on hot
summer days. I would have loved to have been able to come swim."

Gregory shook his head. "We got to swim, but we had to be quiet
because Mom wanted to talk. Can you imagine being out at the pool with
four other kids and you have to swim quietly? No laughter or jumping in

the pool. If the games got too loud, Mom would tell us that it was nearly time to get out or something. Then she'd refill her glass and go back to talking."

Fillian seemed shocked. "You have to be kidding me. I used to look out my bedroom window at your pool and wish I could swim in it, but it sounds like your mother sucked away all the fun."

"She did." Gregory shrugged. "But it was the way it was, and I couldn't do much about it. Arthur did his best to try to run interference for me and would sometimes tell Mom that she could just go inside and that he'd watch everyone. He was a lifeguard by then, and once Mom had gone, then it felt like we could have fun, but we still couldn't make too much noise or Mom would come out and make everyone go home." He set down his glass. "Sorry."

"Don't be," Fillian said. "This is obviously something you needed to talk about."

"Yeah. Gregory has lots of issues," Stevie said as he plopped down into the chair next to Fillian. "The most important of which is, when are you going to figure out that you need to pass the ball instead of always trying to carry it down field?"

Gregory snorted. "I think you're projecting on that one, mate." He was grateful when his food arrived. "I was open three times, and you didn't pass to me."

Fillian rolled his eyes. "You *all* need to pass more. It's how we can throw off the other team." He sipped from his glass as some more of the guys gathered around and the conversation shifted to rugby and away from team gossip.

Gregory checked the time and ate his dinner once it arrived, finished his beer, and then paid his bill.

"Where are you going?"

"I have to get home. My neighbor is watching the kids, and I don't want to take advantage of her good nature and kindness. After all, there's still the entire season left." He said good night to everyone and left, stepping out onto the sidewalk, wondering at what had to have been the weirdest stroll down memory hell he had ever had... even as he wished that things had been very different. More importantly, how did he keep their past from making their present weird? After all, they had to get through an entire rugby season as teammates.

CHAPTER 3

FILLIAN WAS thankful that his work schedule was somewhat predictable, at least for now. He had Thursdays off for practice, and with their matches scheduled for Sundays, he was golden there too. "You have to give your father and me your game schedule so we can watch you play and cheer you on," Mom said as he sat at her table making his way through a stack of her blueberry pancakes. She and Dad spent two weeks in a small town a few hours north every year, and the property had wild blueberries. Mom and Dad picked the berries while they were there, and she froze them to use all year long, making her pancakes something extra special.

"I will." He didn't have a game today, but he had one next week. This Sunday was an extra practice to help get them ready to face the Blue and Red team, or as Fillian thought of them, the carpet guys. And he wanted nothing more than to wipe the floor with them. One thing Fillian was self-aware enough to know: he was very competitive, especially when it came to rugby. "Next week is the first one, and then we have a game each Sunday. Thankfully they're no farther than Hershey."

"As long as they're played while it's light." She put a plate in front of Dad. "Your father can't drive as well at night."

"Verona, my driving is just fine. You're the one who has trouble seeing after dark," Dad groused, even as he threaded his fingers with Mom's. "And I called the eye doctor and made you an appointment."

Mom growled. She hated doctors, saying they were always looking for something to be wrong.

Fillian let the two of them play out their love dance and tucked back into his breakfast. The back-and-forth between them had been going on for as long as Fillian could remember. "If you two are done with your foreplay." He finished the pancakes and drank the last of his coffee.

"Get out of here," Mom scolded with a smile. "You have practice, and your father has things to do."

"I do?" Dad asked, and Mom gave him a list. He rolled his eyes as Mom sat down with her own breakfast. Fillian kissed her cheek and headed out.

"Call me if you need anything." He left the house drove over to the rugby pitch. The guys were already assembling, and Fillian found himself standing around while they talked and gossiped.

"Uncle Stevie," a young voice called, and a boy of about six ran across the field. Stevie scooped him up midstride and swung him around to peals of giggles. "I'm gonna woof," he said, but continued giggling.

"Then woof all over Daddy," Stevie said as Gregory approached, holding the hand of a little girl. Stevie set the boy down. "Do you have a hug for me, Marnie?" he asked, and the little girl came over more cautiously to give a hug and get a lift and a twirl. "You're growing up so fast."

"Yes, I know," she said as though it were obvious. She stood so seriously and stepped back toward Gregory. Both kids looked like miniatures of him, with the same light blond hair. Marnie's was to her shoulders, with a cascade of beautiful curls.

"Marnie, Weston, this is Fillian," Gregory said. "He just joined the team."

Weston looked Fillian over from top to bottom. "You're big. Those carpet bastards are going to have a hard time getting around you."

All the guys nearby snickered, and Fillian didn't know what to say to that. "I hope so."

"Weston, you know you aren't supposed to talk like that," Gregory said.

Weston shrugged. "What? That's what Uncle Stevie said last week. He said the new guy was big and strong and that the carpet bastards were going to get their floor wiped. Didn't you?"

Gregory narrowed his gaze at Stevie, who took a step back. Clearly, teaching the kid bad words was not to be tolerated. "I thought he was in bed."

Weston put his hands on his hips. "I still heard you." Then he turned to Fillian. "Uncle Stevie talks loud when he drinks beer."

"I noticed that," Fillian said. The kid was sharp, no doubt about it.

Weston blinked up at Fillian. "So are you going to kick the carpet bastards' asses?"

Fillian knelt down. "How about this. I'll try if you say 'kick the carpet guys' *booty*.' Okay?" Judging by the looks he was getting from Gregory, Fillian did not want to get on Gregory's bad side, and he had no doubt Uncle Stevie was in for a talking-to.

"Okay," Gregory told the kids. "You two need to sit over there at the table under the tree. I packed things in your bag for you to do, and there are drinks and snacks." He seemed a little frazzled. The kids hurried over to the table. "My mother couldn't watch the kids, so I had someone else lined up to stay with them, but her mother got Covid and she had been around her part of the week, so...."

"Let's get this practice started," Coach called, and they all jogged out onto the field for warm-ups before the practice began in earnest.

ABOUT AN hour in, Fillian was a little winded, and during a break, he went to get a bottle of water. The hair on the back of his neck stood up, and he slowly let his gaze slip all around him. Something wasn't right, and he had learned to trust his instincts. He tried to look past the people playing and walking through to park to see if there was someone who shouldn't be there. Cops were trained to look for the out of the ordinary, the guy standing still in a sea of foot traffic or someone in a jacket in the summer. Kids yelled and played on the equipment on the other side of the park, while families stood near the creek to watch the ducks. All normal behavior. Fillian didn't see anything unusual, and yet that feeling wouldn't go away.

"What are you doing?" Stevie asked from next to him. "Checking things out to make sure no one is crashing our practice? You don't need to be a cop here. You can be yourself."

Stevie meant well, but something was bothering Fillian, and he couldn't put his finger on what it was. Weston sat at the table, and Marnie was just sitting down again, so the kids were fine. They went back to coloring, and Fillian kept searching, even as Stevie yammered on about something. Maybe he was imagining things, but as he continued watching, movement out near the start of the trail through the back of the park caught his attention. He watched as a man disappeared down the trail.

"You want another water?" Stevie asked, pulling Fillian's attention back. Fortunately, whatever it had been, the feeling of being watched seemed to have passed. Fillian took a deep breath and thanked Stevie for the bottle of water, then downed it. He tossed the bottle into the nearby trash can, glancing back toward the kids' picnic table. Then he returned his attention to where the coach was just calling them back to practice.

Fillian started jogging back toward the other players, but he glanced back one more time. Weston stood near the edge of the field, looking anxious, shifting his weight from side to side. Fillian hurried over, looking for Gregory, who had taken his place on the other side of the field. "What's wrong, buddy?"

Weston pointed to the table, where Marnie now had her head down. "She says she doesn't feel good." She had seemed fine a few minutes ago. Still....

"Gregory!" Fillian bellowed, and the entire field came to a stop. Sometimes he loved his cop voice. Even Coach came to a stop, standing still as Gregory hurried over to the picnic table where Fillian had already sat down. "Do you think you're going to throw up?" he asked Marnie, who shook her head. "Did you eat something?"

"Those berries," Marnie said, pointing, and began to cry. Fillian pulled out his phone, dialed 911, and got right through to the operator.

"I need an ambulance in LeTort Park immediately. We're located between the baseball diamond and the play area. Possible poisoning of an eight-year-old girl. This is Trooper Fillian O'Connell of the state police, and I need the ambulance immediately." He stayed on the phone as Gregory comforted Marnie. "Do your best to keep her calm." If what she'd eaten was poisonous, keeping her calm and settled would mean less of whatever she had eaten would affect her. "It's going to be okay," Fillian told Marnie. "Your daddy has you, and help is coming."

Sirens sounded, quickly drawing nearer. The ambulance garage was less than a mile away, and the sirens grew even louder as the ambulance pulled in. Fillian directed them onto the grass and right up to where Gregory sat with Marnie.

His partner was the first to arrive. "Wyatt," Fillian said as he saw the familiar face, "this is Marnie. She ate some of the berries over there. The black ones." Marnie nodded to confirm, and Fillian's partner got some of the berries and looked them over before picking some and placing them in a plastic bag. Then the paramedics got Marnie and Gregory into the ambulance, asking questions along the way.

"I'll bring Weston to the hospital," Fillian offered.

Gregory tossed Fillian his keys. "Take my truck. It has Weston's car seat." Gregory climbed into the ambulance, and the doors closed. The ambulance took off a few moments later. Fillian had worked with the paramedics before, and they were efficient, but they rarely worked that quickly. But like allergic reactions, poisonings were very time sensitive, and they could get whatever information they needed from Gregory while they were en route.

"Is Marnie going to be okay?" Weston asked, shaking a little.

Fillian knelt down. "She is because you got help right away," he said before turning to Coach to explain that he was leaving as well. He gathered his gear and tossed it into the trunk of his car before using the keys he'd been given to unlock Gregory's truck. Once Weston was inside and buckled in, Fillian pulled out and headed toward the hospital. This was not at all how he'd expected the practice to go.

He pulled in and parked, then took Weston's hand as they headed for Emergency. He explained who he was and flashed his badge, which got him entrance immediately. They found Gregory in a small room with Marnie in bed.

"They don't think the berries are poisonous, but they are making her sick. The doctors are still deciding what they're going to do."

Fillian sat down, and Weston climbed onto his lap. "I'm sorry you're sick," Weston told his sister quietly, leaning against Fillian's chest.

"It's going to be okay," Fillian told Gregory softly as he sat next to him, Gregory comforting Marnie and Fillian doing his best to help Gregory and Weston. He took Gregory's hand, holding it gently to try to give his support. Fillian had seen plenty of worried parents at work, and Gregory seemed out of his mind. His gaze kept going to the door, as if he could will the doctor to appear.

"Why doesn't someone talk to me?" Gregory asked just as the doctor came into the room.

"I'm Doctor Rosco," he said, smiling as he approached Marnie. "I understand you ate some berries."

Marnie nodded. "They hurt my tummy."

"I bet they did."

"Am I going to die?" Marnie asked, and Gregory squeezed Fillian's hand, growing even paler.

"No, honey. But the nurse is going to come in, and she's going to give you something that will make you sick. We need to get the rest of the berries out of you." He turned to Gregory. "We could pump her stomach, but getting her to bring it up more naturally is a lot less invasive."

Gregory nodded, still pale and biting his lower lip. A nurse came in with a cup and a pan.

"Weston and I are going to step out. But we'll be right outside if you need us." Fillian smiled at Marnie and met Gregory's gaze before taking Weston's hand and leading him out into the hall.

"They're going to make her throw up?" Weston asked in a stage whisper. "I throwed up once. It was yucky."

Marnie's door closed, and Fillian was grateful that they weren't going to hear what was happening.

"Me too. It's always yucky. But it's how your tummy gets rid of bad things, and Marnie needs to get rid of the berries she ate." He met Weston's gaze. "Why didn't you eat any?"

Weston shrugged. "I wasn't hungry. I ate crackers with cheese, but Marnie wanted berries, so she picked some." He leaned closer, and Fillian held his hand, the two of them standing quietly until the door to Marnie's room opened and the doctor and nurse walked out. Fillian approached the door. He peered inside. Marnie was in bed, her eyes closed. Gregory sat beside the bed, even whiter than before.

"She's going to be okay."

Weston hurried to his dad and climbed onto his lap for hugs. Gregory held him as Marnie rested.

"They got a lot of the berry stuff up. They're going to start an IV to help hydrate her and flush the rest out."

"Like what I had?" Weston asked.

"Yup, just like you." Gregory held Weston closer, closing his eyes. "There's been way too much excitement these past few weeks. Lord knows I need some quiet time with a break from medical emergencies."

The nurse returned, and Marnie woke up as she put in the IV. Fillian was impressed that Marnie held still and didn't cry as she inserted it. The nurse talked to Marnie the entire time, telling her what she was doing, and once she got the fluid flowing, she made sure Marnie was comfortable. "The IV is going to take about an hour or so, and hopefully you'll start to feel better by then."

"Then I can go home?" Marnie asked.

"We all hope so," the nurse told them before checking Marnie's vitals and making sure the machines were set up before leaving the room once more.

"I don't think this is what you expected to be doing on your day off," Gregory said. "You don't need to stay. There have to be a ton of things you could be doing that are more fun than sitting here with us."

"It's fine." Fillian smiled and got a small one in return. Gregory seemed much less tense now that Marnie was on the road to recovery.

"Thanks for being here and for knowing what to do," Gregory said as he smoothed Marnie's hair away from her forehead. "I don't know...."

As Gregory lifted his head, Fillian got a clear view of blue eyes as dark as the depths of the sea, filled with fear. Gregory had been through hell more than once in the past few weeks. He seemed brittle, in a way, and Fillian hoped he could keep it together for the kids' sakes, but he definitely needed someone to talk to. He thought about taking his hand to let Gregory know he was there for him, but he wondered if that was a good idea. Still, how could he just sit still and let Gregory fall to pieces?

CHAPTER 4

GREGORY MANAGED to get Weston and Marnie home after dropping Fillian back at his car in the park. Marnie was in her bed sleeping while Weston played Legos on the living room floor. Gregory sat at the table just outside the kitchen area in their apartment. Somehow he'd been lucky enough to find a two-bedroom unit with a room that had once been a closet that he was able to make up for Weston. There wasn't a lot of space for anything other than his twin bed, a small dresser, and a lamp, but it would do for now. He had lined the walls with shelves about a foot down from the ceiling, where they kept things that Weston wanted to display. If Weston wanted to play with them, then Gregory had to get them down, but so far it seemed to work. What he really needed was for his business to pick up so he could afford a more permanent home.

"Daddy," Marnie called, and he went into her room, which wasn't much bigger than Weston's. "I'm thirsty." He got her a glass of water, and she sat up, took a few sips, and lay back down again.

"Go back to sleep. I'll be right out in the other room. Just rest and don't worry."

"Is Mr. Fillian here? He saved me and knew what to do," she said softly.

"Not right now. He said he was going to get us something to eat." Gregory had told him that wasn't necessary. "I'll come get you when he returns. I promise." Gregory didn't know what he had thought Fillian would be like as an adult. He hadn't thought too much about him over the years. But he was different from the kid Gregory had known, or at least the one he'd made assumptions about.

"Okay." She closed her eyes, and Gregory pulled up the covers before quietly leaving the room. Weston had finished up what looked like a dinosaur and was making a few buildings for it to stomp.

Light footsteps on the stairs were the first indication that Fillian was back. Gregory met him at the door, but when he opened it, he was surprised to find his mother on the other side. "I wasn't expecting you," he said and stepped back so she could come inside.

"Grandma," Weston called, jumping up. He hurried over and hugged her legs. She lightly patted Weston's head before kneeling down for a proper hug.

"Where's Marnie?" she asked, looking around the room with the intensity of a lighthouse beam. Mom never missed anything.

"She isn't feeling well, so she's lying down," Gregory told her levelly. "Is there something I can do for you?" He checked his watch. "Aren't you heading out to a meeting or something?" He had asked her to sit with the kids, but she'd been too busy.

"I have to go meet with the Civic Ladies Association to talk about how to make Carlisle a better place to live. Charles's mother was a member of the group, so an old friend of his family sponsored me as a member." She stood straighter, as though membership was something he should be impressed about. A year after his parents divorced, his mother married Charles Haber. He was a leading citizen in town and had enough money to buy half of it. Charles was a nice enough man, but he spent a lot of his time traveling, often for weeks at a time, and wasn't particularly interested in his step-grandchildren.

"That's very good, Mother." He figured their meeting was more of a social gathering. "You don't want to be late."

She checked the time herself. "I just wanted to see Weston and Marnie since I was in town, so I thought I'd stop by." She plastered on a smile and went into Marnie's bedroom, where she spoke with her for a few minutes before sweeping back through the living room to the door. "This place is so… small. You really should try to get a place more… suitable." She shook her head. "I don't know what Arthur and Stephanie were thinking." She seemed to be starting one of her usual rants about their will and naming him as guardian of the kids. It was a sore spot that she never seemed to be able to let go of. "I'm sure they never thought of their children living in a hovel." She pulled open the door to find Fillian standing in the doorway, transferring a white bag to his left hand, probably so he could knock.

"Mrs. Montrose?" Fillian asked with a slight smile.

She looked at Fillian as though she were trying to place him. "It's Haber now, and I don't think I know you." She was already heading out the door and down the stairs as Fillian followed her with his gaze.

"Wow," he mouthed once he came inside, careful not to say anything in front of Weston, which Gregory was grateful for. His mother had always been distant where he was concerned, not that she had been all that different toward Arthur, except for allowing him more freedom to choose the things he wanted to do. Gregory's activities were planned out for him based on what his older brother had already chosen. Many times he had followed in Arthur's footsteps. Soccer and swimming came to mind. He was signed up and carted off to camps and after-school activities right next to Arthur without ever being asked if he was interested. It had quickly become evident, however, that in soccer he excelled, whereas in the pool, he could swim, but not with the speed needed for competition. Gregory pulled his attention away from his mother's behavior and shook his head to get rid of her lingering presence.

"Daddy," Marnie said as she came into the room in her pajamas, holding a doll under her arm. "I'm sorry." She sniffed, and Gregory lifted his best girl into his arms while Fillian set out the food he'd brought.

"It happens. I'm just glad you're okay." He hugged her exaggeratedly and planted a kiss on her cheek. "In the future, don't eat berries until you find out what they are, okay?" His heart rate sped up just thinking about what could have happened, and he turned to Fillian with a grateful smile, wondering what he would have done if he hadn't been there. Fillian, with his warm eyes and soft smile. The guy he had lived next door to all those years growing up and had never known… or, honestly, taken the time to get to know. He liked to think that they could have become friends. "Do you want a little apple juice and a piece of toast?"

She nodded, and Gregory set her on a sofa that had seen better days and got a light blanket for her. Then he set about making the toast and poured her a glass of apple juice to help ease her abused tummy. Weston went back to his Legos, too busy playing to eat, and Fillian sat down with him to make something.

"Did you have these as a kid?" Fillian asked. "I used to love them." As Gregory brought the juice, he saw Fillian and Weston share a smile as they continued building.

"Those are them," Gregory said. "Mom was a whirlwind when it came to old toys. If we didn't play with them, she would toss them out." Fillian turned toward him, his eyes clouding over for a second, cheeks pinking up a little. The unreadable expression lasted just a few seconds, and then Gregory wasn't sure if it had been there at all. "I had Lego building sets and models that I put together and displayed in my room. One day I came home to Mom looking them over. I knew what that meant, so I hid all of them in a box in the very back of my closet. It went under the stairs, and my clothes made a curtain of sorts, so what I put back there, Mom didn't know about." He grinned. "Over the years, the models came apart, and I put all the pieces in the bag, along with the regular building sets that I had." And at that moment, Fillian and Weston were using those very blocks to have a Lego dinosaur battle. If he still missed his old toys, it definitely wasn't at moments like this.

The toaster popped, and Gregory pulled out the toast, buttered it, and added a little cinnamon sugar before cutting it into quarters and bringing it to Marnie. He sat next to her, holding her gently in one arm, watching to make sure she seemed okay while she ate.

For a second, Gregory closed his eyes and let himself dream a little. This was what he had always wanted: a family of his own. Gregory remembered Arthur and him sitting on the bleachers during swim practice when it was someone else's turn in the pool. They always said that they were going to do things differently than their mom and dad, that they were going to have real families, not the "push their kids off on anyone or anything around" families.

"You're awfully quiet," Fillian said. "Maybe I should leave you alone with them. I don't want to butt in."

Gregory shook his head. "Sorry. I was just thinking, I guess." He was very grateful to Fillian. Marnie had eaten half her toast and set the plate on the table. She sipped her juice and yawned, so Gregory encouraged her to drink the rest of her juice and carried her back to bed. He returned a few minutes later, and Fillian sat next to him on the sofa.

"I don't know what I would have done if you hadn't been there," Gregory said, trying not to think about all the things going through his mind. The past few weeks had been a roller coaster, and…. "What are you doing, Weston?" he asked, realizing that Weston was at the window looking out over the street below.

"Watching the man. He was at the park too." Weston scowled before turning back to the window.

Gregory got up, and Weston backed away from the window. Gregory peered out as shards of ice went up his back. "What the hell?" he muttered.

"Bad word, Daddy. Mama always said not to use bad words. Papa did anyway sometimes," Weston added.

"I know." But this was definitely an exception. He motioned to Fillian. "That's the crazy guy." Gregory had done his best to try to put the incident at the hoarder house behind him. The guy was in jail, or so he thought. Dammit, he was crazy… and they had let him out? What the hell?

Fillian tensed. "Back away from the window." He stood to the side and carefully looked out, then shook his head. "There's no one there now, but you're sure it was him?"

"Yeah, I'm sure." Gregory still saw him each and every night in his dreams, so just seeing him from a distance sent a shiver up his spine. "Did you see him in the park?" Gregory asked Weston, who nodded seriously.

"He was creepy," Weston said. "I saw him watching Marnie and me for a little while, but mostly he watched Daddy." He blinked. "Is he a murder man?"

Gregory stopped dead still, wondering where that term came from, but it was Fillian who answered. "No. He's someone who is watching, and that means you need to watch for him. If you see him again, be sure to tell your daddy."

"Or you?" Weston asked.

Fillian nodded. "Yes. But don't wait until you see me. Tell your daddy, me, a teacher, or anyone you trust right away." Dang, Fillian sure knew how to handle something like this. "Your daddy can call me, and I'll be over to help. This isn't something for you to worry about, though. Your daddy and I know what to do." Gregory appreciated that Fillian was trying to keep Weston calm.

Weston nodded. "I'm hungry." Clearly that was more important to him, which was a relief. He didn't want Weston looking over his shoulder all the time.

"What do you want?"

"Macaroni and cheese. The box kind. Grandma made some the last time we were there, and it was really yucky. She said it was blue cheese macaroni, but it was awful, and it wasn't really blue." He stuck out his tongue. Gregory couldn't blame him. That really did sound bad, especially since his mother was no cook, and God knows how she had made the stuff.

"Can I make you some of the kind I made last time?" Gregory asked. Weston thought about it and nodded, so Gregory got to work cooking the mac and putting together the cheese sauce while Fillian and Weston returned to their Lego dinosaur battle.

"ARE THEY both asleep?" Fillian asked when Gregory came back out to the living room.

"Yes. Marnie is feeling better. Weston is happy, and I think I've been through the wringer." He sat down, sighed, and closed his eyes. "I really don't know what I would have done if you hadn't seen her and known what to do."

Fillian patted his leg. "You would have called for help. The berries made Marnie feel bad, but they weren't poisonous, which is good, and it taught her a lesson."

Gregory nodded. "But my mother is going to make a big deal out of this. I don't know when or how, but she will bring it up when she wants to use guilt to try to get something." He didn't quite know how to explain it to Fillian. "I know I had a lot of things growing up, but that was all I had. My mother was never much of a mom, and she likes things the way she wants them and expects them to be that way." The worst thing was that there was nothing he could do about it except try not to let it bother him.

"You're a good dad, and those kids adore you. That's all you need to worry about. I had great parents, and while we didn't have a lot, they were always there for me, and they still are. So I can tell you that I know what makes a great parent because I was blessed enough to have them, and you fall into that category."

Gregory swallowed hard. "Do you really think so?" It was sometimes really hard when the people who were supposed to be his role models were more like "don't do this" models. He turned toward Fillian and found those warm eyes looking back, drawing him closer.

Damn, he wanted to bask in what they seemed to be offering, but he wasn't sure he had time for anything more than friendship. The heat in Fillian's eyes and the way he licked his lips were so damned enticing. The chills from earlier completely melted away under that gaze, but Gregory had to be strong and think of Weston and Marnie. Their needs had to come first. Taking care of them and making a living took all of his energy, and he wasn't sure he could begin anything else, no matter how much he might want to. His throat went dry. The pipes that carried the steam that heated the building in the winter tinked softly, even though the system had been shut off for some time. Time seemed to slow down as Fillian gradually drew closer.

Gregory's heart beat so hard and loud he was sure Fillian could hear it. Part of him said to pull away, but the building fire in that gaze... for him... held Gregory still. Fillian slid his hand gently around Gregory's neck, the heat from his touch going deep. Gregory held his breath, wondering if this was a good idea.

"Daddy," Weston called out. Fillian's touch slipped away, and Gregory turned to where Weston stood in his bedroom door, holding a stuffed turtle to his chest.

"What is it, buddy?" Gregory asked, standing up.

"I'm thirsty, and my tummy wants a cookie," Weston said.

"Me too," Marnie added as she joined her brother.

"Okay, but after you're done, you need to go right back to bed." He sighed and went into the kitchen, where he poured two small glasses of milk and got a couple of cookies out of the cupboard. He sat the kids at the table with small plates and let them have their snack.

He turned back to Fillian, who had stood as well. "I should get home. I have to work early tomorrow morning. But you need to call me if you see anything, okay?"

"Thank you for everything." He was sad Fillian had to leave, but a little relieved as well. The kiss he was sure had been coming would be put off, and he would have some time to think things through. Though the more he thought about it, the more he realized he'd probably regret it.

CHAPTER 5

FILLIAN WAS all set for the rugby match. It had been a rough week, and he was more than ready for a chance to take out his frustration and pent-up aggression on the other team. Rugby was a release. His job required cool thinking and caution. No matter the situation, he had to remain in control and take charge—didn't matter if it was a traffic stop, a robbery investigation, or a hostage situation. He pulled up to the field and parked his car next to Gregory's truck, getting out just as Marnie and Weston raced around to him.

"I'm all better," Marnie said brightly.

"That's really good. I'm glad." Fillian got a hug from the little girl while Weston waited for his turn. Gregory came around the car just as Weston got his hug.

"Go sit in the stands right over there with Auntie Cherie, okay?" The two kids raced over to the bleachers, and when the woman waved, Gregory went over to speak with her. Fillian headed for the field, and Gregory joined him a few minutes later. "That's Stevie's wife."

"Wow," Fillian said. He knew that Stevie had recently gotten married, but he hadn't expected such a classic dark-haired beauty.

"Admiring my wife?" Stevie asked, his gaze as proud and happy as possible.

"Wondering how you landed her with the mug you got," Gregory retorted, dodging a swipe from Stevie. Fillian laughed.

"Knock it off," Coach called, and the team gathered together. "These guys are not going to be pushovers. They play rough sometimes, and last year…." He growled, because apparently the carpet bastards cleaned their clocks last year, and the coach, as well as the rest of the team, didn't intend to allow that to happen again. "Now, everyone, warm up and stretch. I want hard play, and I don't want any of you injured, and I *especially* don't want any new wives lecturing me about returning their husbands in one piece." He looked right at Stevie, who rolled his eyes. "The game starts in ten. Be ready."

Fillian stretched on the grass and got himself psyched up. Rugby was an exceedingly physical sport, involving strength and endurance. A game was eighty minutes of hard, tough play, and often the fifteen-man team that won was the one that could hold out the longest against their opponents' nonstop aggression.

"Go, Daddy!" Marnie and Weston called from the stands, jumping up and down as Gregory waved to them. "Go, Mr. Fillian!" they added.

Fillian smiled and waved back before finishing up his warmup and jogging onto the field to take his place.

Fillian always loved this time in every game where anything was possible. His heart raced, and he was all business. Rugby was his escape, a chance for him to put aside the pressures of his job as well as man's inhumanity to man that he saw almost every single day.

"Are you ready?" Gregory asked.

"You bet. Let's kick some carpet-bastard ass." He couldn't help thinking about how Weston had picked up on that particular phrase. They got into position to receive the kickoff from the carpet bastards, a whistle blew, the ball sailed through the air, and the game began.

The first forty-minute half flew by, with Fillian tackling two players who seemed especially intent on getting to Gregory. By the time the whistle blew, he was covered in dirt and had scrapes on his legs and a grin from ear to ear. It didn't hurt that they were ahead by ten points, and it was clear to Fillian that a number of the players on the opposing team were beginning to flag.

"You did great," Stevie said to him, slapping Fillian on the back. As a hooker, Fillian came in contact with the ball a lot, and he was one of the players who decided what to do with it and had to react quickly to the other team's strengths. "I don't think they knew what hit them. Gillespie was good, but you have a real knack for the position." He jogged off as the coach called the team together. His speech was a combination of tips for improvement and revving them up for the second half.

Fillian was getting ready to return to the field when he saw Weston bound out of the stands and race over to the side of the field. He seemed so intent that Fillian tapped Gregory on the shoulder, and they both hurried off to the side where Weston stood. "What is it?" Fillian asked.

"That man, the creepy one… he's right over there." Weston pointed, and Fillian looked where he indicated but didn't see him. During the week, he'd confirmed that the suspect was out on bail. "He's gone now."

"I believe you, and thank you for letting me know," Fillian said, still watching the area Weston indicated. The park where they were playing was close to Harrisburg and filled with people. Across the main park road were soccer fields with plenty of spectators for the games. It would be easy enough for someone to melt into the crowd. "Go back and sit with your sister and Aunt Cherie. Let me know if you see him again, okay?"

Weston nodded and sat back down.

"What do we do?" Gregory asked.

"Give me a minute." Fillian stepped aside and called the station for an update. He then called the local police department and explained what was happening, providing as much pertinent information as he had. Once he was done, he returned to where Gregory paced off to the side of the field.

"I called my department and the local police. They're both aware of the situation. If they can get proof of the behavior, then his bail could be revoked and he'll sit his butt back in jail. Keep calm and your eyes open. When I go back on duty, I'll find out what's going on, along with the conditions of his bail. Most judges are not going to allow someone on bail to stalk or harass their victims. Don't worry. He's probably trying to scare you." Though Fillian had to wonder if it was more than that. His mind began to whirl as possibilities arose, but he'd look into them later.

Coach called them back to the game, and Fillian needed to focus his mind on that if they were to have any chance of winning. Usually that was at the top of his mind, but keeping Gregory and the kids safe easily pushed that to the side.

The second half went as well as the first, with the game turning into a blowout just as clouds overtook the sky. By the time the game ended, drizzle coated everything. The guys celebrated with whoops of redemptive joy before agreeing to meet at Molly Pitcher Brewery in an hour.

Gregory collected the kids, and Fillian joined them, not sure what Gregory wanted to do. "We should go home."

Marnie sulked slightly as Weston groaned. "But I want Molly Tots," he said, pooching out his lower lip.

Fillian took a step back. He wasn't going to get involved in this discussion, even though he hoped Gregory would decide to go. Fillian had already figured out that if he wanted to be in Gregory's life, then it was a package deal and the kids came along with him.

"Yeah, Daddy, I want tots too. You played really well, and we cheered real loud. Did you hear us?" It seemed both kids knew how to wrap their daddy around their fingers.

"Okay, but I have to go home and get cleaned up before I can go anywhere, and we all need to get out of the drizzle."

Fillian couldn't help wondering if he could master the pooched lower lip to see if he could get Gregory to do what he wanted... and it had nothing to do with Molly Tots and more to do with getting Gregory alone and personal.

"Then I'll meet you there." He was grungy and needed to clean up as well. The end-of-game drizzle had added mud on top of dirt, and he needed to get it out of places that were certain to chafe. "Don't eat all the tots." He smiled and then hurried home.

AN HOUR later, Fillian strode into the tap room and was directed upstairs, where most of the players and their partners had gathered for the after-game celebration. "You were awesome," Stevie told him, already a few beers in.

"You need to sit down and eat something," Cherie told him. "You can't just drink beer and get all sloppy drunk." She flashed him a scowl, and he took a chair at the table with Gregory and the kids. Cherie joined them, and Fillian took the last seat, across from Gregory.

"You both need to eat more than tots," Gregory told the kids. He went through the menu with both of them, and they chose chicken fingers. Fillian ordered a chicken sandwich and some tots along with a Red Coat.

Thankfully, the guys seemed to understand that Gregory needed to stay with the kids, and they congregated around the table. "That was some save in the last few seconds," Stevie told him.

"That was all Gregory. I passed the ball back to him, and he knew exactly how to press it forward," Fillian said.

"Where did you learn to play like that?" one of the other guys asked. "Did you go to a prep school or something? They don't play much rugby in this area, at least not in schools."

Fillian snorted. "I went to public school here in town. When I was studying law enforcement, I had friends who played, and they taught me the game. One of the guys was from England, and he grew up with rugby. Damn, he was fast, and he could run like the wind. He taught me to weave and dodge like that." He really loved the physicality of the game. Yes, there was strategy and team play, but also sheer physical exertion. All of them together were what he loved.

"I'm gonna play rugby like Daddy," Weston declared.

"Me too," Marnie added.

"Girls don't play rugby," one of the guys said.

Gregory hit him with a glare that froze the air in their immediate area. "Tell that to Sharon McClure. She played with us in college, and she could tackle harder than most of the men. She could also move the ball a heck of a lot better than Chester did tonight."

Fillian knew exactly who had made the offending comment. "So, Marnie, if you want to play, I'm sure your daddy would be happy to teach you when you're a little older." Gregory beamed over her head, and Fillian nodded slightly, pleased that Gregory was happy.

The server brought orders of food, and the kids settled in to eat. "Wait until it cools down a little," Fillian told Weston as he reached for one of the steaming tots. He spread them out and then slowly began to eat his own dinner, sharing his cooled tots with the kids to give them something to munch on.

"I have to go," Marnie told Gregory, and he took her down the stairs to the bathroom. While they were gone, what started as sharing goofy smiles with Weston ended up as a funny-faces contest, with the guys joining in. Weston ended up gigging and nearly snorted soda out of his nose.

Fillian kept looking at the stairs, wondering where Gregory and Marnie were. Weston began eating again, and Fillian grew more worried, wondering if he should check on them, when Gregory, holding Marnie's hand, returned with Gregory's mother behind him.

"…and you brought the kids to a bar." She had built up one heck of a head of steam.

"That's enough, Mother," Gregory said. "Go back and join your husband and leave us alone." He looked about ready to explode.

"Are Grandma and Daddy gonna fight?" Weston whispered, and this was no stage whisper, but one filled with real fear. The rest of the team heard the exchange, and they all turned and stared at Gregory's mother, some even moving in behind Gregory. Fillian slipped out of his seat to stand next to him.

"You have an entire rugby team on edge. I think you should go back where you came from," Fillian said, watching as Mrs. Haber straightened her shoulders. He wondered if she was going to put up a fight, but she turned and went back down the stairs, the tension clear in her posture.

"Go on back to your dinner," Gregory told Marnie gently, and she climbed back into her seat before she and Weston began talking softly between bites of their tots.

The mood of the entire evening seemed to have changed, with a pall hanging over it. "Well, who knew we'd get a show with our beer?" Stevie chimed in. The guys laughed, and the sour mood popped like a soap bubble.

"What's up with her?" Fillian asked. "The kids aren't at the bar, and there are other families here having dinner. There's nothing wrong."

Gregory's rigid posture didn't shift. "She's threatening to fight for the kids. Mom thinks she can provide a better home for them. She and my stepfather live in a big, fancy house with every convenience known to man, including a housekeeper, a pool, and huge rooms for Marnie and Weston. She thinks she'd be able to provide them with more than I can. But there was a reason Arthur and Stephanie chose me to raise their children. He didn't want them to grow up the way we did, with everything money could buy… and nothing else." He sighed softly as he took his seat once more.

Fillian moved and took the now empty seat next to him, holding his hand under the table. The guys had shifted throughout the tap room, with small conversations and occasional jolts of laughter cutting through the din of intermingled conversations.

"Just because she wants something to happen doesn't mean it will. There have to be grounds, and she would have to go a long way to prove that you aren't fit to raise the kids, and she can't do that." He squeezed Gregory's fingers under the table.

Damn, growing up, he always thought Gregory was the lucky one. He'd look out his bedroom window to the sparkling swimming pool and all the toys and games Gregory had and long to have just some of the things he did. But all those material things came with a huge price. Fillian realized he was the lucky one. After giving Gregory's hand another squeeze, he pulled his away and ate his dinner.

"THANK YOU, Mom," Fillian said into his phone half an hour later, standing on the sidewalk out in front of the tap room. He needed a few minutes without the wall of sound coming at him.

"What are you thanking me for? What did you do?" The mirth in her voice was instantly calming.

"Nothing. I met Gregory Montrose a while ago. He and I play rugby on the same team and… well… just thank you. It's too much to go into right now, but… yeah. Thank you for being good parents, for truly caring about me… for everything."

"Okay…. What is it that's getting to you? And don't try to pass this off as nothing. I'm your mother." That warning tone always made him stand straighter. A late summer breeze swirled around him. "I know better."

"Gregory is raising his brother's two kids."

"Yes, I know. I saw that Arthur and his wife died a few years ago. I was worried that his mother would get her hands on them so she could treat them the way she did Gregory and Arthur. We always worried about them."

"They're sweet kids, Mom. And Gregory… well, I envied him, but…." Those old feelings and assumptions, as well as his growing attraction, left him in an emotional jumble.

His mother chuckled. "And you like him." He could always count on his mother to see things clearly and to be able to tease him with only a few words, using that all-knowing tone mothers had. "And those kids." He could almost see her smile. "So why did you call me?"

"I don't know, other than Gregory's mother made an appearance, doing her best impression of Cruella de Vil, and it made me want to thank you." He turned to look into the restaurant, where patrons sat and talked. "I should get back to them. We're at Molly's, celebrating our win."

"Then I'll let you go to spend time with your friends. But you should come to dinner and bring your friend and his kids. I'm tired of cooking for just your father and myself."

"Okay. I'll ask him." He said goodbye and went back inside, passing Gregory's mother at a table for six with a group of people. She glared at him as he passed, but Fillian paid her little attention. There was nothing he could do about her, and he didn't want the guys to think he left them.

"Everything okay?" Gregory asked when he returned to the table. The bills had been presented, and Fillian snatched up both of theirs and handed the server his credit card.

"It's fine. I was talking to my mother, and she wanted me to ask if all of you would like to come over for dinner sometime. Mom loves to cook a big meal, and with it being just her and Dad now, she doesn't get to very often."

The kids had settled down and were yawning. "I think that would be nice. Let us know when and what we can bring." He smiled a little. "I need to get these two home. It's getting on their bedtime."

"Okay." Fillian followed Gregory out of the tap room.

"You don't need to go. I'm sure the guys will be more than happy to talk, drink, and celebrate the win for hours yet." Gregory was already looking toward where he'd parked the car.

"I'm on duty early tomorrow morning. There are some ongoing issues with the freeway and excessive speeding, so I'm going to be sitting by the side of the road handing out tickets." Fillian shrugged. "Whoever said being a state police officer was exciting and glamorous knew nothing about the job. It's hours of sitting around for a few minutes of action." He drew closer. "But I'll message you tomorrow with a few dates that we can get together for dinner with my parents."

Gregory swallowed hard. "You really want me to meet them... with the kids?" His reaction seemed strange, and Fillian wondered why, but now was not the time to ask.

"You already know my mom and dad, and yeah. They will be head over heels to meet these two." They walked toward Gregory's truck. Weston and Marnie ran ahead to the back door, and Fillian took a chance and drew right up to Gregory. "Stop worrying and just relax a little. I know you have the kids and that they have to come first. That's the deal with being a parent. But that doesn't mean that you need to be alone forever or that you can't have someone in your life." He closed the distance between them and kissed Gregory quickly, just to give him a taste of what was possible. "I'll talk to you soon." He turned and hurried west toward his car, smiling to himself.

CHAPTER 6

GREGORY AND Fillian had settled on the following Tuesday as the night for them to have dinner with Fillian's parents. The thing was, they still lived in the same house, and Gregory found it strange to return to the old neighborhood. The house he had grown up in looked much the same, though the landscaping had been updated and the yard was immaculate. The huge porch where he retreated when his parents were fighting looked amazing, with wicker furniture and even a porch swing. He wondered if the pool was still in back and if the family who lived there had children.

"Come on in," Fillian said as he stepped out the front door. "Mom is putting the finishing touches on dinner." He held the door, and Gregory led Weston and Marnie inside. The house was much the same as he remembered from the very few times he'd been inside: homey and lived in. This was a place that exuded warmth, from the living-room fireplace to the scents drifting in from the kitchen. None of his memories from the house next door included any of those feelings.

"Gregory, it's so good to see you," Mrs. O'Connell said as she came out of the kitchen. He almost held out his hand, but she took him in a hug, and he closed his eyes. It had been quite a while since he'd been held so gently and caringly.

"I'm glad to be here. Thank you, Mrs. O'Connell," he said softly as she released him.

"Please call me Verona." She smiled, looking down at the kids. "They both look just like your brother." She got so serious for a second and then shook her head slightly. "Now, do these two have anything they don't like?"

"Just blue cheese mac and cheese," Gregory told her, and chuckled when she made a yuck face.

"Who makes that?" Verona asked.

"Grandma," Weston piped up. "She says it shows good taste, but it's yucky."

Marnie stayed close to Gregory and seemed to be going through a shy moment. He kept his hand on her shoulder and let her decide when to come out of her shell.

"Well, there won't be anything like that. I made a beef roast with mashed potatoes, some green beans from the garden, and some rolls. I didn't make them from scratch, though. I get those at Costco. Jim, are you finishing up?"

Fillian's dad came down the stairs. He looked much the same, only with a few extra pounds and more snow on the roof than the black hair Gregory remembered. "Dad, you remember Gregory. And these are Weston and Marnie."

Gregory got a firm handshake, and each of the kids got a smile. "It looks like we're ready to eat."

"What were you doing?" Fillian asked.

"I got a new job. I substitute teach at the high school. I took a couple of classes, and they took me on. I teach three or four days a week, and it's great. Lately I've been teaching algebra, and I'm having so much fun. I don't think their regular teacher is very good at explaining things so they can really understand it. I've been working with them for a week, and I have another week before the regular teacher comes back, so I've been working on sheets to help make sure they have the basic principles down pat."

"That's pretty cool," Gregory said. "I used to hate math, but now I use it each and every day, and I never really think too much about it, I just do it."

"Daddy does 'lectricity," Marnie said.

"That's really important," Mr. O'Connell told her. "Otherwise we can't turn on the lights and we'd all sit around in the dark with nothing to do." He smiled, and Marnie moved away from Gregory slightly. "What do you like to do?"

"I draw and color. Weston plays Legos and makes things," she answered. "I want to take dance class too. Daddy says that I can start in the fall."

"What kind of dance?" Verona asked. "I took ballet when I was a little girl. I was pretty good at it too."

"I didn't know that," Fillian said. "Is that why I'm such a good dancer?"

His mother snorted and scowled at him. "You're a terrible dancer. Every time he tried, he stepped on my feet," she added, and then invited everyone into the kitchen and got them settled around the table.

Gregory didn't know what to expect. Growing up, when there was some sort of family meal, which wasn't very often, his parents were quiet. His mother mostly heated up food, and once Gregory was older, she left him to his own devices. There was food in the house all the time; he just had to make it. As a result, he became a decent cook, but nothing he ever made smelled as enticing as the table of food in front of him.

"How much would each of the kids like?"

Gregory helped Verona make up plates for each of them. Marnie took a few tentative bites and then dug in. Weston wasn't as hesitant. Gregory wondered if Fillian's family was going to think he never fed them by how fast they ate. "No one is going to steal your food, and there's plenty."

Verona cut the meat and passed plates. From there, everything was passed, and Gregory was in culinary heaven.

"Do you like being an electrician?" Jim said, probably as a conversation starter.

"Yes. I completed my journeymanship three years ago, and I have my own business now. Though there are a few construction companies that are looking for full-time help."

Jim met his gaze sternly. "Work for yourself if possible for as long as you can. I know there are disadvantages, but at least you can take the jobs you want."

"Lately, it's been the jobs no one else wants," Gregory said softly, not wanting to complain. "Though things are picking up, and I've been working steadily for the past few weeks. It's hard with the kids and childcare."

"What do you do?" Verona asked.

"The kids spend time in a program at the Y. There are camps and a day care that they're enrolled in. They also have after-school programs during the school year." He took a bite of the roast, which was amazing. "It's always a bit of a jumble putting all the pieces together, sometimes with various programs."

"Your mother doesn't help?" Verona asked.

Gregory cleared his throat. "My mother has her own ideas about how things should be, and they aren't mine or what Arthur and Stephanie wanted for them." He skirted the issue and found himself eating more quickly just because the dinner was so amazing. He couldn't remember ever having a meal like this one.

"Mom is an amazing cook," Fillian said softly. "She tried to teach me some of her secrets, but I just don't have the knack for it."

"That's because you never stayed still long enough to really learn," Verona said without any heat. In fact, her tone was almost proud. "You always blazed your own path." Yeah, she was a proud mother. "Is the food okay?" Verona asked both kids, who nodded and kept eating.

Jim and Verona talked a little about their day. Fillian leaned close and spoke softly.

"I found out a few things about our person of interest. He was called before the judge and told to stay away from others in the case. His bail wasn't revoked, but he was given a warning."

Gregory leaned in too. "Do you think that will make any real difference?"

"It should if he doesn't want to spend months in jail waiting for his trial," Fillian said.

Gregory wasn't sure that this guy really cared. He had tried to tell the police how the guy had acted, but it was hard to describe. Mostly it had been things that Gregory thought and felt—conjecture rather than facts. The man seemed scattered and at loose ends, like all the stuff in the house could somehow keep him grounded. "I know. But…." He leaned closer. "I guess we'll have to wait and see." He was really worried that this wacko would try to hurt him or the kids. He certainly had a fascination with Gregory. "I just want him to go away and leave us alone." Every time he showed up, he made Gregory feel more like a victim, and he hated that.

Fillian rested his hand on Gregory's leg, the heat seeping right through his chinos. "It will be okay. I was able to talk to some of the senior guys, and they called in a few favors from the local police and alerted them to the issue. So it isn't just us but the Carlisle department that's on the case."

"What are you whispering about?" Jim asked.

"Nothing, Dad," Fillian told him. "Mom, this is amazing, really."

"Yes," Gregory added. "It really is."

Weston cleaned his plate and asked for more meat, while Marnie wanted more vegetables and potatoes. Verona beamed, and Gregory helped the kids with small portions.

When dinner was over, Gregory tried to help clean up, but Verona would have none of it and shooed everyone out into the living room. He sat next to Fillian on the sofa while the kids sat on the floor with coloring books that Gregory had brought along. He had learned quickly never to go anywhere without something for the kids to do.

Once they were settled, Gregory leaned back and found himself comfortable and relaxed. Fillian took his hand, while Jim flipped through the television stations until he found one of those cooking competition shows. The kids ignored it, but the show seemed to work for the adults. Verona joined them and scowled at Jim, who flipped off the TV, making the room quiet.

Gregory knew he should feel awkward at the silence, but he didn't. Fillian leaned a little closer, and Gregory reveled in something he never seemed to have in his life: quiet.

"I guess I have to ask. Are the two of you dating?"

"Verona," Jim said, rolling his eyes. "Anyone can see that they are." He shook his head. "And before you get yourself all worked up, leave the two of them alone, okay?"

She snapped her head around to Jim. "Is it wrong for me to want Fillian to have someone in his life?" She looked at her husband as though he were crazy.

"No. But there's no need to push," Jim said levelly and with a slight smile. "This whole exchange is being pushy."

"And neither of you would do anything like that," Fillian interjected, rolling his eyes before turning that gaze on Gregory with an innocent smile that made him wonder just how innocent he really was. "Just ignore them, okay?"

"Well, you did bring me and my kids to dinner, so I figured you were serious about things, but I didn't know how serious." He decided to play along and have a little fun. "But if meeting the parents is some sort of huge relationship milestone, then maybe you and I should…."

Fillian put up his hands. "I know you're having fun with me, all of you, and you can stop now. God, if I would have known." At least he didn't seem upset.

"What's going on?" Marnie asked.

"Nothing, sweetheart. I was just teasing Fillian a little." He shared a smile with her and then glanced at Fillian, resting his hand on his leg.

The house phone rang, and Verona went into the kitchen to answer it. Her voice trailed in, getting louder. "What do you mean there's a man watching the house?" Her tone grew sharp, and Fillian got to his feet and hurried to the front window. He peered out and then headed outside as he pulled out his phone.

"Stay here," Gregory told the kids and followed Fillian. As he reached the door, Fillian was coming back inside. "Was it him?"

Verona was still on the phone, talking to whoever had called her. "It's okay. Thank you for letting us know." She ended the call. "Louise says that whoever they were hurried down the sidewalk toward Bedford as soon as they saw the front curtains move." She sat back down.

"You need to tell us what's going on," Jim said. "Why is someone following you?" He looked at Fillian. "Is this some sort of police protest thing?"

"It isn't me that's involved," Fillian said levelly. "It's a suspect who's following Gregory. I was hoping to get a good look at him so I could have the evidence necessary to get his bail revoked." Tension radiated from Fillian so strongly Gregory could almost feel it. "I hate that I can't make this go away."

"You have to work within the boundaries of the law. You can't do anything else," Jim said, and Gregory found himself nodding. He wouldn't want Fillian to do anything else. "Has he actually done anything or made threats?"

Gregory nodded slowly. "He has, and he seems to show up wherever I am… watching, like he wants us to know that he's there. I think he may have done more, but I can't prove it."

"He's creepy," Weston cut in. "But I'm not scared of him. I'm big now." Marnie nodded.

Gregory was relieved that the kids weren't afraid. After all, he was scared enough for all of them. All he kept thinking about was what would happen if this guy got his hands on Weston or Marnie.

"I'm glad, but remember that you promised to tell your daddy or me if you see him again," Fillian said, and both Weston and Marnie nodded.

"Can we talk about something else?" Gregory asked. He needed something to take his mind off this situation. All he'd done was take a job and then turn down a guy who wanted something he had no right to.

How was he supposed to know that he'd end up picking up a stalker? Though after he saw the condition of that house, he should have refused to go inside and gotten the hell out of there.

"What do you want to talk about?" Verona asked, turning to Fillian. "I have plenty of stories about this one as a child."

"Like us?" Weston asked. Verona nodded, Fillian groaned, and Weston grinned. "I wanna hear." And just like that, Verona told a story about Fillian, watermelon, and a very wet diaper.

"Mom, is this really necessary?" Fillian asked.

"At least your mother has stories to tell about you," Gregory said, and Fillian nudged his shoulder and let his mother continue.

As she regaled them with story after story, laughter filled the house, and Gregory realized that this was the type of family he wanted—and wanted the kids to be part of. This happiness and closeness had been missing from his childhood, and he didn't want Weston and Marnie to have the same kind of upbringing.

After a dessert of chocolate cake, they all moved back into the living room. Marnie and Weston sat next to Gregory and Fillian at first, but soon slipped onto the floor as Verona brought out some of Fillian's old toys. Soon they were putting pegs into the old Lite-Brite, making pictures with light and having a grand old time.

"What is the plan with this stalker?" Jim asked once the kids were occupied. "You know that he isn't going to be content with just watching. This guy wants something."

Fillian slipped his hand into Gregory's. "We know. The thing is that he may not even know what he wants, at least not yet. And the guy, while acting creepy, hasn't done anything other than watch. He hasn't even tried to talk to Gregory. I know it's unsettling, but there is nothing illegal about standing on the public sidewalk. That's what's so frustrating. I have the sheriff's department as well as the local police on alert, but other than that, my hands are tied until he actually does something."

And that was what had Gregory scared. But it seemed there was little they could do about it… at least until something happened.

CHAPTER 7

"WHAT ARE we going to do?" Fillian asked fellow troopers Casey Bombaro and Wyatt Nelson. They met near exit forty-nine on eighty-one. Both men were mentors to him. Not only were they more seasoned troopers, but both were gay, and their experience had helped him navigate the sometimes old-fashioned brotherhood of officers. "He's got two kids, and I'm not sure how to protect him."

"The suspect is on bail, so he's already on shaky ground. You'd think he'd leave well enough alone and keep his head down." Wyatt shook his head. "But we all know that sometimes rational thoughts and actions just don't happen."

"There are limits to what we can do. The local police and the sheriff's department have jurisdiction over the town itself," Casey added.

"I know," Fillian said. "But this is frustrating as all hell. He isn't hiding what he's doing, and we could probably make a case for attempted witness tampering, but he never says anything. He just watches, and he seems to be following Gregory around. Last night Gregory told me that he was on a job in South Middlesex and saw him hanging around." Fillian grew more frustrated each time Lawrence Little was spotted.

"We're here for you," Wyatt said. "And for them. But our hands are tied until he does something illegal. I'm assuming that you've kept records of when he's been spotted."

"Yes. And I turned them in to the DA, but they don't have enough to go to the judge to have his bail revoked yet." It was the most frustrating thing Fillian had ever experienced, and that included hours sitting by the side of the road to catch speeders. "I know we have to follow procedure and the law, but there are times when…." He closed his eyes and forced himself to regain control of his emotions. Just the thought that Lawrence could be out there right now watching Gregory or the kids made him more than a little angry. They didn't deserve this.

"The one thing we all learned in the academy is to keep our eyes open and to pay attention to detail. That's what you have to do here." Wyatt reached through the open window of his cruiser and got his cup of coffee, then sipped it. "You can't let him get under your skin. It's pretty obvious that you like Gregory, but what would you be doing if this was just another case?"

Fillian nodded. He'd take notes, add to the case file, and wait. But this wasn't just another case—this was Gregory, Weston, and Marnie. Somehow, without him thinking about it, all three of them had gotten under his skin and into his heart. "You know, that's it. I've been worried about Gregory and the kids, but I haven't been doing the other side of my job. I need to find out where Lawrence is living." This was so stupid and basic. He should have thought of that earlier, but he was otherwise distracted.

"All right. He has to list his address with the court since he's out on bail."

"And the place he was living exploded, taking two other homes with it. I'm willing to bet that he listed that as his residence, and he can't be staying there." Maybe this was the information he needed. "The investigation is still active, but I'll take a trip out there and see what's going on." Fillian would also check with the court to see what they had for an address before he went.

"Sounds like a plan. The biggest thing is to keep your head about you and look at things logically," Wyatt told him.

"Did you do that when you met Quinton?" Fillian asked.

Wyatt chuckled. "Well… I did my job and things worked out, but it's hard, and you know it. We're police officers, but we're people too, and our emotions sometimes get the better of us. I sometimes think we're hardwired to try to protect, especially the people we care about. I know I'd do anything to keep Quinton and Callum safe, no matter what." They both looked at Casey, who nodded. "But remember that logic and good police work are going to get you a lot farther than flying off the handle."

Fillian sighed. "I know that."

"Okay. So do your job the best you can and keep your wits about you," Casey told him, clapping Fillian on the shoulder. "Finding out what's really going on and getting the information you need on the suspect are going to do more good than the worry and fear ever will." He finished his coffee and handed Fillian the cup. "Rookie takes care of the trash." He grinned and climbed back into his cruiser, then took off down the highway.

Fillian rolled his eyes, took Wyatt's cup as well, and tossed both in the rest area trash can before heading down the road and across town toward the location of the original call. He wanted to take a look at what was left of the house Lawrence had been renting.

Along the way, he did a wellness check that was called in and found a retiree in her recliner. It had broken and tipped back, holding her at an odd angle and separating her from her phone. Fillian helped her out of the chair and got her phone back in her possession. "Are you sure there isn't someone who can help you?"

"I'm fine as long as I leave that old chair of my husband's alone. I always told him to get rid of it, and now that he'd dead I don't have the heart to throw it away. But I'm not going to sit in it again." She used her cane to see him to the door.

Fillian called back to Dispatch to report before continuing on.

He pulled into the property's drive. There was very little left of the house other than the foundation and charred debris. Fillian turned off the engine and carefully got out of the cruiser. The wind blew through the trees that surrounded the clearing, the scent of fire permeating the air.

There was no one around, and he slowly made his way up to where the house had been, looking into the charred mess of the house and what had been inside. Fillian walked the perimeter, checking for any sign that someone had been there recently, but he found nothing. The garden shed had been charred but still stood, the door hanging open on a single hinge. He checked inside before moving on. As he headed back toward the car, Fillian noticed a path through the trees to the west.

He cautiously checked through the brush and then stepped down the path, on his guard. It led a few dozen yards away from the road before opening up into a small clearing, where he found a makeshift tent with a plastic bag of clothes and another bag with a sleeping bag. Fillian checked through the things without disturbing them before heading back down the trail to his car. At least he knew where Lawrence had been living, and while it was likely he didn't have permission to squat on the property, he was technically living at the address he'd given the court.

Back in the car, he backed out of the drive and onto the road and headed toward town—but then he received a call to reroute to a major accident scene on the freeway.

FILLIAN WAS dog-tired when his shift ended. He drove to Gregory's, pleased to find him at home.

Gregory answered the door. "How was your day?"

Fillian smiled at him. "Good. I went out to the scene of an accident, and I know where your stalker is living, but he wasn't there."

"What about his car?" Gregory asked. "He had a car when I worked for him."

"I didn't see it. I suspect that he's living in it when he isn't at the camp. Did you see him anywhere today?"

"No, thank goodness. I kept looking for him, though."

Fillian looked around. "Where are the kids?" The apartment was unusually quiet.

"At the Y for a day camp. I need to go pick them up in a few minutes. I just stopped here to change clothes and get cleaned up."

"Then I should head on home myself," Fillian said.

Gregory moved a little closer. "You know, you could come with us. I promised the kids that we could have hamburgers for dinner and then ice cream." He smiled, and Fillian placed his hands on either side of Gregory's face and cupped his cheeks. Then he closed the distance between them and kissed Gregory hard until he groaned softly against Fillian's lips.

"I'd really like to lick something other than a cone," Fillian whispered.

Gregory shivered under his touch. Fillian then backed away and smiled.

"You really know how to tease a guy," Gregory said softly. "Sometimes I wonder if you're for real."

"Of course I am. We grew up next door to one another."

"Yeah, but…." Gregory paused, biting his lower lip. "I keep wondering if I can believe that this is real. I mean, I have two kids, and most guys aren't interested in taking on that kind of commitment. Then all of a sudden, my life changes and here you are."

Fillian stroked Gregory's cheek. "And you think I'd play games with you?"

Gregory shrugged. "I don't know what to think. I want to believe in this." He placed his hand on Fillian's. "I really do. But it's difficult."

"No, it's not. All you have to do is let yourself accept what's standing right in front of you." He smiled slightly, looking into Gregory's deep blue eyes. He wanted to kiss him again, but he was afraid to push too hard. "We'll take things slow."

"Yeah," Gregory breathed. "We have to pick up the kids."

Fillian nodded and let his hand drop away. Then he left the apartment with Gregory behind him.

Fillian rode in Gregory's truck to the Y. A group of kids sat in the shade with their backpacks next to them. Gregory parked and got out. Weston and Marnie hurried over, and Gregory spoke to the attendants, who logged them out. Fillian got out and strode up to the attendant.

"We're all set," Gregory said.

"I'll be there in just a minute," Fillian said before speaking to the young woman with the clipboard. "I don't want to bother you, but I'm with the state police." He showed her his identification. "I just want to know if you've seen anyone hanging around the kids, watching them."

She swallowed hard. "No. We've spent much of the day in the gym inside or out here on the playground, and the area is fenced. We check the kids in when they get here, count them when they go out, and do the same when they return inside." She showed him her clipboard. "And we check them out again when they leave."

Fillian nodded.

"Has there been a complaint or a problem?" The girl's hand shook a little as she asked.

"No." Fillian smiled, trying to put her at ease. He hadn't meant to go complete police officer on her. "Just keep your eyes open. We've had some issues with people hanging around places where kids are. Just keep watch, okay?" He thanked her and returned to the car. He shared a smile with Gregory and got back in.

"Is everything okay?" Gregory asked.

"Yes. It's all fine." At least for now. He didn't think Lawrence had followed the kids to the Y, but he wanted to be sure. He didn't think he was interested in the kids—he thought he was fixated on Gregory—but that was just a theory. "Let's go eat."

"Yay," the kids said in unison, and Gregory drove them to the diner on the edge of town.

THE FOLLOWING evening they had rugby practice. Gregory brought the kids because he didn't have someone to watch them. They moved one of the park picnic tables nearer to the practice field so the kids could be close to them and so it would be easier to watch them between plays.

It was pretty clear that they didn't want to be there. The kids were grumpy, and once they got down to practice, Gregory seemed distracted. He almost tripped over his own feet, and Fillian found himself watching Gregory more than paying attention to what he was doing. "What's going on?" he asked while Coach worked with one of the sections.

"My mother," Gregory growled.

"What did she do?" Fillian had wondered if Gregory's stalker was back. He hadn't been seen in a few days, so Fillian had hoped Lawrence had moved on. It seemed logical that he would get tired of Gregory when someone else captured his imagination.

"She was supposed to watch the kids while I was at practice. Mom has been asking to take the kids shopping for school clothes, which would be a huge help. She was supposed to take them this evening. That way they wouldn't have to sit at the table for a couple of hours. They were looking forward to it, but she backed out at the last minute because she had forgotten an appointment to get her nails done and didn't want to reschedule. All she would have had to do was pick up the phone and get a different time. Is that really so hard? Maybe I'm dumb, but shouldn't her grandchildren come before a manicure?"

Fillian was pretty sure it was more than that to Gregory. "It's okay. We can take them shopping if you like. I have Sunday off." He leaned closer until his forehead touched Gregory's, their gazes locking. "We'll figure it out."

"I know. But they were looking forward to it."

Gregory was truly upset, and Fillian wanted to make him feel better. He slipped his hand round the back of his neck and held it there, and within seconds, the world became just the two of them in this little bubble that grew hotter by the second. Fillian swallowed hard, completely forgetting where he was.

"Get a room," one of the guys shouted from behind him.

Fillian rolled his eyes and pulled back. "We should get back to practice," he said softly. "But don't sweat it. We'll figure it out." He gently patted the back of Gregory's neck before letting his hand slip away. Instantly Fillian missed that touch and the warmth from Gregory's gaze, and he was in the real world again, which didn't hold a candle to one where it was only him and Gregory.

"Get your heads out of your butts," Coach told both of them. Fillian nodded and hurried back onto the field, and practice continued.

During each break, he looked over at the kids and scanned the area around the park. He kept expecting that hair-standing-on-end feeling, but it never came, and he never saw anyone hanging around watching the kids or the practice. As practice continued, Gregory loosened up and they were able to play some really good rugby.

"Are you done yet?" Weston half whined when Fillian hurried over to the table to get some water during a brief break.

"Not too much longer," he answered. "Why don't you and Marnie each draw a picture for your dad? He's been a little sad, and I know that would cheer him up, okay?" He figured giving them something to do would be help the time pass more quickly.

They both smiled and lowered their heads to make their pictures. Fillian finished the water and jogged back to the practice. "They okay?" Gregory asked as he picked himself up from a tackle. He was grinning and covered in dirt.

"Yes. But they're bored and reaching the end of their patience," Fillian told him. "They've been really good, though." Those kids were pretty amazing as far as he was concerned.

Gregory smiled as he looked toward the table, but after a few seconds, his expression fell. "What is she doing here?"

Fillian turned to look. Gregory's mother strode across the grass in high heels, her flowing coverup blowing in the breeze like a royal blue sail. She went right to the table to stand with the kids. Gregory jogged over while Fillian stayed behind, wondering what sort of trouble she was trying to stir up.

"You leave the kids sitting here alone while you're out there running around like a schoolboy?" His mother's voice carried on the breeze. Fillian's anger rose, and he wanted to go over to back Gregory up, but he knew it would only escalate the situation.

"The kids are fine. Fillian and I...." Gregory turned away and his voice was lost.

"Let's clean up and put things away," Coach said, calling it a day. "But you all had better bring your top form this weekend or we're going to get our heads handed to us."

Weston got up from the table and raced out onto the field. He practically barreled into Fillian. "Grandma is being mean to Daddy." He hugged Fillian's legs.

Fillian ruffled Weston's hair. "Let's go see what's going on." Weston took his hand, and they walked back to where Gregory stood, his body rife with tension, every muscle taut.

"I think it's time for you to go," Gregory told his mother between clenched teeth.

"I'm going to take the kids with me," she pronounced.

Gregory was clearly shocked, but he recovered quickly. "No, you're not," he countered, glaring at his mother, tension building even higher.

"You obviously aren't looking after them. They're here at a table while you're over there on the field. How is that looking after them? The last time you did this, Marnie got sick because you weren't paying close enough attention." She waved her hand like she was dismissing whatever Gregory said. "I don't know why Arthur and Stephanie thought you could raise their children, but you clearly can't, and—"

"Because they didn't want you," Gregory snapped. "They knew you were a terrible mother, and they didn't want their kids raised the way Arthur and I were." He leaned closer. "They wanted someone who would care for them and not leave them in the care of babysitters, the cleaning lady, hell, anyone who would watch us while you were out doing God knows what." Gregory clearly had a great head of steam. "And as much as you like to think you're some kind of mother of the year, what you want and think hardly matters. So go home and leave us alone." He leaned closer as Fillian strode over to him. "If you want to see them again, ever… then you need to change the attitude."

"I have rights," she snapped, drawing back her hand.

"Not here, you don't," Fillian said gently. "There is a fallacy that grandparents have rights. They don't. Not over a legal parent, and like it or not, that's Gregory."

"You're mistaken," she said, turning on Fillian.

"I don't think so, and don't you dare hit him." He could see the anger in her eyes and the way she had already pulled her hand back. "I will arrest you for assault and you can spend a couple days in jail." Fillian wasn't going to mess around. "Now, as Gregory said, it's time for you to go. You've caused enough of a scene in front of the entire rugby team, as well as your grandchildren." Maybe reminding her of everyone watching would get her to back away.

"Just go home, Mother. You don't get to make demands here. And whatever case you think you're making isn't being helped by this display.

Now, I have to get the kids home so they can have dinner, because that's what parents do. And they don't try to feed kids blue cheese macaroni." He turned and began getting the kids ready. Fillian waited until Gregory's mother stalked off, leaving depressions in the dirt from her high heels.

"Jesus…," Fillian breathed as he waited for her to get in her silver Acura and drive away.

"Can Grandma really take us away?" Weston asked as Gregory held him and Marnie, both kids upset.

"No. You're going to stay with me. That was what your mom and dad wanted, so that's what's going to happen." Gregory sounded confident, and Fillian put his hand on his shoulder just to let him know he had his support.

"But Grandma was mad," Marnie said. "And she's mean when she's mad."

Gregory hugged the kids more tightly. "It's okay. She's mad at me, not you. And that's okay. She can be mad at me all she wants, but I'm not going to let either of you go. You call me Daddy, and that's what I'm going to be forever and ever. I promise you that."

Fillian wanted to shake Gregory's mother, but he stepped back and let Gregory have a few minutes with the kids while he said goodbye to the other players.

"Watch out for him," Stevie said. "She's a real terror when she wants to be."

"I know, and I promise I will," Fillian agreed. After the last of the guys left and the cloudy day shifted to mist, he returned to where Gregory was speaking quietly with the kids, who had settled down. "What do you all want for dinner? We can cook."

"Can I help?" Marnie asked.

"Of course. You both can." Fillian met Gregory's grateful gaze. He had clearly been through the wringer. "We can stop at the store and get some of your favorite things, if that's okay with your daddy."

"Ice cream and cupcakes?" Weston asked.

"Sure," Gregory agreed, and once he got the kids in the truck, Fillian followed him over to the store. They got a cart and wheeled it through the aisles.

"I don't know why she has to be that way," Gregory said in a whisper as the kids stood in front of the freezer case to pick out the flavor of ice cream they wanted. The cart already had chicken and beef in it, along with cupcakes, eggs, and a few other essentials. "She wasn't a good mother to Arthur or to me, and my father wasn't much better. They had their own lives and made very little room for us. For the longest time I thought that sort of family dynamic was normal. But watching your family and your mom and dad showed me that there was something different. At least from the outside."

"I'm sorry," Fillian said, not sure what else there was to say.

"And now she wants to raise Arthur's kids the same way she raised us. Mom isn't interested in raising these kids any more than she was interested in raising me and Arthur. I won't put the kids through what we went through. I know Arthur wouldn't have wanted that." He stopped the cart and got some bags of frozen veggies as the kids came over with a carton of double chocolate brownie ice cream.

"Can we have this?" Marnie asked.

"If you want," Gregory told her before adding it to the cart. "Is there anything else we need? If not, we should get to the checkout so we can go home and get dinner started. It's a little late, and you both need baths and to get ready for bed right after we finish dinner." He seemed worn out, so Fillian took charge of the groceries before getting them checked out and following Gregory home.

"HOW ABOUT chicken?" Fillian offered, and that seemed to be a hit with the kids, so he made dinner and got them all fed before Gregory took an extra-long time to put the kids to bed.

"Are they okay?" Fillian asked from the sofa. He'd cleaned up the dishes and had been waiting for him.

Gregory took a seat next to him. "Yeah. What my mother said scared them to death. Weston asked if they had been bad, and Marnie cried. I've done my best to try to keep the strain with my mother from them. I wanted the kids to have a good relationship with both their grandparents, not that they see my dad very often now that he's moved to North Carolina. But when she acts like that, I can't do anything other than keep the kids away from her."

"Was she always so self-centered?" Fillian asked. "Wait, I guess she was from what you've told me, but was she always so vehement?"

Gregory shrugged. "I think my mother blames me somehow. Arthur was always her favorite. He was the one that Mom used to take to a few of her meetings sometimes. He was the one who could sometimes make her understand that we didn't like being shuffled off all the time. Especially as he got older, Mom would listen to him. She never listened to me." He sighed and then shrugged. "At least I got them comforted and calmed down. Hopefully they'll sleep and the memory of what they saw and heard will fade."

"I don't know about that," Fillian said. "I get the feeling that your mother isn't one of their favorite people." He had noticed how they didn't get excited and run over to her when she came around. They tended to hang back. There was no excitement to see her at all. "But we can talk about something else if you like."

Gregory shifted so he was looking more in Fillian's direction. "Oh thank God," he breathed. "Anything but her." He rested his head on the back of the sofa. "Sometimes I feel like there's a box around me that keeps getting smaller and I'm being squeezed into a tighter space all the time. My mother wants to try to take the kids from me, or at least use that threat as leverage for whatever she wants, and then there's this crazy hoarder guy who doesn't want to leave me alone. Though I haven't seen him lately, it doesn't mean he isn't there. Maybe he's being more careful right now, I don't know. I'm on edge all the time, and at work…."

"How *is* work? Are you busy?" Fillian asked, trying to give Gregory an opening if he wanted to change the subject.

"I'm busy, but it's mostly small jobs, and I wonder if my stalker is going to show up or something. Then there's the kids, and I wonder if they're safe."

Fillian hugged him, and Gregory shook in his arms. "You know the worry about the kids just means you're a good parent. Your mother is only interested in what she wants, while you're the one concerned about Weston and Marnie. That says a lot." He held him tighter and closed his eyes, hoping that the act of comfort would sink in a little for Gregory.

It was becoming clear that Gregory had spent a lot of his life alone—or at least on his own. His parents weren't supportive and seemed interested in their own needs rather than those of their kids. Fillian was lucky in that regard, and he was grateful to his mom and dad every day. As a kid, he had been jealous of Gregory for all the material things he had, but as an adult, he knew he had been the true lucky one. "It will be all right."

"I wish I had your confidence," Gregory said softly, pulling back from the hug. It surprised Fillian how dull and tired Gregory seemed, like all his energy had been sapped away. Under most circumstances, Gregory was energetic. On the rugby field, he ran from end to end countless times and still had the juice to celebrate with the kids and include them when the team won. He was an amazing man, and yet in this moment, he seemed at such a low ebb.

"You will. I think you need to get some rest. You have work tomorrow, and I have to be on shift first thing." Even as the words passed his lips, he didn't want to leave. Fillian stroked Gregory's cheek, and he leaned into the touch, closing his beautiful eyes.

"I just wish that simple, gentle moments like this could go on forever," Gregory whispered.

Fillian leaned closer, and Gregory lifted his chin. Their lips met gently. Fillian only meant to provide comfort and reassurance, but Gregory pressed into the kiss, deepening it. He went along with Gregory, giving him what he needed, and soon Gregory's fingers slid through Fillian's hair, the kiss growing hotter and more desperate as Gregory shook in Fillian's arms, pouring more into the kiss, taking Fillian quickly down the road to desire.

"I need…," Gregory whispered.

"I know. But is this a good idea right now? You're vulnerable, and I won't take advantage or let you do something you might regret." No matter how much he wanted to take Gregory into his bedroom, strip the man naked, and blow their minds.

Gregory growled deep in his throat and lunged at Fillian, kissing him as he pressed him back on the sofa cushions. Damn, he seemed to have found his energy now, and it ran rampant all over Fillian, not that he was complaining.

Fillian managed to pause Gregory and got to his feet. Gregory stood as well, watching Fillian, looking deeply into his eyes as though he were searching for something. Then he took Fillian's hand and led him toward the bedroom.

Fillian had to wonder what Gregory truly wanted, even as his heart beat faster and his breath quickened. Gregory was stunning in old jeans and a T-shirt that had seen better days, both of them hugging him tightly. Fillian took a deep breath as Gregory sat on the side of the bed and looked down at his shoes.

"Talk to me," Fillian said gently. "Look me in the eyes and talk to me. Tell me what you want." He gently touched Gregory's chin just so he could look into his eyes.

"I… I need to check on the kids," he said and hurried out of the room.

Fillian sighed and took his place sitting on the side of the bed, wondering if he should go home. He had had a tough relationship before, and at the moment, Gregory reminded him of Jeffrey. He was a nice enough guy, but Jeffrey had issues—lots of them. His parents had been very strict, watching his behavior, keeping him on the straight and narrow. At least that was what they thought they were doing. What they did was build up enough guilt in their son that he'd wanted to be with Fillian badly, but would back off again as guilt took over. Fillian had endured six months of the back-and-forth because he'd liked Jeffrey, but he couldn't take the hot-and-cold-running boyfriend. It was just too much.

Gregory returned, closing the door.

"Are they asleep?" Fillian asked.

"Yes. Marnie was holding her doll, and Weston had his turtle." He lowered his gaze again. "They were so peaceful and quiet. It was like that crap with my mother hadn't happened."

"Kids are resilient, and you have to know that you had nothing to do with that. It was all on your mother. You can't let her behavior get to you, if for no other reason than you have to be the adult in the room for those two." He pointed toward the other rooms. "You can't let her get you down because you have to be strong for them."

Gregory nodded. "But who's strong for me?"

Fillian stood up, took a second to lock the door, and tugged Gregory into a kiss, pressing them together, holding Gregory as tightly as he could while kissing him with everything he had. Gregory closed his arms around him, and Fillian pushed Gregory back to the bed and then down onto the mattress. It was time that they put all their worries away, at least for a little while. Gregory needed a break, and Fillian was more than happy to provide.

"Is this what you really want?" Gregory asked as Fillian leaned over him. "I'm the parent of two kids, and I'm a mess."

"Maybe, but you're my mess," Fillian growled and took Gregory's lips once more, and within a few seconds, he felt Gregory give himself over to him. Fillian was determined to make Gregory's decision one of the best he'd ever made.

"So you really think I'm a mess?" Gregory quipped.

Fillian rolled his eyes. "What I think is that you need to stop thinking about all that." He met Gregory's gaze, holding it in his own. "It's time you try to let it all go." He released Gregory and took his hands, raising them over Gregory's head. "Put your hands together and hold them right there." He let a little police officer creep into his voice.

Gregory swallowed. "Really?"

Fillian growled deep in his throat. "Yeah." He tugged Gregory's shirt from his grip and pulled it over his head, then wrapped it around his hands. He didn't tie him or anything—Gregory could get out of the hold if he wanted. That wasn't the point.

He took a few seconds to look Gregory over, his flat belly pale and dusted with light brown hair that disappeared into his jeans. Damn, he was stunning. Fillian took a second look before placing his hands on Gregory's skin, slowly running them up his belly and chest, the muscles twitching under his touch. "You need to relax. You know I would never hurt you."

"Uh-huh," Gregory groaned softly.

"Then trust me. Put your head back, close your eyes, and just let yourself be." He ran his hands up Gregory's sides before trailing them over his pecs and tweaking both nipples, earning a soft moan. Damn, that was sexy, and he did it again, making Gregory quiver. "Sensitive...," he whispered before going in for a taste, swirling his tongue around the now tight buds, giving them a little pinch that only made Gregory shake more.

"Fillian," Gregory groaned as Fillian slipped his hands back down his belly and snapped open the top of his jeans. He let the fabric part, Gregory thrusting his hips forward. Fillian kissed him hard, pinning Gregory to the bed with his lips, letting his hands roam over the denim.

Gregory was big, long, and hard as hell. He whimpered, pressing into Fillian's hand. Kissing him harder, Fillian eased down the zipper but otherwise left his pants right where they were. He was intent on taking his time, though Gregory seemed in a hurry. "Just relax. There's plenty of time for everything. You and I are behind a locked door"— Fillian had made sure of that—"and it's just you and me." He kissed him again. "Breathe deeply, in... and out.... Just concentrate on that. In... and out... yeah. Let the oxygen get to your head and get rid of everything negative." He kept his voice low. "Close your eyes."

"Okay," Gregory whispered. Fillian cradled his head in one arm, letting the other roam down his belly, teasing him as he tasted those succulent lips. "But I want...."

"I know you do, and you'll get everything you desire... but slowly. No rushing and no worries." Damn, he wanted Gregory to have a chance to breathe. His life had been running at top speed, and Fillian had had a front-row seat for the past few weeks. The man needed a break and a release. Fillian intended to give him both. "Do you think you can live with that?"

"You really are a sadist, you know that?" Gregory said, his lips curling upward slightly.

"Actually, I'm not. And don't even think about calling me a tease, because I'm not that either. Remember, a tease doesn't put out, and I have every intention of getting you so hot that when you do come, you're going to worry about your mind melting." He kissed away further words, sliding his hand down, cupping Gregory through his boxers.

The whimper against his lips was priceless. Fillian kissed him harder before pulling away. He smiled down at Gregory, loving the view of the sexy man laid out before him.

Slowly, because he had some mercy, he tugged off Gregory's shoes and then his socks. He caressed his feet, running his thumbs over the pads. Then he slid his hands up his legs before pulling the jeans down and off and letting them drop to the floor. "You know, you're magnificent."

Gregory scoffed. "No, I'm not. I used to have time to work out, and now I carry kids and eat when I can, and I'm getting flabby."

Fillian leaned over him. "Don't give me any bull." He leaned closer and sucked at one of Gregory's nipples, then moved down his belly.

"Fillian," Gregory whined. "Damn, you're going to kill me."

"I wouldn't want that." Fillian tugged off Gregory's boxers, leaving him naked and gorgeous, his cock stretching toward his belly. "Is this what you wanted?" He gripped his length and stroked slowly.

Gregory sighed, putting his head back. "It's been a long time...."

The hot length in his hand jumped at the attention, and Fillian smiled before he leaned forward, parting his lips and taking Gregory between them. He sucked him deep, then held still before easing off, doing it over and over. The sounds Gregory made were glorious, as was the way he reacted. The man was a live wire filled with energy and tension. "Then it's time you had someone to care for you." Fillian pulled off his shirt and let Gregory get a good look at him. Then he toed off his shoes and slipped his pants down his legs.

"Talk about magnificent," Gregory whispered. "Damn...."

Fillian knew he looked good—he worked hard at it, and keeping fit was part of his job—but the heat in Gregory's eyes was more than ample reward. "Like what you see?"

Gregory nodded, his gaze staying on him. That alone was exciting, but Gregory groaned and freed his hands, then sat up to tug Fillian to him before burying his face against Fillian's skin, inhaling deeply.

Fillian carded his fingers through Gregory's hair. "What do you want?" he whispered. Gregory lifted his gaze. "What will make you happy right now?" He stepped back and tugged Gregory to his feet, standing toe to toe with him. "You need to tell me."

Gregory shook his head. His face turned cherry red. "We don't talk about that sort of thing."

Fillian closed the distance between them. "In here, we talk about everything. Nothing is off limits, and there is no shame or worry. This is a safe place no matter what." He wrapped Gregory in his arms and propelled him back against the bed. Gregory tumbled onto the mattress once more. "Close your eyes and tell me what you want."

"To forget," Gregory answered.

Fillian didn't need any more elaboration as he kissed Gregory into silence. If the man wanted to forget, he could make that happen. "Anything else?" Fillian cocked his eyebrows. "Tell me what it is you like."

Gregory blinked at him.

"Are you a pitcher or a catcher? Do you have fantasies about a little pain with your pleasure?"

Gregory shook his head. "Nothing like that. Just...." His words tapered off. "I like being a catcher," he finally said.

"Good, because I really like to pitch." He got Gregory comfortable, his head resting on the pillows. He really was stunning, and Fillian's mouth watered just looking at him. "I like to be the one in charge." He held Gregory's hands again. "But what I like most is seeing the fire in your eyes and hearing those little whimpers you make when something feels good." He licked one of Gregory's nipples, then sucked lightly. "Just like that."

"You think you know me already?" Gregory asked.

Fillian smiled. "I know some things, and the rest are going to be my pleasure—and yours—as I find out."

When he kissed Gregory again, it was like lightning shot between them. The electricity was undeniable. Gregory shook with it, and Fillian found his own control slipping. There was something about Gregory that made him want to make him happy. But it was more than that. He knew that Gregory had the potential to touch his heart, and that was frightening.

His past relationships hadn't ended well, and he had a tendency to pick the wrong guys. But this felt so right here. Gregory even *tasted* right, his skin salty sweet, his lips wet but not too wet, the pressure perfect... and he tasted like ambrosia. Fillian slid down Gregory's body, licking a trail down his chest and belly, loving the way his breath hitched. Damn, Gregory was responsive. He held his breath in anticipation, then moaned steadily as Fillian took him between his lips and sucked his long, thick cock farther and farther, sending quivers of excitement through him. It only made Fillian want to push him more.

"Fillian," Gregory whimpered urgently, carding his fingers through Fillian's hair, shaking intensely. He knew that tone of desperation, and Fillian sucked harder, his own desire rising at the sound. There was nothing sexier than a man nearing the intense relief of climax, and Fillian reveled in it as Gregory grew closer to the precipice. "I can't...."

Fillian didn't want him to. He bobbed his head as his mind clouded and pure instinct took over. He drew Gregory to the edge and held him there before taking him over. As Gregory tumbled into release, his own quickly descended on him, and Fillian swallowed hard as he throbbed through his own climax.

Gregory lay back on the bed, breathing deeply, spent, his eyes closed. Fillian lay next to him, unable to move. He listened to Gregory's breathing, grateful the apartment was otherwise quiet. At least their intensity hadn't made enough sound to wake the kids.

Gregory slipped under the covers and pulled them up over both of them. Then Fillian rolled over, cradling Gregory in his arms, wishing he could stay all night. It felt wonderful to have someone to hold and to be held back.

"Night," Gregory whispered and kissed him gently. "Do you think we should talk about what just happened?"

Fillian held him tighter. "I don't know that we have to now. Just close your eyes and rest." The last thing he wanted was to dissect what had just happened. Not that he regretted it; he didn't. But being with Gregory came with complications, and whether he was ready for it or not, he had just taken a further step to embroiling himself in them. He tried not to think too deeply.

"You should take your own advice and try to get some sleep. I know you have to get up for your shift early in the morning, and you're going to need your rest if you're to help keep yourself and everyone else safe from evildoers." He smiled slightly.

"You make me sound like a superhero." Fillian liked the sound of that, even if it was far from the truth.

"Maybe you are."

"And what would my superhero name be?" He smirked, wondering what Gregory would come up with.

Gregory yawned and sighed softly. "I don't know. You could be the Gay Crusader, fighting for truth and justice with a gun that shoots sparkles and sprinkles." He nestled closer.

"Yeah… well… I'm no superhero." He closed his eyes and tried to rest, but there was too much going on in his head. Still, after a long day and with another ahead of him, sleep finally came, and he let himself fall into it. All his worries and doubts would still be there when he woke, and there was nothing he could do about them now.

"Sure you are," Gregory said, just loud enough for Fillian to hear.

CHAPTER 8

"Do you have a game today?" Marnie asked.

"I do," Gregory said. "Do you and Weston want to come?" His mother had offered to sit with them, but he wasn't willing to forget or trust her after what she had said the last time they'd met or forgive her for her harshness. The truth was that she had called a few times and been nice for the past week, but that didn't mean that her intentions had changed.

"Yes."

"Are we playing those carpet bastards again?" Weston asked with a grin. "I know you can beat them."

"That's enough of that language," he scolded, reminding himself to have a talk with Uncle Stevie as well as the rest of the guys about what they said in front of the kids. He didn't want them talking like that. "And no, we're playing the Lancaster Comets today, so we have to get dressed because we're going there." He smiled gently.

"Is Mr. Fillian going to be there?" Marnie asked.

"I don't know." Fillian had been very busy the past few days. They had sent a few texts back and forth, but that was all. Gregory was starting to wonder if taking things to a physical level had been a mistake—a step too soon. Though he thought things had been intense between them, and amazing, when he'd woken the following morning, the bed had been empty and cold, meaning that Fillian had left some time before. "Go get ready to go. It's supposed to be a nice day today." He already had his bag with his uniform. He packed a cooler with drinks and snacks for the kids and took that down to the truck.

By the time he was done, Weston and Marnie were dressed, and they made the hour drive east to Lancaster and the large park on the edge of town.

"There's a playground. Can we go?" Weston pointed as they walked toward the field.

"If you like," Gregory agreed. "But only for a little while. The game will start in half an hour, and I need to have you nearby."

Weston sighed as though all the unfairness of the world rested on his shoulders. "Okay." He and Marnie ran off, and Gregory carried his gear and the cooler toward the field, keeping an eye on the kids.

"Where's Fillian?" Stevie asked as he dropped his stuff near the metal stands. "I thought he would ride with you."

Gregory shrugged. "No idea."

Stevie's eyes widened. "Is there trouble in paradise? I thought the two of you were thick as thieves." He shook his head.

"Don't be a smartass," Gregory retorted. "And for God's sake, watch what you say around the kids. Weston has picked up some interesting turns of phrase, and I don't want him to get any more." He just knew Uncle Stevie was responsible.

"Fine. I'll be careful about what I say in front of your kids. Shit, damn, piss, fuck, fuck, poop, wanker, bugger, ass. Motherfucker!" He smiled as Gregory rolled his eyes. "Gotta get it out now or else it builds up." He turned as that grin became wicked, and Gregory wondered what else he was going to be subjected to. "Look who's here. It seems you'll get your chance to figure things out." He winked as Fillian set his gear next to Gregory's. "I'll leave you alone so the two of you can get your sh… stuff together… and you can stop moping like a lovesick teenager," Stevie added in a stage whisper before darting off.

"What was that about?" Fillian asked, following Stevie with his gaze.

"I don't know," Gregory answered flatly. "The game starts in fifteen. I need to change and check on the kids." He turned and pulled off his shirt, took out his jersey, and put it on. Then he jogged to the playground. He leaned on the fencing, watching them. It was better than talking to Fillian at the moment.

Until he'd seen Fillian, he hadn't realized how hurt and angry he was. They had slept together, and then Fillian had snuck out of bed like a thief in the night. Yeah, Gregory knew that he couldn't stay, but the least Fillian could have done was wake him up to say goodbye. Instead, he'd left, which made Gregory feel dirty and more than a little embarrassed, especially by the way he'd acted. Then, over the next few days, Fillian hadn't texted or called. He'd answered Gregory's messages, but that was it. Gregory couldn't help wondering if he'd done something wrong. That voice in the back of his head kept telling him that he had rushed things and scared Fillian off somehow.

He focused on the kids and sighed. Maybe it was too much to expect that any single guy would take on someone like him. Asking a guy to accept him as well as two young kids was a hell of a lot. Gregory had thought Fillian liked all of them, but maybe that was too much to hope for.

"Daddy," Weston said as he raced over, "I wanna stay here while you play your game."

"I know you do, but you have to come over where I can see you." He didn't want to bring up Lawrence and frighten him, but the play area was too far away, and even though Lawrence hadn't been seen around for the past week, it didn't mean that he had given up. Every day without him showing up only raised his hopes that he had moved on and had found someone else to fixate on a little more.

"Daddy," Weston whined, pooching out his lower lip. "The games are so long." He made it seem like the entire world was going to end or that his head would explode if he had to watch the whole thing.

"We brought things for you and Marnie to do, remember?" Gregory said.

A hand settled on his shoulder, and Gregory tensed. He knew it wasn't Fillian. The touch was wrong. He turned quickly. "Hey, Cherie."

"Stevie sent me over to remind you the game starts in a few minutes and Coach is going to want to talk to all of you before the game."

"Thanks. Marnie, Weston, we need to go back to the field."

"I can stay here with them for a while," Cherie said. "You can let them play and run out all their energy."

"Are you sure?" Gregory asked.

Cherie smiled and ran her hands over her belly. "It will be good practice for me. Stevie and I aren't telling a lot of people because it's still early, but I'm due in January." Now that Gregory looked closer, her smile was a little brighter, and her eyes shone.

"Congratulations."

"Go on before Coach pops a button. I'll bring the kids over in a little while," Cherie said, and Gregory thanked her before calling Marnie and Weston over and telling them to be good and to mind Aunt Cherie. Then he over and joined the guys.

"Glad you could join us," Coach growled. "Now, let's get down to brass tacks. These Lancaster guys mean business. They've beaten everyone else so far this year and clobbered the carpet bastards a few weeks back, so we're going to need everyone to put their heads, bodies, and asses in this game." He glared at Fillian and then at him. "Got it?"

"Yes!" they all replied together.

"Now go out there and kick some ass." They broke apart and got into position, and play began.

Gregory didn't have time to think about the kids, because if he did, there was a Lancaster guy ready to take him down. The play was rough, dirty, and damned gritty. The Lancaster men played loosely enough with the rules to make the game extra physical. Gregory's team had plenty of ability and strength to counter, but it made for a hard game that tested the endurance of every player.

Early in the second half, Fillian had the ball and was about to pass to Stevie when he was tackled hard. A second and then more opposing players piled on. "Shit," Gregory said under his breath, pulling one of the players and then another off Fillian while Stevie ripped the jersey off a third when he yanked the back of his shirt to keep him from joining in.

Whistles went off everywhere while the coaches and refs pulled men off Fillian, who somehow had managed to come up with the ball.

"You okay?" Gregory asked him. Fillian groaned, and Gregory helped him to his feet. "Catch your breath while they sort all this out."

Fillian nodded. "Jesus. What kind of truck hit me?" He continued taking deep breaths.

"Are you sure you're all right? That was one hell of a hit and jam-on." Gregory let Fillian breathe and turned away, checking for Cherie and the kids, who had joined the rest of the spectators on the stands. He waved as Lancaster was assessed a penalty for roughness. Gregory's team were already slightly ahead, and Fillian made good, which added padding to their slight lead, but Gregory knew it was only going to increase the physical play of the Lancaster team. He could feel it deep down.

Play resumed, and sure enough, the level of physicality increased. It was clear that this was going to be a game of endurance. "Hold the damned scrum and let's kick some ass," Stevie growled as they huddled together, ready to go at the other team.

"Go, Daddy!" wafted over the field as the rest of the onlookers grew quiet. Gregory looked at Fillian, who gave him energy, so in their push down the field, he dug deep, grunting and setting a grueling pace that the other men matched, overwhelming the Lancaster team, setting up another score. That seemed to break their spirit, and while the game continued to the finish, there was no doubt who the victors were going to be.

"Beer to celebrate!" Stevie called as the guys backslapped and lifted Gregory onto their shoulders.

"Put me down or you'll hurt yourselves," Gregory chided. They complied, and the celebrations continued.

"See you back in town. Molly's at six," Stevie called, and the guys whooped and put up another cheer before gathering their gear and heading to cars. Gregory got his things together as Weston and Marnie hurried over, and he hugged both of them.

"Let's get to the truck, okay?" He was tired, revved up, and just wanted to get home. He got the kids in their seats, thanked and hugged Cherie for looking after them, and then headed for home.

Marnie and Weston fell asleep in the back seat after about fifteen minutes, giving Gregory time to think—not that anything fell into place.

"Can we get Molly Tots?" Marnie asked as he exited the freeway at the edge of town.

"I think I just want to go home, okay? I'm really tired. I'll make some dinner and we can all watch a movie together with popcorn and stuff." They loved movie nights, and Gregory wasn't up for being social, especially if Fillian was going to be there. The more he thought about it, the more it felt like he was pulling away, and the last thing Gregory wanted was to have some huge talk about how it was all too much. He understood, but he'd let himself get his hopes up, and he felt stupid about that. Moreover, he didn't want to have to stare across the tap room at Fillian all evening. "I'll make you tater tots with cheese and bacon." He wasn't above a little bribery to get what he wanted.

"Okay," Weston huffed, while Marnie wiggled in her seat, clearly happy. Gregory was just relieved.

He got them home and parked in back to carry the cooler and his gear upstairs. He got the laundry going and the kids settled at the table before hurrying off to shower. He had no idea how long he would have before they argued about something, so even though they were coloring and happy, he grabbed clean clothes and jumped in the shower, then washed quickly to get the dirt off.

The hot water was so damned tempting. It felt good, and he wanted nothing more than to spend a few minutes under it. His mind was already conjuring up images from the other night with Fillian leaning over him, his strong compact body glistening with a light sheen of sweat.

A crash from the other room pulled him back to reality. He turned off the water, grabbed a towel, and wrapped it around his waist before peering out the bathroom door. "What was that?"

"Weston knocked over the crayons," Marnie said. Both kids were on the floor, picking them up and putting them back into the plastic container.

"I tried to find the blue one, and it was all the way on the bottom," Weston explained as someone knocked on the door. Marnie hurried over and opened it before Gregory could stop her.

"Hey," Fillian said to her, and Gregory knew the second his gaze lifted and it fell on him. "Gregory," he said softly, a little breathily. "I came to see if you were joining the others, but from the looks of things, I guess you all are staying in."

"Daddy is going to make cheesy tots, and we're going to make popcorn and watch movies." Weston hurried over and took Fillian's hand. "You can sit here and watch with us."

"I think Fillian was planning to go celebrate with the rest of the rugby team," Gregory said, his skin heating under Fillian's gaze. "I'm going to get dressed. I'll be back out in a minute." He figured he'd give Fillian a chance to escape without a bunch of drama. Gregory dressed in light sweats and a T-shirt before returning to the living room, where the kids sat next to Fillian as they all watched *Teenage Mutant Ninja Turtles* cartoons.

"Aren't you going out with the guys?" Gregory asked.

Fillian stood and joined him in the kitchen area. "Is that what you really want me to do?"

Gregory shook his head. "Don't play games with me," he retorted. "You snuck out, and then you go mostly silent on me for days. Now you show up like nothing happened. I don't know what you want or what you're looking for. I know you're busy and so am I, but…."

Infuriatingly, Fillian nodded. "Then why don't we talk once the kids are in bed?"

Gregory nodded and went back to making the kids their dinner, trying to cook and keep his attention on the food rather than on Fillian.

LAUGHTER FILLED the room as Gregory made up plates and took one to each of the kids. He also made one up for Fillian and handed it to him before sitting down to eat and start *Mulan*. It was Marnie's favorite, and tonight was her turn to pick. In the next round he was going to have to make sure that both kids chose different movies or his head was going to explode.

"Are you sure you don't want to watch something else?" Gregory asked, trying a final time.

"I wanna watch *Mulan*," she reiterated.

"Do we have to?" Weston whined, looking up with pleading eyes Gregory understood very clearly.

"We'll watch *Mulan* this time, but not again," he told Marnie before starting the movie. "I'm going to make popcorn." At least he had an escape.

Fillian got up to help him. "I take it movies are a flashpoint."

Gregory got the first bag of popcorn in the microwave. "Marnie always wants to watch this one, and it's getting a little old for the rest of us. All I can say is that at least it's not *Frozen*. I ended up deleting it from the player before I went crazy." He put on some butter to melt and got out the large popcorn bowl as well as some napkins. "But it seems she's just as fixated on this one."

"I guess she likes it," Fillian said. "It does have a strong girl lead."

"I know, and I want her to be strong, but I also don't want my brain to melt. Not that it really matters. I'll make some popcorn, and they'll be ready for bed when the movie is over and I can put on something else… and it was her turn." He smiled as Mulan sang her first song on screen.

Once the first batch of popcorn was done, he made a second and added it to the bowl, then lightly poured over melted butter while tossing the popcorn, watching Fillian as he leaned against the counter. "Why are you still here? Honestly. I could almost feel you putting distance between us, and if that's what you want to do, it's okay. You have a right, but I can't have an off-again, on-again kind of thing. Being with me means being part of the kids' lives as well as mine, and they deserve some stability."

"I get that. But it's a huge step." Fillian shifted his weight. "After… last time, I got to thinking, and…." He sighed. "Look, I needed some time to think."

Gregory could well understand that. "Yeah, me too."

"I love the kids. They're great, and they seem to like me." He smiled at them as they sat entranced in front of the television. "And I like you too. You're really sexy, and we seem to have a good time together. But I keep wondering where the bad stuff is. There's always something hidden somewhere, and I keep wondering when something is going to happen and everything will fall apart, because it usually does for me. So I tried keeping my head clear so I could figure it out, but all I did was think about what you and the kids were doing." He shrugged. "I missed all of you."

"And that was bad?"

"No. It meant I was looking for trouble rather than just taking things as they were. I kept wondering if I had done the right thing, and I still keep asking myself if I'm getting in over my head." Fillian watched the kids while Gregory filled glasses of ice water.

"Did you come up with any answers?"

Fillian shook his head. "Not really. I guess I was looking for something that didn't have an answer. I mean, no one knows what's going to happen next. And the more I thought about things, the more I thought about you and the more I missed you."

"Then why didn't you call or let me know? Maybe I was asking the exact same questions. Did you think of that?" He made sure the kids weren't paying attention to them. Then he turned back to Fillian.

"I was scared. I can handle chasing a speeder down the highway at a hundred miles an hour, but just the thought of Weston or Marnie being unhappy makes me want to do whatever I can to make things better. I've never felt that before… for anyone. Do you know how frightening that is?" Fillian rolled his eyes. "Of course you do."

"Yeah, and I understand the fear. Those first months I had the kids, I barely slept. I'd lie awake worrying that I was going to hurt them or do something to scar them for life."

"They adore you," Fillian said.

Gregory set down the bowl on the counter. "Every time one of them calls me Daddy, it warms my heart. When I first got them, they both called me Uncle Gregory. Then over time Weston started calling me Daddy Gregory. I never pushed either of them. Arthur was a good father, and I didn't want to take his place. But I'm not afraid to tell you that the first time they each called me Daddy, I went into the bathroom and cried. I did it for Arthur, because he never got to see them grow into the amazing people they are and will become. And… being daddy to anyone was something I never thought would happen. Part of me even felt guilty, because maybe I was taking Arthur's place. But then I realized that he would be pleased that his kids were happy. That was all Stephanie and Arthur ever really wanted for them." He sighed, pulled out an old wooden tray, and put the popcorn bowl and the glasses on it.

"I think you're a great dad," Fillian said, moving closer before Gregory lifted the tray. "And I promise I'll try to be a better boyfriend." He kissed him, and Gregory returned it.

"Just don't cut me out."

Fillian nodded and kissed him again. Then Gregory took the tray in and they all sat down to watch the rest of the movie, with Fillian's hand slipping into his.

CHAPTER 9

FILLIAN HAD stayed through the movie, and once the kids said good night and Gregory put them to bed, the two of them talked about the state of things—what they both wanted and hoped for. Not just in a relationship, but what they really dreamed of. Gregory hoped that someday he'd be able to grow his business into a major electrical contracting firm. It seemed Gregory wanted to be in charge of major projects, which Fillian thought was ambitiously awesome. "I want to be able to send the kids to college and give them a real start in life."

Fillian had shared the fact that he wanted to make captain and be in charge of one of the state police posts or even head of the department. "But there's so much politics at that level."

"Politics is everywhere," Gregory told him. "Don't let that stop you from dreaming." Eventually Gregory had put on another movie—one for them—and they sat together, just the two of them. They still paused the movie a few times to talk a little, but talking to Gregory felt right, and part of Fillian wondered just what he'd been so worried about.

The following morning, Fillian rode out to where he believed Lawrence was living. Once he arrived at the scene of the fire, he noticed a number of changes. The area around the house had been cleaned up considerably, with a lot of the debris cleared away and parts of the old structure knocked down, likely for safety reasons.

He parked and cautiously made his way along the path back to where he'd found the camp a few days earlier. But it had been cleared out. The tent and sleeping bags were gone, along with the rest of the gear. All that remained were a few bits of trash and a lot of flattened grass.

"Dammit," he swore under his breath. His last few shifts he had been run off his feet and hadn't been able to get out here, but it seemed he was too late and Lawrence had moved from the one spot Fillian had hoped he'd find him. Fillian checked around the area just to make sure Lawrence hadn't merely moved his camp before leaving the area.

"Can I help you, Officer?" a man asked as Fillian stepped out of the woods. "Mason Carpenter," he added as an introduction. "I take it you're looking for my camping tenant." He scowled as he turned to what was left of the house.

"Yes. He's been causing some issues." Fillian purposely kept his answer vague. "I found the camp last week and was hoping he might come back to it. When was the last time he was here, Mr. Carpenter?"

"Thursday." So three days ago. "The men I hired to shore up the place reported where he was camping. They ran him off and told him that they were going to need to clear his area, and if he didn't want everything flattened.... The men said he gathered his stuff and was gone fast. I don't know where he is, but good riddance." There was clearly no love lost between the two of them.

"Were you aware of the condition of the house?"

"Yes. That's why I was in the process of evicting him. His mother was the original tenant, and she'd been here for years. Nice lady. He moved in with her to take care of her, and I guess he intended to stay after she passed. I didn't think anything about it until two weeks ago, when I came out because he said there was a problem with the electrics. I saw the mess and knew I needed to get him out. I started eviction proceedings and called an electrician...." Fillian knew the rest. "Then, when I have the place cleaned up, I find him camping on the property."

Fillian nodded. "Do you have any idea where he might have gone?"

Mr. Carpenter shrugged. "No idea. The men said he took off. By the time I got here, the camp had been cleared out. I'm trying to secure the place as best I can and make sure no one gets hurt until the insurance company is done with their investigations. Then I can clear the land and figure out what I'm going to do next."

"Has there been a determination as to what caused the fire?" Fillian had looked up the fire marshal's report, but it was still ongoing.

"He had tanks of propane in here, and he was using them to cook. Since he never threw anything out, the old tanks were in there too, apparently. We were all lucky everyone was out of the house when it went up. Lots of people are looking for him. The insurance company wants to talk to him, and I want some answers too."

"I bet you do." Fillian couldn't blame Mr. Carpenter for being upset with Lawrence. The guy wasn't exactly one of Fillian's favorite people either. "If you see him again, please give me a call." He handed him one of his cards. "I'd like to speak to him as well."

"I will," he agreed, and Fillian went back to his cruiser. At least there was some explanation as to why he hadn't been around. But deep down, Fillian had a pretty good idea that Lawrence would be back, and his gut told him that he wasn't going to be content to simply watch for much longer.

"WHAT HAS you so worked up?" Wyatt asked as they met on the median of the freeway. They were both on duty to control speed on highway eighty-one.

"I thought I had a lead on the guy who has been giving Gregory a bad time. I'd found his camp, but not him. Now the camp is gone."

Wyatt nodded. "Look, for now, let this go. If he hasn't been hanging around, then maybe he figured out that his bail was in jeopardy and he had a chance to cool down. You said he hadn't been seen in a while."

"I know. But I want to make sure Gregory and the kids are safe. I hate the thought—"

Wyatt cut him off. "This is personal for you, but you can't let it get that way. It's easy to take things too far, which is what you're on the verge of right now. Unless there is a report of him breaking bail and we have solid evidence, it will be seen as you overextending yourself, especially with Reynolds. The captain is a stickler for procedure, and going out on a limb for personal reasons isn't going to endear you to him. You've been with us just a few years, and in his eyes that still makes you a rookie."

"Yeah. But the guy didn't have permission to live on the property, and before the explosion, he was being evicted from the house. Is that enough of a parole violation?"

Wyatt sighed. "Possibly. But there would be questions about your motive for checking on him in the first place. There hasn't been a formal report, has there? Gregory told you he hasn't called it in, so that makes a difference as well. Like I said, the best thing to do is to back off on this one until there is something more for you to go on."

Fillian knew Wyatt was right, but that didn't make it any easier.

"If the guy is violating his bail, then wait until we get a formal report and look into it closely. You already have information to go on, so track it down then. And if Gregory is concerned, then he can make a formal report. That would mean you were covered."

"I suppose you're right." As much as he hated to admit it. "Fine. I'll back away." Hopefully Lawrence would decide to keep a low profile.

Wyatt received a call, so he rolled up his window and pulled out into traffic, heading back toward town with his lights on. Fillian expected he'd receive one as well, and seconds later he was right behind him, the two of them heading toward Shippensburg to an accident that threatened to shut down the entire freeway. Traffic was already backed up for two miles by the time they wove their way through the stopped cars and trucks to reach the scene of destruction that involved two cars, a tipped-over semi, and a camper in pieces covering both southbound lanes.

It was a mess. First fire trucks were called to ensure that the semi, which had ended up on its side, didn't burst into flames with the diesel all over the highway. Then ambulances arrived to help the wounded, followed by interviews and evidence-gathering to try to piece together what happened. Traffic had to be diverted off the highway and onto country roads around the scene. And that was only the beginning. Once the mess was cleared up and the freeway opened again, there would be a mountain of paperwork and reports to write and submit. Finishing all that work took Fillian until just before the end of his shift.

To say he was tired was an understatement. During the day he had received a few messages from Gregory that he had answered briefly to let him know that he was at an accident scene. The messages had stopped, but he knew Gregory was probably at home with the kids, so he stopped at the diner along the way home and picked up some soup and sandwiches for all of them before stopping by the apartment.

Fillian climbed the stairs. Raised voices reached his ears as he approached the door. Fillian knocked loudly, and the voices hushed. Heavy footsteps approached the door, and it opened. Gregory stood there, his shoulders slumped. He opened the door farther so Fillian could see his mother, fire coming from her eyes, hands on her hips, one hand in the air like she had been lecturing Gregory.

"What is he doing here? You and I need to finish talking about these kids," she snapped.

"Where are they?" Fillian asked Gregory.

"With the neighbor. They're playing with her son for a little while," Gregory explained.

"That's none of his business," Gregory's mother snarked as she drew forward. "Gregory and I have things that we need to get straight, so whatever you want, I'm sure it can wait until later."

Damn, she was an even bigger piece of work that Fillian had thought. "I thought you and the kids might want to join me for dinner, so I stopped by the diner and got soup and sandwiches." He went over to the counter. "You can have them later when you're ready." He didn't think it was his place to get in the middle of things.

"No. My mother is under the illusion that she is the mother of all mothers and that she gets to decide how Weston and Marnie are raised and who they get to see." Gregory turned back to her while Fillian got a glass of water in the kitchen area. "At best you were an absent mother for me and Arthur. At worst, if someone had called Child Services, we would have been put into care for parental neglect. Nannies are one thing, but you were never around. And you have the nerve to come in here to lecture me about what Weston and Marnie are doing? I was granted full custody in the will and ultimately by the court."

"We'll see if that lasts," she snapped back.

Fillian set down his glass and stood next to Gregory. "You really want to go there?" he asked. "These are your grandchildren, and going down this road is only going to end up with you never seeing them again. The kids are already growing scared of you, and I've seen the way you act around them... and how you treat your son."

"And you think any court is going to listen to someone like you?" The sneer was inescapable. Was she stuck in the sixties or something?

Gregory shook his head. "The court isn't going to listen to you any more than anyone else, and you have to have a valid, legal reason to challenge the will. Furthermore, you've threatened to call Child Services, but again, you have to have a reason for that call... and you don't. So your choices are to live within the rules that I set as Marnie and Weston's parent, or not see your grandchildren. They will not be staying at your house overnight, and they will not visit unattended. Those are my rules."

Fillian thought both of them were good ideas. Who knew what she would try to do if given the chance?

"And as for whatever else you have to say, I think it's best we end this conversation before we both say something we'll regret." Gregory was remarkably controlled, which Fillian found sexy. He returned to the kitchen so Gregory could see his mother out and he could get thoughts of how hot he found Gregory at that moment out of his head. Arguing with one's mother was not supposed to be a turn-on for anyone. Maybe there was something wrong with him.

"You can't just push me aside like this. I won't have it. These kids can't continue living in this small apartment with homeless people sitting out on the sidewalk eyeing the building like they're about to move in and take over."

Fillian paused to parse what she had said. He went to the window and peered out the front. Sure enough, the "homeless" guy Gregory's mother described watching the building was Lawrence. He was leaning against one of the buildings across the street, surrounded by a small pile of belongings. Fucking great. Fillian was just close enough to see the way Lawrence smiled and then flipped Fillian a single-finger salute before picking up his things and slowly moving on down the sidewalk. Great, just great. Lawrence was getting bolder and now wanted them to know he was there. Fillian let the curtains fall back into place.

One of the frustrating things about his job was that no matter what he thought he knew, he had to be able to prove any accusation he made, especially in this particular situation. Fillian wanted to charge down there, pull Lawrence aside, and find out exactly what he hoped to gain by all this. But Gregory and his mother were still in a heated battle over the kids, and Gregory needed his support at the moment.

"Gregory, I will not have this. Your brother wanted more for his kids than living in a place like this!" The disdain rolled off her tongue with such ease it made Fillian even angrier.

"What Arthur wanted was someone to raise his kids with love and as much care as possible. He knew I would do my very best for both of them, and he knew I'd love them and put them first in my life. Can you honestly say you'd do that?" The way he looked at his mother, daring her to argue, sent a shiver through Fillian, and he turned away because this was so not the time. But Gregory's strength was attractive, there was no doubt about that.

"How dare you!" The anger rolling off her was palpable. Fillian cleared his throat, fearing she would slap Gregory, and he wanted to remind her that he was there.

Gregory shrugged and walked to the door. "Good night, Mother. The kids need to eat dinner, and you need to go home and cool down. I'm tired of your demands. I know you thought you were some kind of mother of the year, but you never were. You were mostly absent, off in your own little social-climbing world." He shook his head, and she at least had the sense to leave.

"This isn't over," she said as a parting shot.

"What are you now, some kind of supervillain?" Gregory asked before closing the door. "Sometimes that woman drives me absolutely crazy. She came in here and told me that she was going to take the kids for two weeks. She and my stepfather want to go to Florida this winter, and they were going to take Marnie and Weston with them. There is no way I'm letting her take them anywhere. She used to take Arthur and me to Disney once a year, and she would leave us with a sitter so she and my father could do what they wanted. I literally could see into the parks while we sat in the hotel room. I won't have her doing that sort of thing to them."

"Hey, it's okay. I wouldn't let her take them either. What if she decides that she's going to take them to Florida and then doesn't come back? Or worse? Your permission for them to go leaves built-in delays before people take action. Besides, if you ask me, this has nothing to do with the kids and everything to do with control and who will make the decisions."

"Of course that's it. Mom was always about being the one to make the decisions and controlling what everyone did and how we all looked. I had to join the right clubs and meet the right kids. She signed me up for lacrosse one year because one of the kids of some lady she wanted to impress played. I was terrible at it, but I was stuck. To top it off, I didn't become friends with the person she wanted, and that only added more pressure from her." Gregory checked outside the door. "I need to get the kids."

"Then I'll heat up the soup and get the food out," Fillian said. He went to the kitchen and warmed the soup in the microwave while he got out sandwiches.

"Did you and Grandma fight?" Marnie asked as she came into the apartment. "I heard yelling."

"Your grandmother and I had a disagreement. But it isn't something you need to worry about," Gregory explained. "And Fillian brought us some soup for dinner."

"There's sandwiches too. I got chicken with noodles and beef with rice," Fillian said. He asked them each what they wanted and made up bowls. "Did you have a good time with your friend?"

Weston went off talking about all the things they did. Apparently Mickey had a ton of army men and they played some kind of battle game. Marnie played Barbies with Bernice. Both kids seemed happy.

"Are we going to have movies and popcorn?" Weston asked. "'Cause I wanna watch something."

"*Mulan*," Marnie said.

"Actually, I got something new for you. I don't think you've seen it, and we can all watch." Gregory caught his gaze, and Fillian nodded. "It's *Encanto*. It's supposed to be very good."

"I saw it at Marsha's house once. I liked it, but not as much as *Mulan*." Apparently Marnie had a one-track mind when it came to her movies. Still, Fillian was grateful for something else to watch.

"Is Grandma going to be mad at us?" Weston asked. "We saw her when she left. I was looking out the window, and she looked mad. Like that lady who wanted to wear dogs in the Dalmatian movie."

"Cruella de Vil," Marnie supplied.

"Yeah, her. She looked mean and mad." His gaze fell to the floor, and he shifted his weight like he was nervous. "Did we do something?"

"No," Gregory said. "If Grandma was angry, it had nothing to do with either of you. I promise." He gathered them both in a hug and held them tightly.

Fillian left the three of them to have their moment while he took the bowls to the table and placed the sandwiches on plates.

"I love both of you, and I would never let anything happen to you."

By the time Fillian had everything at the table and had poured glasses of ice water, they were all seated.

"After dinner, you need to take baths and get ready for bed. Then we can all watch the movie and have popcorn." Gregory's gaze met his, and Fillian could tell he had questions. Fillian nodded to mean that they would talk once the kids were out of earshot. Until then, Fillian ate his soup as seriousness seemed descended over all of them. The kids ate quietly, and he and Gregory had this eye conversation going on that told him absolutely nothing.

Weston sneezed, sending soup flying all over him. While Gregory helped him clean up, Fillian turned away to keep himself from laughing. He could tell Gregory was doing the same, but thankfully the dark mood had shattered. Once he was cleaned up, Weston began asking about the movie, Marnie talked about one of her dolls, and even Gregory's shoulders seemed to lose some of their rigidity.

"ARE YOU both done?" Gregory asked when the kids started to fidget. "If so, take your dishes to the sink, and then you need to get your baths. Who goes first?"

"Me," Marnie called and hurried to the sink with her dishes before running to her room.

Weston pooched out his lower lip and sighed.

"It's okay. You'll get your turn," Gregory told him.

Weston sighed. "But she takes forever."

"Go put your dishes in the sink, and I'll make sure she doesn't take forever."

He nodded and carefully took his bowl and then his plate to the sink. "You won't start the movie without me, right?"

"I promise," Gregory told him, and Weston hurried to his room. "I need to run bath water and stuff. Are you going to stay, or do you have things you need to do?"

"I'll watch TV if that's okay." Fillian took care of his dishes and let Gregory handle what he needed to. Fillian checked out the front window to make sure Lawrence hadn't returned before settling on the sofa with a rerun of *Young Sheldon*. He loved that show, but he'd already seen the episode, so he half listened to the television and the sounds of the family as he calmed down from his hectic day.

"Are you sleeping?" Weston asked as he climbed onto the sofa next to him in Sponge Bob pajamas. Marnie joined them in a Mulan nightgown. Gregory made popcorn and turned out the lights before starting the movie.

Fillian didn't remember much of what happened. He pretty much fell asleep less than half an hour in, closing his eyes as fatigue took over.

"Okay, munchkins, it's time for you to go to bed."

Fillian sat up, blinking a few times, wondering where the time went. He said good night to both kids and got a hug from each of them. Gregory put them to bed and rejoined Fillian a while later.

"Weston had a ton of questions, and Marnie wanted yet another story." He sighed. "But they're in bed and I hope asleep."

"Good." He turned away from the side of the window, careful not to move the curtains. "I hate to bring bad news, but our friend was outside watching the building. He continued on, but he wants us to know he's there. The guy isn't hiding any longer."

"Which means…?"

"I don't know. He isn't afraid, and we're no closer to knowing what it is that he wants. But I think you need to make a formal complaint."

"And say what? That he's watching us? That we see him on the sidewalk?"

Fillian turned to look at Gregory straight on. "He's out on bail, and you were hurt by him. If nothing else, then his behavior is being put on the record. We had hoped he would stop, but apparently he isn't." He was afraid Lawrence's behavior would escalate. "I didn't want to say anything in front of your mother, but she noticed him on her way in."

"I see." Gregory grew paler through the conversation. "What do I do? I want the kids to be safe."

"So do I."

"Okay. I'll call tomorrow and report him to the local police and let them know what's been happening. You'd think the guy was already in enough trouble, but no, he has to decide to harass me because I wasn't interested in him." He shook his head. "What is it with me? I didn't do anything when I was in that house with him. All I was trying to do was get my work done so I could get out of there." He shivered.

Fillian slid closer and put his arms around him. "You didn't do anything wrong, and you deserve to feel safe on the job and in your own home." Just like he deserved a mother who wasn't completely self-absorbed and more concerned with her own wants than supporting her son. But he kept that to himself because he didn't want to bring up the argument between Gregory and his mother. She was a real piece of work, and Fillian wondered if she wasn't escalating in her own way as well.

"Maybe I shouldn't let my mother in, then." Gregory snickered.

"I'm glad you can make jokes about her."

Gregory shrugged. "What am I going to do? She's always been this way. When she doesn't get what she wants, she fights and bickers until most people just give up because it's easier than fighting with her. I won't do that. Marnie and Weston are too important for that."

Fillian nodded. "You know her better than I do, but do you think she'll make good on some of her threats?"

"I don't know what she'll do or how much she thinks she'll get away with." He quivered in Fillian's arms. "But I will fight her with everything I have. This is all selfishness on her part."

"I get that." Fillian was already trying to think a few steps ahead.

"When Arthur and Stephanie were killed, I was in a much smaller place. I managed to find this apartment in a short time, and because of the adoption and stuff, Social Services was involved. They inspected the place and everything. My mother was all up in arms then because it wasn't a house and because it was too small… or their rooms weren't big enough. She actually tried to ingratiate herself with the social worker, though it didn't work then and it isn't likely to work now. But Mom could cause trouble, I'm sure."

Fillian sat up. "I'm not sure what I can do to help. Do you know who you worked with during the transition?"

Gregory got up and went to his room. He returned with a small box, sat down, and began going through it. "I know I have his business card in here somewhere." He continued rifling through it. "Here it is." Gregory handed it to him.

"I know Donald. He's a good guy, and his husband is a police officer in town. Carter Schunk. I worked with him once on a cooperative effort between departments last year. It was some thefts in the area that crossed jurisdictions…." He stopped himself. "You don't need to know the details." He held the card, his mind flowing quickly. "Do you mind if I make a phone call and see if I can get some help on both fronts?"

Gregory shrugged. "I don't want to bother anyone."

"I won't if you don't want me to. That's why I asked." This had to be Gregory's decision.

"Do you think they can help?"

"For now, it will be a friendly call," Fillian said and pulled out his phone. He looked up Carter's number, checked the time, and made the call.

"Fillian," Carter said brightly. "What's up?"

"Sorry if it's too late, but I have a little bit of a problem, and I need some assistance. This isn't official or anything."

"I told you if you needed something to call, and I meant it. What's going on?"

"Well, I have a friend who's having some trouble. He was at the house that blew up a few weeks ago between Carlisle and Newville. He was my neighbor growing up, and he's having some issues."

"Is this about the suspect on bail who might be harassing his victim?" Fillian should have known Carter would be up to date on everything. "Is he still doing it?"

"Yeah. I saw him outside his building tonight. He knew I saw him too, and he doesn't seem to care. The thing is, it's victim harassment, but it's hard to prove anything." Fillian turned away and lowered his voice. "The guy was assaulted and managed to get away before the house blew up. And now he's being harassed. It stinks."

"I agree. Tell your friend to get a picture of him if possible, preferably from the apartment. Note down dates when he's been seen and where, stuff like that. Give me something solid, and I'll take it to the court here immediately. It's best if you let us do it, because that way you aren't involved and it will make the case stronger."

"Thanks." He sighed. "We'll have something to you as soon as we can get it." He cleared his throat and then told Carter about the issues Gregory was having with his mother. "Donald handled the original placement."

"Hold on," Carter said, and Fillian figured he was talking to his husband. "Okay. Donald said he can stop by first thing in the morning on his way to the office to talk to you." He thanked them and said goodbye, then set the phone down on the table.

Gregory looked around. "Do you think the place looks good enough?"

"It's clean, each of the kids has a room of their own, they're well fed, happy, and loved. It's all that Donald—or anyone except your mother—could possibly wish for," Fillian told him, slipping an arm around Gregory's shoulders, drawing him closer. "And if your mother should register a complaint, then Donald is going to have a sterling visit report on file with the department." He could already see some of the worry slip from Gregory's posture. "You have nothing to worry about."

"I hope so," Gregory said.

Fillian leaned in and kissed him gently. "I've wanted to do that ever since I got here."

Gregory sighed, leaning against him. "One thing is for sure, the kids are definite blockers, if you know what I mean."

Fillian leaned even closer until their foreheads touched. "If I just wanted sex, there are plenty of places that I could go to get that. I'm here for so much more. You make me happy, and the kids… well, as long as they're in my life, I think it's going to be exciting, and I know it will never be dull. Just thinking about you when I'm at work is enough to make me smile."

"But you know it's a lot to take on."

Fillian pulled back. "If that's your way of saying that you aren't interested…."

Gregory shook his head. "No. It's just that…."

"I know what it means. Bath nights instead of evenings in bed. It means getting up to make breakfast before sending the kids to school instead of lying in bed that extra half hour. It also means vacations to Orlando instead of a couple's retreat to Club Med. I'm well aware of what it means. But I also know that I'd have a family of my own, and my mother would be over the moon to have grandchildren. It means doing things as a family for the next twelve to twenty years. I'm well aware of all of it. So don't use that as an excuse. If you aren't ready or don't want a relationship, then that's one thing, but don't use them as an excuse. That isn't fair to the kids, me, or yourself."

"Maybe you're right." He looked toward the closed bedroom doors. "I worry about them, you know. What if I mess things up? What if I leave them with some sort of complex?"

"And what if you show them that love and care can come in many different packages and that it doesn't matter who the people are or what they look like?" Fillian said gently. "That's what counts. That they're loved and that they know it, no matter what. The rest will come out in the wash."

"How do you know? Look at the role model I had. What if I become exactly like her?"

"Just asking that question means you won't. Now, go check on the kids, and I'll put on something we can watch for a while before we go to bed."

CHAPTER 10

GREGORY WOKE with Fillian wrapped around him. He was warm, but in the best way possible. The window toward the side of the building was open, a breeze blowing through. Carefully, he extricated himself from Fillian's embrace, pulled on his robe, and went to the bathroom. Once he was done, he got a drink of water and peeked in on each of the kids, who were sound asleep.

On returning, he went back through the living room. Something wasn't right. He looked around and didn't see anything, but when he inhaled, something was wrong. The room smelled strange, like the faint scent of an old cigarette. Gregory checked the door, where the scent grew stronger. After unlocking it and pulling it open, he found the hallway outside filled with smoke. He slammed the door closed again and raced back to the bedroom.

"Fillian, there's a fire."

"What?" he asked, sitting straight up.

"The hallway to the front door is filled with smoke."

Fillian jumped out of bed and leaped into his pants. "Fire extinguisher?"

"Under the sink in the kitchen," Gregory said.

"Good. Call 911 and get the kids out the back way—now." He raced out of the room, and seconds later the front apartment door slammed. Gregory swung into action, making the call and waking the kids, taking them each by the hand and getting them out the window in Marnie's room before helping them descend the back fire escape. Chris, the single lady who lived above them, met them along the way, and the four of them made it to the ground, where they stood under one of the parking lot lights as sirens drew closer and stopped out front.

"Should we go around?" Chris asked as they stood together. She held the leash of her poodle mix, which both kids were lavishing with attention.

Gregory was wondering the same thing when a fire department vehicle pulled up to where they waited. "Is everyone out?" the huge firefighter asked as he approached.

"Yes," Chris answered. "There are only the two apartments and everyone is accounted for, including the kids."

"Excellent. The fire appears to be out, and it seems it was confined to the entrance just inside the door. Someone set fire to a pile of papers in the trash can, and it was already out when we arrived."

"Fillian must have gotten to it with the fire extinguisher," Gregory said with relief. "Is he okay?"

"Yes. He's fine. The fire was out before we got here, and he had the door open to let the smoke out. We're checking the rest of the building just to be safe, but you should be able to return in a little while."

"Did the bad man do this?" Weston asked. "The one who keeps watching Daddy?"

"I don't know," Gregory answered. "Fillian and the firemen will figure it out. I'm pretty sure of it." God, he hoped so. He could already feel his anxiety growing. He had never had issues with nerves, but now it seemed like he was watching around himself wherever he went and having trouble concentrating as his mind spun over possibilities. It got more unsettling by the day.

Gregory held both kids close, an arm around each of them, as he waited with Chris and the firefighter for some sort of word on what was happening. Finally, Fillian strode around the corner and right up to him, still in just his pair of jeans. "Everything is okay. It seems it was a trash fire with more smoke than anything else."

Weston let go and wrapped his arms around Fillian's legs. "Are you sure it wasn't the bad man?" He held Fillian tightly.

"It will be okay. It was an accident," Fillian said, meeting Gregory's eyes over Weston, telling Gregory that the truth was something different. "The firefighters are getting the smoke out, and then we can all go back inside and you can go back to bed."

"But what if more fire comes and we get burned up?" Weston asked, making Marnie cling to Gregory.

"I don't wanna burn up," Marnie said.

Gregory squatted down, hugging her tightly. "I'm going to be there, and so is Fillian. Neither of us is going to let anything happen to you. I promise." He took a deep breath, refusing to let his own worries transfer to the kids. He had to be strong and solid, because that was what they needed him to be.

"You can all go back inside," the firefighter said after receiving a message.

"Thank you," Fillian responded. He led them around to the front, where the firefighters were packing up and getting ready to leave. Gregory thanked them as he passed and went inside.

The entrance area still smelled strongly of smoke, though the air itself seemed clear enough. The trash can had been removed, and the paint was charred and blackened near where it had been, with a trail of soot running up the wall. Gregory figured it could have been much worse, and it probably would have been if Fillian hadn't been so quick to jump into action.

Inside the apartment, the scent had almost totally dissipated. Other than a slight residual odor that open windows would quickly blow away, the smoke didn't seem to have caused any damage. "Come on, you two, let's get you back to bed."

Fillian carried Weston into his room and helped him into bed, and Gregory did the same with Marnie. She settled right down after Gregory promised again that he wasn't going anywhere. He partially closed her door and returned to the small hallway. Fillian spoke softly to Weston, comforting him, before saying good night. Damn, there were few things as heartwarming as a man taking the time to comfort his son. Gregory gave Weston a kiss on the forehead, and then he and Fillian left the room.

"What do we do now?" Gregory asked, knowing he wasn't going to be able to go back to sleep right away. He was too wound up. Every noise in the building was going to have him sitting up in bed.

"Come on." Fillian led him to the sofa. "When I got down there, the papers were burning, and if the trash can had been closer to the wall, it probably would have caught fire. I was able to put the flames out with the fire extinguisher and open the door to let in fresh air. By the time the fire department arrived, it was pretty much over."

"So you think it was an accident?" Gregory asked.

Fillian shook his head. "I smelled what might have been lighter fluid or something like that. It wasn't gasoline, I don't think, but it had a petroleum smell, and there was black smoke along with the rest, so some sort of accelerant was used. The fire department took the can with everything in it, and they'll see what they can find out."

"So it looks like someone tried to set our home on fire," Gregory said.

Fillian pulled him into a tight hug. "Or scare you. Look, they set the trash on fire downstairs. The fire department is going to notify the building owners, and I'll suggest that they check the main door and make sure it's better secured. They should install a smoke detector out there as well."

"Who would want to do something like this?" Gregory asked. He tried to think of people who hated him. "Weston asked about the bad man, which I believe is Lawrence, my stalker and all-around sicko. I can't help wondering if he could be behind this." He shook his head. "What could this guy want from me?"

"The fire department will investigate thoroughly, and I'll make sure Carter knows what happened." Fillian took Gregory by the hand and led him to the bedroom. "You need to try to get some sleep, because Donald is going to be here in a few hours."

"I know." Gregory didn't know what was worse, the fire or the fact that he was going to look like hammered shit in the morning. Who knew what Donald was going to think. "You know I won't be able to sleep."

"I'll stay up and make sure nothing happens. You try to sleep." Gregory hung up his robe and got into bed. Fillian slipped out of his pants and joined him, remaining sitting up. "I'll be here, and I promise not to let anything happen to any of you." Fillian leaned over and kissed Gregory hard. "I want so much to make love to you right now, but that can wait. Just try to sleep."

Gregory burrowed under the covers and did his best to quiet his mind. When he rolled over, Fillian placed a hand gently on his hip, letting Gregory know he was there, and eventually he fell into a fitful sleep.

"DONALD IS going to be here soon, and I can hear the kids getting up," Fillian said what seemed like minutes after Gregory closed his eyes. Gregory climbed out of bed to find Fillian dressed. "I need to go in for my shift, but call me if you need anything and I'll get over here as quickly as I can." Fillian kissed him and then quietly left the apartment.

Gregory dressed quickly and met the kids in their PJs, rubbing their eyes. "Is the apartment all burned?" Weston asked as he went through it, looking everywhere as though his toys had spontaneously combusted.

"You're silly. The fire was out there, and it's gone now," Marnie said in her know-it-all voice.

"Everything is fine. But you need to go get dressed, and then I'll make you breakfast before I take you to day camp." He had a job this morning and wanted to get there by eight thirty.

Fortunately he had breakfast sandwiches in the freezer, and he put them in to heat. He poured juice and set out plates as the kids joined him. They'd just sat down when the knock came. He answered the door and let Donald inside.

"I understand you've been having a few issues," he said, looking around.

"Yeah. As you saw, we had a bit of excitement last night. The fire department and police are looking into it. But my mother has been creating problems, and I suspect she might make some complaints and cause some trouble."

"That's what Carter told me." Donald wandered through the apartment. "Honestly, if every home visit looked as good as this one, I'd be out of a job." He peered into the refrigerator and then the freezer before closing the doors again. "Our criteria are pretty basic: food, clothing, shelter that's safe, and kids that are cared for. I don't see anything out of line here, and I didn't expect to."

"Would you like coffee?" Gregory asked. He poured himself a mug and a second for Donald when he nodded. "My mother is so used to getting her own way that she thinks the rest of the world should bend to her will. I don't know what bee has gotten into her bonnet all of a sudden, but I have an idea it's because I'm dating someone."

"I see," Donald said. "You know you're allowed."

"Yeah, I know. But my mother is another matter. And well, Fillian just seems to get under her skin." Gregory couldn't help smiling. "And he stands up for me and the kids so she can't steamroll over us." Maybe that was the real key to everything with her. This was a battle of wills, and she was determined to come out on top.

"I can't help with any of that, but both Weston and Marnie seem to be happy and well cared for. I needed to perform a routine follow-up visit, so this will serve as that, and I will make sure it gets entered in the files today." He spoke quietly with both Weston and Marnie before heading toward the door. "I wish all my visits were this easy." He paused at the door. "My only concern is around this fire. Do you know who might have set it?"

"We don't," Gregory said. "I've been having problems with a stalker that the police are following up on, and I would tend to assume that it was him, but I don't really know." And that made him even more nervous. If it was Lawrence, then he was sure the police would figure it out and find him. But what if it was someone else? Then what was he supposed to do?

"I'm sure that all the authorities are looking into it," Donald said. "But it has to be frightening."

"It is. The kids were up part of the night, and they keep asking questions and are scared. To top it off, my mother was here making a scene yesterday, and the kids heard part of it. Now they keep asking if Grandma is going to take them away." He shook his head. "What they need is stability and care, not all this chaos."

"I agree. And the best you can do is shield them from it. As I said, the kids seem to be happy." He shook Gregory's hand.

"Thank you for coming," Gregory told him.

"You're welcome. Now I'm off on some appointments that I'm sure are going to be much less pleasant than this one." He left, and Gregory closed the door and returned to the kitchen.

"Let's finish up so we can get you both to the Y before I have to go to work," Gregory said.

Weston looked up from eating, his eyes huge. "What do we do if the man who set the fire tries to burn that down too?"

Gregory knelt between them. "If either of you sees anything, you tell one of the counselors right away, okay? And if you see the man you did before, the one that was watching, you tell them and ask them to call me right away." He hugged each of them. "Now finish eating and then get your backpacks." He hated that they had questions like this. Kids shouldn't have to worry about men setting fires or watching for people who were watching them. They should be able to play and be kids. He sighed and got ready for work before leading the kids down the stairs and around to the truck in the parking lot in back. After getting them inside, he drove to the Y, where he checked them in, said goodbye, and headed off to his job site, wondering if he was doing the right thing by leaving them.

GREGORY'S WORK hadn't been the same since the attack and subsequent explosion. Gregory liked being an electrician, and he was good at it, fixing issues other people missed. He took pride in his work and strove to always provide value to his customers. But in the past few weeks, he had felt jittery at every job site and kept an eagle eye on everyone around him. He knew it was to be expected and that his mind wasn't going to just let him go back to the way things were, but he wished it would. The jumpiness was driving him out of his mind.

"Do you need anything to drink?" his elderly client asked him, and Gregory nearly jabbed himself with his pliers.

"No, I'm okay," he breathed, trying not to act as though she had scared him within an inch of his life. "Thank you." What he needed to do was get this line of wire rerun so he could finish hanging the ceiling fan. The wiring itself had burned out because of an electrical storm, and Gregory was fixing the damage to the old house. This place had a mishmash of wiring, some modern with other bits dating to the building of the house in the early 1900s. "This should be the last of the really old wiring in the house."

"That's a relief. My husband never wanted to do anything with the lighting because he said it was best not to disturb what was there." She sat in one of the white wicker chairs that had to be as old as she was… and just as well cared for. Mrs. Carthage was a lady who always looked her best.

"He was right. But its time had come." He pulled the wiring through the wall from the junction box he'd installed, to the ceiling, feeding the wire as he went. This job would be easier with help, but he managed and was pleased once he had the gray wiring where it belonged. Gregory made the connection at the junction and checked that everything was as it should be before turning his attention to the light fixture. He got everything hooked up and the fixture set up. Then he tested everything before putting on the covers. "That should do it."

He checked everything again and told Mrs. Carthage which switch operated the fan and the light. She took a turn and smiled. "Thank you. I've had this fan for a while, but I…. I heard about what happened to you a few weeks ago and I didn't think…." She paused again.

"I'm okay. He didn't hurt me, and I was able to get out before anything happened." That wasn't totally true, but she didn't need to hear the unpleasant details, and Gregory didn't need to go over them again. He'd done that plenty of times, including almost every night when he closed his eyes.

"Well, that's very good." She smiled at him. "Because I was wondering if you'd have time in your schedule in the next few weeks for a few more things." She led him out into the backyard and explained that she wanted to add lighting. She laid out what she wanted.

"It's quite a job. Would it be okay if I came back in a few days to take some measurements, and then I can give you an estimate?" This would keep him busy for days.

"Of course," she said with an excited smile. "I'm having a family reunion here toward the end of the summer, and I'd like to have it done by then."

Gregory was about to tell her that would be no problem when he caught movement at the back of the property toward the alley. He turned to see Lawrence standing in the open gate, staring right at him. Gregory was close enough to see the intensity in his eyes.

"Young man, what are you doing here?" Mrs. Carthage asked. "This is my yard, and that gate should be closed." She stared daggers right back at him, but Lawrence didn't move and he didn't speak. He just stood there, watching. "What do you want?" she asked again, heading toward him.

"It's all right," Gregory told her, standing between them to keep her from getting close to him. He had no idea what Lawrence would do to her. He was clearly out of his mind. "What do you want?" Gregory asked him.

"I'm calling the police," Mrs. Carthage said, and Lawrence stepped back, turned, and walked down the alley, leaving the gate hanging open. "Who was that?"

"The man we were talking about a little while ago," Gregory told her.

"The blow-up-his-house one?" she asked.

Gregory nodded. "He's out on bail, and he keeps following me around." At least this time he had an independent witness. "I'm going to need to report this to the police." He pulled out his phone and called the number Fillian had given him. He got voicemail but left a message for Carter to return his call. "Thank you," Gregory said to Mrs. Carthage after he hung up and strode to the back of the property. He checked outside to make sure no one was hanging around and then closed the gate and made sure it was properly secured. Mrs. Carthage was on the phone when he returned.

"That's right. He was watching us, and I know who he is. Lawrence… something. He's on bail, and you need to stop this man from scaring people." Whatever response she got made her smile. "Excellent. Thank you." She hung up. "Now you have a report from me too. They said they were going to pick him up. That should be enough to revoke his bail." If Gregory didn't know better, he would swear she was being smug.

"Well, thank you." He pulled up his calendar on his phone. "I'll be here next Tuesday to take measurements, and then I can give you an estimate. It should take about three or four days, and I can get you in my schedule for early August. Does that work?"

"It's perfect, thank you. I want some lighting with some interest."

Gregory pulled up her number and texted her a name. "That's the electrical supply store in Harrisburg. They carry a number of things. Go ahead and pick out what you want before Tuesday, and I can use all of that information in my estimate."

She was happy as Gregory gathered up his tools and the remainder of his supplies. He made sure everything was clean, took things to the truck, and accepted her check for payment. After thanking her for everything, he headed to his next job, glad he had enough work to keep him busy.

By the end of the day, Gregory was energized, especially when he got a message from Fillian. *Carter just informed me that Lawrence Little has been picked up for violating the conditions of his bail and he's back in the county jail. He will see the judge tomorrow, where we hope his bail will be permanently revoked.*

That's good. Thank you.

The CPD got multiple complaints, and it seems he was located and taken into custody outside your building. Further proof that he'd been harassing you.

That's really nice to hear. Tension from his shoulders and back slipped away, and he took a deep breath, closing his eyes. He sent Fillian a smiley face. Maybe he could finally leave this incident behind him and get on with his life. He was tired of looking over his shoulder and worrying that Lawrence was spying on his kids.

We have practice tonight, so I'll see you there. My mother said that if you'd like, she'd be happy to watch the kids tonight so they don't have to wait on the sidelines. Here's her number. You can give her a call. He sent his own happy emoji, and Gregory drove to the Y to pick up Marnie and Weston.

"Fillian's mom offered to watch you tonight so you don't have to go to practice with me. Is that okay? You can go with me if you want, but she was nice enough to offer, and you wouldn't have to wait around for me."

"Yes," Weston said right away.

Marnie was more circumspect. "Do we have to?"

"No," Gregory told her before getting in and starting the engine. "You can come to practice with me and sit on the sidelines if you want. But you'll be alone for most of the time." He wasn't going to force her.

"Okay."

Gregory rolled his eyes as he turned out of the parking lot. "Which do you want to do?"

"I'll go to Fillian's mom's. She was nice, I guess."

Weston was way more excited. "She knows what kids like to eat." Typical boy, thinking with his belly. As soon as Gregory got the truck parked, he took a few seconds to message Fillian and then hurried the kids inside, where they got their bags and he changed into practice gear before hurrying back out and over to the neighborhood where he grew up.

CHAPTER 11

"CALM DOWN. He said he was coming," Fillian's mom said from behind him. "You must really like him if you're this nervous."

"Mom, don't go there," Fillian said, letting the curtains fall back into place.

"What?" she asked gently. "You are nervous, and I know you. You like Gregory, and there's nothing wrong with it, so why are you acting like you're some sort of emotionally repressed idiot? You weren't raised that way."

"True, but Gregory was. You know who his parents were, and his mother is still a real piece of work."

His mom put her hand on his shoulder. "That only means that it's more important for him to hear how you feel than for most people. If I'd had that woman for a parent, I think I'd have grown up to be some kind of affection sponge, soaking it up wherever I could get it."

"Then you get it. What if I scare him off?"

His mother shook her head. "I'd say being honest about your feelings is the best way to go. His mother was all about playing games. She'd ask for what she wanted, then use reason, guilt, you name it. Games were a way of life when he was growing up, so don't play them." She went to the window. "They're here."

He turned in time to see the truck pulling to a stop. "How do you do that?"

She just smiled and shrugged. "I'm a mother." As if that explained why she always knew someone was arriving before they actually got there. He had always thought his mother had great hearing, but the fact that her doctors were talking about hearing aids blew that theory out of the water. "Do you have your gear? Practice starts in twenty minutes, and you're going to need to get over there to warm up."

He rolled his eyes. "Yes, Mom." He grabbed his gear and opened the door as Gregory and the kids hurried up the walk.

"Come on in," she said to the kids after Gregory gave his mother and Fillian each a hug. "I made you pasta for dinner, as well as a pan of brownies." She sure knew how to win them over. They hurried inside without looking back.

"I take it Mom is a hit," Fillian said with a smile.

"Of course she is," Gregory said. "Let's get to practice." He returned to the car and they drove the few blocks to the park, where the rest of the team was gathering. "I appreciate you letting me know about Lawrence." He took Fillian's hand. "He showed up at one of my jobs today, and my client was none too happy. I think it was her complaint that finally got the police to pick him up."

"They couldn't find him," Fillian said. "After he packed up, there was no known address. We kept watch because they put out a notice, but he never returned to the property where you first encountered him. They got lucky that he decided to sit outside your building."

Gregory groaned. "So does it take luck for the police to do their jobs?" he snapped. "The guy has been stalking me for weeks and he set fire to shit in my building and no one does anything. I sit up all night just to listen in case someone comes back, and everyone else is just sitting around doing nothing." His voice grew higher, and Fillian felt his defenses rise.

"No, we aren't, but we can't perform miracles," he snapped back, but then he calmed himself. "I know you're scared, but he's in custody, and it's likely he'll stay there until his trial now. It's up to the judge, but I honestly don't see them letting him out if this is how he behaves. I'm sorry you had to go through all of this, but hopefully it's over, and after…." He was about to say *his trial*, but he trailed off because Gregory would have to testify, and that wasn't going to be a great experience for him either.

"I know," he said.

"And if you're frustrated, then take it out in the practice. That's what these guys are for." He lightly kissed the back of Gregory's knuckles.

"Somehow I don't think the guys are going to thank me for wanting to rip the head off anyone who gets in my way," Gregory told him.

"Then take a minute and relax. Everything is going to be okay." Fillian was grateful that the past few weeks had come to some sort of resolution. Having Lawrence still out there, free and able to bother Gregory, had started to get to him, building up more tension and worry until the guy would explode, and that wasn't going to help him or the kids. "I'm not going to let anything happen to you."

Gregory shrugged. "How can you stop it? How can any of us? The guy lit a fire in the building, and all we could do was put it out and run outside. What if he gets out and does it again, only this time we don't get to it in time?"

Fillian didn't correct Gregory. He thought it likely that Lawrence had started the fire to freak him out, but there wasn't any proof that it was him. Logic said Lawrence did it, but they didn't have any evidence. "Hey." He gently held Gregory's hands. He'd known the blowup was going to come eventually. All this drama had taken a toll on Gregory, and it seemed that it was all coming to a head. At least it wasn't in front of the kids. "I don't know what to tell you other than you aren't alone."

Gregory sighed and nodded. "I don't know what to do."

"Just let it go if you can. The comedown is always the hardest."

Gregory tilted his head slightly.

"When I'm in the middle of a situation, I'm on. Last year there was a man who had taken two kids and was holding them at gunpoint. Everyone was calm and collected during the entire thing. I was sent around to the back to see if there was any other way into the house. I got in through the outside basement entrance and then came up through the house. I was able to get the kids and take them back through the basement and out of the house before the perpetrator knew they were missing. After that, they took him into custody. It was easy... until it was over, and then I fell to pieces as soon as I got back to Mom's. I was fine while all of it was going on, but after it was over...." He sighed. "That's what you're going through right now. All the possibilities are running through your head and scaring the hell out of you. But none of them happened. You got the kids out of the building, and they're fine. Right now they're at my mother's filling up on her pasta, brownies, and milk. And after that, Mom has games and other things for them to do. She may even bake cookies with them."

"They'll come home...."

"In a sugar coma and happy as anything. Mom knows what kids like, and she's been dying for grandchildren." Fillian leaned over the seat. "There's nothing for you to worry about except the fact that Coach is going to have a fit if we don't get out there and join the others."

Gregory chuckled. "And none of us wants to piss him off."

"Nope." He kissed Gregory and then opened the door to get out.

"If you two are done making out, do you think we can get on with the practice?" Coach called, his hands on his hips.

"We're ready to go." Fillian jogged to the sidelines and began stretching, watching Gregory as he did the same, unable to take his gaze off him. Not that he wanted to. Gregory was stunning, and the more time they spent together, the more Gregory felt like his—like he was meant for him. The problem was that Gregory had a lot on his plate.

"Fillian," one of the guys called, pulling him out of his daydream. "Get your butt over here. We need to practice the scrum, and for that we need you."

Fillian finished his stretch and jogged out to where the others were waiting with Gregory behind him.

"Let's do this. We need to beat Shippensburg if we want to have a shot to make the league playoffs," Fillian told the guys. "And I wanna win. After all, then we get to drink more beer." A cheer went up, and they got to it.

"MR. FILLIAN!" Weston called as he raced across his mother's living room. Fillian caught him and lifted him into the air. "I found them, look." He pointed to the pile of Legos on the floor. "Your mom said if I looked I would find them, and I did."

Fillian set him down.

"Those were mine when I was your age." He remembered building everything from houses to airplanes with them. He got some most Christmases, and it wasn't until years later that he realized his mother had scoured garage sales and Goodwill stores to find them. They were only loose bricks. The other kids in school got whole building sets, but that didn't matter so much.

"Grammy says that I can play with them whenever I come here," Weston said, looking at Gregory, who seemed confused. "She said we could call her that."

"Of course you can," Gregory said with a smile. It had taken most of the practice, but Gregory seemed in better spirits. It was good to have a chance to run off tension and worry. "Where's Marnie?"

"In the kitchen." Weston pointed before settling back on the floor to play. Gregory went on through, while Fillian sat on the sofa watching

Weston play and Gregory greet Marnie with laughter. That was an amazing sound to hear.

"You wanna see what they've been doing?" he asked Weston, who nodded. Then Fillian stood, and Weston raced into the kitchen with Fillian following. His mom and Marnie had baked and iced cutout sugar cookies. There was icing all over the counter, Marnie's fingers, her apron, and even her face, because his mom's cookies were just too good not to eat.

"We were having fun and got a little carried away," his mother explained as she began wiping up the mess and putting the dishes in the sink.

"It looks like you both had fun," Gregory said with a smile. He looked different, his smile brighter, his shoulders a little straighter.

"We did," Marnie said. "She and I did it together."

Gregory nodded. "Your mom used to love to bake. She made the best carrot cake." He swallowed hard.

"She did?" Marnie asked.

"Yeah. She also used to love to cook for the holidays. We used to have Christmas brunch at her and your dad's house because her cooking was so good." Gregory hugged Marnie, and Fillian could tell he was far away at that moment.

"Do you think I'll be able to cook like her someday?" Marnie asked, so seriously.

"I'd say so," Fillian's mom said. "It takes a little time to learn, but you have the makings of a real baker." She continued cleaning up, and Fillian began loading the dishwasher for her. Once it was full, he started it.

"Thanks," he said softly while Gregory got the kids to gather their things. "This was really nice of you to do for them."

"I didn't do it just for them," she said softly, her gaze going to Gregory and then back to him. One thing about his mom, she wasn't particularly subtle.

"I get it, Mom," he said with a smile. "Are you all ready to go?" he asked as she scurried to pack up some cookies for the kids and gave them each a hug. Then they got everyone loaded into the car and truck and headed back to Gregory's. Fillian parked and followed Gregory and the kids up the stairs, where everyone came to a halt outside their door.

"What the hell?" Gregory turned to Fillian.

A note was stuck onto the door with tape: *I'm watching you.*

"Don't touch it," Fillian said as Marnie reached for it. "Unlock the door and let me go inside first to make sure no one is there."

Gregory unlocked the door with a shaky hand, and Fillian went inside, listening carefully.

He heard nothing but checked from room to room before looking out back to the fire escape. Nothing seemed to have been disturbed. A pile of Legos lay on the coffee table, and the bedrooms hadn't been touched. Nothing inside the apartment seemed to have been disturbed.

"It's okay, guys. No one is here. Check your rooms and let me know if anything is missing." Fillian pulled out his phone. He called Carter, who verified that Lawrence was still in jail and had been since he was picked up. "So what the hell is going on?" He explained to Carter what they found when they got back.

"I'm on my way. Don't let anyone touch anything if its not too late."

Fillian rolled his eyes, even though Carter couldn't see him. "It's probably too late. I'll see you in a few." He ended the call and found Gregory in Marnie's room, both kids on the bed, with Gregory holding them.

"I'm scared," Marnie whispered. "I don't want to be here anymore."

"Mr. Carter is going to come over, and then we're all going to go to my house, so get your jammies and things together."

"Can we take our sleeping bags?" Weston asked.

"Yes. If you want, you can camp out in the living room," Fillian said. "Mr. Carter will be here soon, and then we'll go once he's done." Gregory seemed out of it, but at least the kids got excited. They gathered their things, and finally Gregory stood and went to his room.

Fillian answered the door when he heard footsteps on the stairs. Carter pulled on gloves, took down the note, and placed it into an evidence bag. He also examined the door and the area around where the note was taped. "I don't know what sort of fingerprints we can get, but the note itself might tell us something."

"I thought so. If you need resources, let me know," Fillian said. "With Little in jail, I thought this crap was over." But it seemed that the situation was more complicated than he originally thought. "And now we're all wondering who else could have a grudge against Gregory." It felt like they were right back at square one. "I'm taking him and the kids to my house. They're scared and upset, especially after the fire and now both of them seeing the note."

"Good idea. I'll get on this as soon as I get to the station," Carter said.

"The most frustrating thing about all this is that I can't do much about it. I want to dig in and investigate who the hell could do this, but…."

Carter nodded. "You have to go by the rules, especially since you're involved. Besides, your job is to take care of this family. That's where you're needed. I can check out this note, and I'll look more closely into the fire to see if there's a connection. I really thought we had our man with that one, but if there's someone else out there, then we need to look at everything once more." Fillian was thinking the exact same thing. "Did anyone get into the apartment?"

"I don't think so. The door was still locked, and they haven't found anything out of place. If I didn't know better, I'd say this was just a trick someone was playing to try to scare them. I mean, there was no real harm done other than entering the building. They taped a note to the door meant to intimidate and then they went no further."

Carter shrugged. "Both of us have seen weirder things. Is there any value in having me speak to them?"

"I don't know. Gregory was with me at practice all evening, and the kids were at my mother's." He couldn't help smiling when Carter smirked.

"So not only have they met your parents, but your mom is babysitting. That's quite the step." Carter chuckled when Fillian scowled at him. "Okay, I know you don't want to jinx it. Let me get to work on this and I'll be in touch." He held up the evidence bag before descending the stairs.

Fillian returned inside. The kids sat on the sofa with their BB8 and Ariel suitcases, along with their sleeping bags.

"Where's your dad?" Fillian asked. Both kids pointed to his bedroom. Fillian nodded and went inside to where Gregory sat on the side of the bed.

"What if I'm putting them in danger?" he asked softly. "Whoever is doing this is after me, and what if they hurt the kids?" His voice cracked.

Fillian sat next to him. "This isn't your fault. It's the asshole doing this shit, and you are not allowed to feel guilty. You can worry all you want, but guilt is not allowed. I swear I will figure out who's doing this and rip their nuts off. But this is their fault, and there is nothing you've done to bring this on." He hugged Gregory tightly.

"But what if something happens to the kids?" Gregory asked.

"You're a good parent, and nothing is going to happen to them." Fillian hated that someone was making Gregory doubt himself. "Remember that whatever happens is not your fault." He held Gregory tightly for a while. "Now you should get packed. The kids are out there waiting for you with sleeping bags and everything."

"They love camping," Gregory said.

"Me too. Maybe before the summer is over, we could take them. I have a tent big enough for all of us," Fillian offered. "And maybe you and I could sit out under the stars after the kids have gone to bed." He felt Gregory shiver against him. "Now get packed. And just so you know, you won't need a sleeping bag. I have a king-size bed, and there is plenty of room in it for you."

He left Gregory to pack and checked on the kids, who were still sitting on the sofa, Weston holding the container of cookies from Fillian's mother, looking at them and licking his lips.

"Those are for later," Fillian said. "And didn't you fill up on cookies and dinner at Mom's?"

"Weston ate lots," Marnie said.

"But I'm still hungry," he added.

Fillian sat down across from them. "It's okay. I remember when I was your age and I was always hungry too. Especially for cookies."

"And did Grammy make you cookies and stuff… all the time?" Weston asked, his eyes wide, like Mom had the oven on a conveyor belt. "You were really lucky."

"And so are you, because she sent some home." He ruffled Weston's hair as Gregory joined them. Fillian got up and helped the kids with their gear. Then they trudged out of the apartment. Gregory locked it, and then down the stairs and into the cars they went.

Fillian checked to make sure no one was watching before leading Gregory and the kids around the alley to his house. He had Gregory park in the garage, and he pulled up just outside. Once parked, he led the way into the backyard along the garden path to his back door.

"Do you do the cloak-and-dagger thing much?" Gregory teased as he let them all inside.

"Normally I don't have to. I'm a cop, and people are usually respectful. But you never know." He closed and locked the door. "Go in the living room, and you can lay out your sleeping bags where you want them," he told the kids. He took the container of cookies and set it on the counter. He had no illusion that they would last very long in Weston's hands.

They rushed through and staked out their sleeping areas. Fillian turned on the television. "Whose turn is it to pick?" he asked.

"Marnie's," Weston said, his expression falling. "Not *Mulan* again."

Marnie thought for a few seconds, a finger at her lips. "*Cars?*" she asked. "I like Lightning McQueen." Weston whooped, and Fillian located the movie and put it on.

Fillian took Gregory up to his room so he could get settled in. Then he returned to the kitchen and made a big bowl of popcorn. This was a family who loved the stuff, and at a time like this, comfort food was called for. At least that was what his mother would do, and who was he to argue with her? He brought in bowls and gave each of them one, then made up one for Gregory, who joined him on the sofa.

"How long will it take before Carter has anything?" Gregory asked quietly as the movie played.

"It might take a day or so. I want to check tomorrow to see if I can get permission to speak to Lawrence. I really think we need to know why he was acting the way he was." Something wasn't right, and Fillian hated a mystery with a passion. After all, Lawrence's behavior made no sense, especially since it got him thrown back in jail with revocation of his bail. People weren't always rational, but they usually didn't behave so counter to their own interests. If Lawrence had kept his head down, he would have been better off.

"Do you think you'll be allowed to?" Gregory asked.

"I don't know. It will be up to the chief of police. I'll ask Carter tomorrow and see what he thinks. It isn't going to do any harm to speak to him, and anyway, there is the possibility that Lawrence could refuse to talk." That had happened before, and he would be fully within his rights.

"So what else? Me and the kids can't stay here forever."

"Maybe not, but you can for a few days. They can stay out of sight, and you can all feel safe." It would be supremely stupid for anyone to try anything at this point. But then, stranger things had happened. He slipped an arm around Gregory and drew him close, inhaling his rich scent. "Just try to relax and enjoy the time with the kids. Everything else will work its way out."

"Do you really believe that?" Gregory asked.

"Yes. We'll figure things out. There's something going on that neither of us understands, but now we know to look for something else. Part of what we thought was Lawrence was someone else." He leaned closer. "I have to ask, is there anyone you've really pissed off lately?"

Gregory shook his head. "Who would want to treat me this way? I really don't know of anyone. I mean, they broke into the building just to leave a note on my door."

"And that doesn't sound like anyone you know? Someone who would go to any length to get what they wanted?" Fillian met Gregory's gaze, watching as his eyes widened, and the idea that had niggled at the back of Fillian's mind for a couple of hours got picked up by Gregory, who kept shaking his head slowly.

"My mother? You have to be kidding me. You think my mother would do this?" Gregory snickered. "My mother would never get her hands dirty like that." He paled, and his eyes went even wider. "You don't think she somehow got in touch with Lawrence?" He shook his head hard. "No way. I'm going off the deep end. I know my mother likes to get her own way, but for her to hire a criminal to harass me is just too much to be believed."

Fillian chuckled, because it seemed farfetched to him as well. But if it made Gregory laugh, then it was worth it. He was pleased to see Gregory smile, but Fillian also made a mental note to try to rule that woman out. He knew more than most that sometimes people did things no one could imagine.

"Do you really think… my mother?"

Fillian shrugged. "I'm going to try to rule her out. At least then there isn't any doubt." It was kind of sick that Gregory could suspect that sort of thing of his own mother. Though knowing her from his time as a kid as well as the few times he'd met her in the past few weeks, Fillian was going to need convincing that she wasn't behind all this.

By the time the movie had ended, the kids had settled down and were quiet. Fillian put on *Planes* as a follow-up, and they watched and eventually fell asleep. He turned out the lights and lowered the volume. Then he and Gregory watched the rest of the movie before tucking in each of the kids and leaving the room, with the light on in the kitchen in case they woke up.

"Are you sure you're okay with leaving them down here?" Fillian asked.

"Yeah. Neither of them is likely to wake up before morning, and I have to be up early because I have a busy day. I'll take them to the Y on the way."

"I have a shift as well. But you need to keep an eye out tomorrow and call me right away if you see anything unusual." He held Gregory's hand, leading him up the stairs. "I just found you, and I don't want anything to happen to you." He swallowed hard, realizing just how important Gregory and the kids had become to him.

Fillian let Gregory use the bathroom first and then cleaned up. He returned to a dark room with Gregory under the covers.

"I love this bed. It's so comfortable."

"Me too." Fillian slipped under the covers and right up against Gregory, loving the heat washing off him. "But you know what I like more? You in it." He ran his hand over Gregory's belly. "I like having you right here with me. Especially with the house quiet like this. I love the kids—they're pretty amazing—but I love our time like this too. Just you and me." He slipped closer to Gregory, kissing him gently at first but with quickly growing ardor.

Gregory returned his passion, holding him tightly. "I feel like I'm going to break apart sometimes."

Fillian understood. He ran his hands down Gregory's back and over his firm ass. "I know. But you're safe, and so are the kids." He held still before pulling back a little. "I know you've been through a lot lately, and we don't have to do anything tonight. I didn't invite you and the kids over here so we could have sex." Fillian grinned as he leaned over Gregory. "Well, not *just* so we could have sex."

"That's better," Gregory teased.

"You're here because I want to keep you safe, more than anything else. The rest is…." He closed the distance between them. "You have to know that you drive me crazy sometimes. I see you, I watch you, and all I want is to pull you aside, let the kids fend for themselves, and have you all alone."

"I see," Gregory said with a smile. "My dad bod really does it for you, huh?"

Fillian patted Gregory's belly. "This is no dad bod. And let me tell you, you do it for me. But I never know how to behave in front of the kids." He snickered when Gregory snorted. "I don't mean that. I mean, I want to be affectionate, but I don't know if I should in front of them."

Gregory paused. "I think it's good for them to see that we care for each other. Stephanie and Arthur were affectionate to each other. It was clear that they loved each other deeply, and I think kids need to know that kind of deep affection is possible. Lord knows I never got that kind of example from my parents. Can you imagine my mother being all lovey-dovey under any circumstances?"

"No, but I can see your mother breathing on flowers and her breath coating them in ice. Or maybe we could hire her out to the international community as the cure for climate change." The last thing he wanted was to talk about her again, but Gregory had brought her up. "Sorry."

"I wish I could argue with you, but I can't. I had everything growing up except affectionate parents. They were definitely more interested in themselves and their own wants than they were in anything or anyone else." Gregory sat up. "I always thought that maybe the divorce could be good for both of them. It was for Dad. He's remarried, but to a very different kind of person from Mom. She's nice and takes good care of him. They're truly happy." He sighed. "God, why am I such a complete downer?"

"Because you have a lot on your mind." Fillian put his arm around him and rested his head against Gregory's shoulder.

"But I don't want it. I keep hoping for you to take it all away," Gregory said.

Fillian grinned and leaned closer, capturing Gregory's lips. "Then let me do just that."

CHAPTER 12

GREGORY WRAPPED Fillian in his arms, doing his best to let go of his worries and just be in the moment. Fillian was hot, and the way he touched Gregory made him forget about everything and everyone. Gregory slid down under the covers, holding Fillian, his solid weight pressing down on top of him. There was something comforting about having Fillian on top of him, like nothing could reach him as long as Fillian was there.

It also meant that as Gregory slipped his hands down Fillian's back, he could grip that amazingly tight and hard ass. Fillian groaned before covering his mouth with his, kissing Gregory hard, ramping up the heat between them until all Gregory could think about was Fillian. He became the very center of his attention, and Gregory let it all go.

"Damn, I love kissing you," Fillian whispered before kissing him again. "You taste like salt and even a little butter from all that popcorn, but also you." He kissed away Gregory's ability to speak and splayed his hands against his side.

Gregory held Fillian tightly in case he split into a million pieces. His heart pounded and his breath hitched as Fillian slid against him, their cocks pressing to one another. Gregory thrust upward for more purchase, and Fillian gave it to him, rocking slowly back and forth. This was almost more than Gregory could take.

"Fillian... I feel like a teenager."

"Is that a happy, excited teenager... or a stiff breeze kind of teenager?" Fillian asked. "Because I'm a mixture of both right now."

"Me too," Gregory admitted. Something about Fillian really got him going. He could feel him not just physically, but on the inside. Fillian made him feel warm and safe and want things he didn't think he could ever have, at least not since he got the kids. Gregory had never dreamed that he'd find someone who would be willing to not only be part of his life, but the kids' as well. That was a lot to ask. And hell, the kids liked Fillian, Gregory was falling in love with the guy, and.... He stilled as the full realization of his thought slammed into him.

"Is something wrong?" Fillian asked, looking deep into his eyes, blinking slowly.

"No. At this moment everything is right." He smiled and tugged Fillian down, kissing him hard, taking possession of those lips. He wanted Fillian to know how he felt, and words didn't seem quite adequate.

"Are you sure?" Fillian asked.

"Oh yeah," Gregory groaned. What he truly wanted had suddenly become clear. Fillian wanted to protect him and the kids, and Gregory wanted to do the same in return. Now he just needed to figure out who had it in for him and get them to back off. Hopefully then Gregory could have everything he'd ever wanted. He looked up at Fillian and fought a sigh.

Fillian kissed him, pulling Gregory out of his doubt and back into the blissful brightness of passion. It didn't take long for him to find himself in a haze of desire that left him oblivious and uncaring about anything other than Fillian and what he was doing to make him feel like he was on top of the world and the very center of the universe.

And when Fillian slid downward, trailing his lips over Gregory's skin, he closed his eyes, taking in every single sensation as Fillian drew closer to his aching cock. He held his breath, waiting, praying… until Fillian closed his lips around his length and Gregory sank into delicious, wet oblivion. Fillian had a talented mouth. He could kiss breath-stealingly well, and damn, the man could suck cock like nobody's business.

The last guy he was with before getting the kids hadn't enjoyed that part of things, but Fillian seemed to revel in it—and in leaving Gregory breathless with aching need. He gripped the bedding, kept his eyes closed, and held on tight while Fillian drove him out of his mind, a state that Gregory hoped would never end.

"Fillian," he croaked, trying desperately to keep himself under control, but he was losing it fast.

Fillian backed away. "Am I doing something wrong?" He smirked, his lips a little crooked, mischief shining in those amazing eyes.

"God no." Gregory breathed deeply and tugged Fillian upward, bringing their lips together. "You make me feel like a teenager again, and I never thought that was possible."

Fillian chuckled. "Then let me get back to it. I want you to feel that way. Hell, I want you to think that anything is possible, because it is."

Gregory rolled Fillian over on the bed.

"And I want you to know that you—" Gregory's voice broke, and he ended up growling instead. "You make me feel like I can do anything." He kissed Fillian before returning the favor, taking his length between his lips, burying his nose against his skin. Fillian gasped, and Gregory sucked harder, wanting Fillian to feel like a teenager as well.

"Gregory," Fillian whispered as he backed off. Then Gregory took him deeply again, bobbing his head, the taste of Fillian bursting on his tongue. Damn, he loved that feeling. Fillian's soft groans filled the room, driving Gregory forward.

Soon they moved together, Fillian thrusting upward and Gregory sliding his lips down to meet him. Fillian groaned louder, his movements becoming less regular, and Gregory knew he was getting close. He refused to stop, loving the moans that rang off the walls until Fillian gasped, his breathing shallow and desperate.

"Gregory, I can't...," Fillian muttered between clenched teeth.

Gregory took him all the way as Fillian tumbled into his release, Gregory swallowing his salty essence before slowly pulling away, smiling at Fillian as he gazed up at him with wide eyes full of wonder.

Gregory lay still, their gazes locked together. "Are you okay?" What the hell. "Did I break you?"

"Kind of," Fillian groaned before pulling Gregory into his arms.

"Look, you don't have to—" Gregory started.

Fillian cut him off by manhandling him onto the bed. "Damn, you were sexy as hell, and you blew my mind." He grinned before taking Gregory to the hilt, sending all the air whooshing out of his lungs. His eyes crossed, and once he was able to inhale it took all his willpower not to groan at the top of his lungs and wake the entire damned house. Gregory liked getting his cock sucked, but this was more than that, more intimate and special. Gregory closed his eyes for a second and just let the sensation of wet heat flow through him, but it wasn't until he opened his eyes that the wave of passion slammed into him. It was the sight of Fillian, strong and so sure of himself, taking him between his lips—a beautiful sight that absolutely stole his breath.

Fillian pulled away for a second, and Gregory tugged him to his lips. They kissed deeply before Fillian slipped back down and slid Gregory's cock into his mouth until Gregory's entire body vibrated and he lost control, giving himself over to Fillian and floating on the clouds of their shared passion until he tumbled into a release that left him soaring in Fillian's strong arms before coming back down to earth.

"Good God," Gregory muttered.

"You can say that again," Fillian whispered in return before kissing him. "You need to come with a hotness warning label, sweetheart, because you nearly blew my mind twice." Fillian held him tightly, and Gregory snuggled down under the covers while Fillian slipped out of bed.

"I'll be right back." He pulled on his robe and left the bedroom, then returned a few minutes later after a few stair creaks that told Gregory where he'd been. "Everything is locked up, and both kids are sound asleep." He slipped out of the robe, his golden skin glowing in the small bit of light from the street. He got back into bed and tugged Gregory into his arms. "Go to sleep. Nothing is going to happen while you're here."

Gregory nodded and closed his eyes, drifting off more quickly than he could remember in quite a while.

FILLIAN INSISTED that Gregory and the kids stay at the house for a few days, and Gregory didn't argue. He'd slept like the dead knowing Fillian had his back and would keep them safe. He tried his best not to think about whoever had left the note as he helped Fillian make breakfast the following morning. After eating, Fillian went to work, and Gregory took the kids to the Y before heading to his first job. It was raining, which for Gregory was a bit of a relief. The kids would be spending their day inside in the gym and activity rooms, which meant, at least to Gregory, that they were safer. The kids were excited when he signed them in, and they took right off for the activity room set up as an awesome obstacle course with tunnels and stuff.

Gregory wished he could stay, but he had back-to-back jobs. Both of them seemed to work out. He had the materials he needed, and everything went smoothly. Fillian texted at lunchtime to make sure everything was okay. Gregory hadn't seen anyone hanging around to watch him, and he answered that everything was fine. *I'm going to stop at the apartment after work to get the kids some more clothes.*

Do you want me to meet you there? Fillian texted.

I'm fine. I'll call if anything is wrong. He got a smiley face as a response and then went back to rewiring Mr. Phillips's basement, which was going to take the following day to finish up. Everything seemed to be going well, which Gregory refused to think too much about because it was then that things usually went to crap.

I changed shifts and got this weekend off. Do you want to go camping with the kids? And just like that, with a single message, things got even better. Gregory answered right away and started making lists in his head for what he would need to get.

At the end of the day, before picking up the kids, he returned to the apartment, parked in front, and unlocked the door. As he climbed the stairs, the faint scent of smoke still hung in the air. When he reached the landing, he stopped, looking at his door with a folded piece of paper taped to it. He reached out to take it but stopped himself and called Fillian instead.

"There's another note on my door," he told him as soon as he answered.

"I'm on my way, and I'll call Carter. Did you touch it?"

"No. I don't even know what it says, but it was waiting for me when I got here." He tried not to think about it. "The locks on the front door weren't broken or anything."

"Let me make that call. I'll be there in five." Fillian hung up.

Sirens sounded less than two minutes later, growing closer before stopping outside the building. Gregory let Fillian and Carter in and followed them up the stairs. Carter pulled on gloves and took down the note, then showed it to both of them.

Don't think you can hide from me, it read. *I will find you... all of you.* It was printed in red magic marker.

Gregory read it and turned to Fillian. "What the hell is going on? Someone is as crazy as shit, and I'm tired of it." He could only shake his head.

"It seems to be the same paper as the last note, and the writing looks about the same." Carter pulled out his phone and compared the note to a picture.

"Do you want me to let you in?" Gregory was determined to hold it together as he unlocked both locks on the door. Fillian and Carter went inside, and he carefully followed behind, letting them look around.

"Does it look like anyone has been here?" Carter asked. Gregory looked through the place, checking out the kids' rooms as well as his own. "The locks don't seem to have been messed with, and there's nothing disturbed."

Gregory went through his room and even checked under the bed, but as far as he could tell, no one had been inside. He was pretty sure of that. "I don't think anyone's been here. I can't see that anything was taken or damaged, and I don't get the feeling like someone has come and gone." He sat down in the living room. "So it seems like they got into the building and left the note."

"Let's put a small camera in the hallway. We can install it over the front door, looking up the stairs. If someone comes in again, we'll be able to see them. We'll need the landlord's permission," Carter added.

"I can get that," Gregory offered. "They're good people, and they want this to stop as much as I do." It seemed like a simple solution.

"I have one in my car," Fillian said. "It's small enough that no one is going to see it unless they're specifically looking for it." He left and returned while Carter went out as well. Gregory stayed where he was, his anger building. He was so tired of all this shit. Whoever was doing this deserved to be hung up by his balls.

Footsteps on the stairs pulled him out of his anger. "I don't see anything out front. I'd say that whoever got in used a key. I'm assuming you have one to the outer door, and so would the other tenant, as well as the landlord. We've already spoken to them because of the last incident. I doubt Chris would let anyone in. The other tenant was away for a couple days the last time, and your landlords were visiting in Virginia. All verified." Carter read from his notes. "So… do you know of anyone else who has a key?"

"I've never given one to anyone," Gregory said.

"Did you loan your keys to anyone at some point?" Carter asked.

Gregory thought a minute. "I mean, I let Fillian use them once, but he gave them back." He knew he was being a smartass, but giving out copies of his house keys was something he didn't do. Not with anyone.

"Okay. Someone likely has a key to the outside door but can't get any further and is using that access to try to scare you."

Gregory stood taller. "It isn't going to work. I'm tired of all this, and I'm damned sick of feeling afraid all the time. I'll move or add eight locks to the door, but I'm keeping the kids safe, and I'm not letting this crazy sicko dictate my life." He wanted to hit something, but he unclenched his fists and sighed. "Lawrence is still in jail, right?"

"Yeah. It's definitely not him."

"Can I speak to him?" Fillian asked.

Carter shook his head. "Afraid not. He doesn't want to talk to you, and the chief doesn't think it's a good idea either because of your personal connection to the case. I was able to speak with him, though."

"And...?" Gregory asked. "Way to bury the lede." He was getting cranky.

"There isn't much to go on. He admits to following you around because he's kind of obsessed with you. We are currently having him evaluated to make sure he's competent to stand trial. But he denies setting the fire in the stairwell or leaving notes anywhere. In fact, when I brought up those things, he got angry... on your behalf."

"Could it be an act?" Gregory asked.

"I don't think so. He admits to thinking he had a chance when you were at his house and to following you around town. But he was actually perplexed at the other things, and like I said, he was upset and angry. So I think we have two people involved. The camera is installed here, and I'd say it's best if you stay with Fillian for the time being, but make a show of coming back here on occasion. Be careful when you head to Fillian's—make sure you aren't followed."

"And park in my garage so no one sees the vehicle."

"Yeah, I know. But why come back here?"

"Because we want whoever is doing this on camera, and to do that, we want them to think you and the kids are here. Otherwise they will probably try to find out where you are." Carter turned on some lights and made a point of standing near the front window, keeping his side or back to it. "If you have any timers, put a couple lights on them and make them overlap, or get those Wi-Fi lightbulbs that you can turn on and off with your phone."

"Okay." It seemed like a lot, but if he got them, then he could have lights go on and off in the rooms throughout the house.

"We can pick some up and get them installed," Fillian offered, and Gregory agreed.

"What else do I need to do?" Gregory asked.

Fillian came closer. "The most important thing is to keep yourself and those kids safe, and we're going to do that. You stay at the house, and call me when you arrive at and leave a job. Or text me where you're going."

"Like I'm a kid?" Gregory asked.

"Just so I can know you're okay," Fillian said gently. "I'd feel better if you weren't alone, but this way I can be there with you in a way."

Gregory sighed. "Okay." When he put it like that, how could he be a dick about it? Even if he kind of wanted to. "Let me get some things for the kids and then I can go pick them up." He checked the time and hurried to Weston's room, then packed some additional clothes for him and then Marnie, knowing they probably wouldn't be happy with what he picked out, no matter what he brought back to Fillian's. He also got a few things for himself before joining the others in the living room.

Both of them were on the phone, and Gregory took the clothes down to the truck. When he came back up, they were still on the phones. Fillian wrapped up and joined him.

"Is there anything else you need? Carter is following up on the last note to see if the lab found anything."

Gregory nodded and leaned close to Fillian. "You know you look really sexy in your uniform." He winked. "Do you think you could frisk me sometime?"

Fillian smiled. "That could be arranged." They watched each other until Carter hung up.

"Okay. First, you two are sickeningly adorable together. Second, they didn't find anything on the last note. No fingerprints, just a few slightly oily smudges. Whoever put it up probably used gloves, maybe the driving kind, because the oil was a leather moisturizer. I'd suspect we'll find the same thing with this one."

"Leather gloves in the summer, like that isn't suspicious," Gregory chimed in. "Who the heck wears gloves in the summer?"

"They don't, unless they're planning to break in somewhere. Whoever it was came prepared, or at least they thought they did," Carter said. "Let's get out of here and let the cameras do their thing." He led the way, with Gregory double locking the door on his way out.

OF COURSE he had brought the wrong clothes or the wrong shoes. Marnie wanted her pink ones, while Weston just took what Gregory gave him and tossed it into his bag before going back to the video game he'd been playing. Fillian had found an old console in one of the closets and set it up.

"It's okay," Gregory told Marnie. "It's just a few days."

"But I wanted the pink ones."

Gregory stayed patient. "Did you tell me that?"

"No."

"Then how was I to know? I brought you what I could find. Now, you can mope all you want, but it isn't going to change anything." If he lived through their teenage years, it would be a miracle. "But I do want to tell both of you that Fillian got the weekend off, so we're all going camping!" He hoped that the cheers and excitement meant that the drama over shoes was forgotten, at least for now.

"Where?"

"Can we go to a place with lakes and stuff?" Weston asked.

"Yes. There will be a place to go swimming. I promise." He caught each of them in a hug, happy they were happy.

"HEY, WHAT'S with the pasted-on happy face all evening?" Fillian asked once Gregory slipped under the covers. He wore boxers because he wasn't sure that one of the kids wasn't going to come in during the night. In fact, he half expected it. Marnie had moved from the living room to the guest room, and Weston was still camping out, but on the floor in the office. They were both asleep the last time he checked, but this was a strange place for them, and if they woke, they'd look for him.

Fillian, on the other hand, wore nothing, and Gregory slipped his arms around him and copped a feel of his tight backside.

"I guess as much as I tried, I couldn't just let this whole note thing go. Who does crap like that?" Gregory asked.

"I've been giving it some thought, and I keep wondering the same thing. There has to be a reason for all of it. Is there a client who might have taken something wrong and thinks you spurned them? Some dispute over a bill?" Fillian shrugged. "I'm running on empty here." He slid closer. "Is there one of the guys on the team who might be jealous? It's a pretty mixed bag of guys. I know it sounds weird, but I'm grasping at straws."

The thought had never occurred to him. "I doubt it. If anything, they'd be upset because of the kids. I used to go out with the guys all the time, but I haven't done that nearly as much since I got them. Marnie and Weston like to go to Molly's, but it's expensive, and I don't want them in a place like that all the time. So I go out occasionally, and that hasn't changed recently." He yawned and closed his eyes. "I hate thinking about my friends this way. I've known some of those guys for years. I'm closest to Stevie... but can you see him doing something like this?"

Fillian shook his head. "Not really. These are guys who have an outlet for their frustrations. They don't keep them bottled up inside. This note writer... I get the sense that they are a whole mess of pent-up resentment. That somehow they think you don't see them, and it's spilling over into over-the-top behavior. That isn't the guys on the team. Not that it couldn't be, I suppose, but I don't see it." His expression grew even more serious, and he pursed his lips. "There is one person we haven't talked about again, and I think we need to. Your mother." He winced as he said it. "She wants the kids and has said more than once that they should be staying with her."

Gregory shook his head. "I know Mom thinks that Arthur and Stephanie should have left her with custody. But my mom is more likely to hire a lawyer to do her dirty work. If she thought she had a chance, she'd go the legal route. My mother doesn't leave notes, and setting a fire would endanger the kids, and she'd never do that. I really believe that."

"I had to bring it up because...." Fillian bit his lower lip.

"I know you did, and I'm not shocked or mad at you for it." He rested his head against Fillian's shoulder. "I hate this, looking at my friends as though they could be stalkers. Trying to think who might have a thing for me or something." It was giving him a headache.

"Who says that this has anything to do with having a 'thing' for you?" Fillian rolled him on the bed and pressed Gregory against the mattress. "As far as I know, there is only one guy who has a thing for you... and it's me. I'm not counting Lawrence."

"As far as you know." Gregory asked as he batted his eyes at Fillian until they both broke down into laughter.

"You are cute *and* sexy," Fillian said before kissing him and running his hands over Gregory's side, making him laugh.

"You aren't supposed to tickle," Gregory said, chuckling lightly and squirming away.

"I heard you," Weston said from the door, and Fillian pulled up the covers to his neck.

"We're sorry, buddy," Gregory said as Weston made a jump for the bed.

"Are you playing tickle monster? I wanna play too," Weston said as Gregory caught him.

He lifted him onto his arms and stood up. "It's too late for tickle monster. We were just talking." He left the room and took Weston back to the office. "It's time for you to go back to sleep." He set him down in the office, and Weston slipped back into his sleeping bag. "Are you okay now?"

"Yes, Daddy. I love you."

Those words never failed to touch his heart but always brought a pang of regret. Gregory adored those words, but when he heard them, he couldn't help thinking that Arthur should be the one hearing them. He pushed that thought away, hugging Weston before he got settled, and Gregory partially closed the door as he left the room. Then he checked on Marnie, who was sound asleep, before joining Fillian in bed.

"Sorry," Fillian said softly.

Gregory slipped back under the covers. He rolled onto his side and pressed himself to Fillian's wide back. "Not your fault. It happens sometimes." He couldn't help sighing.

"What's running through your head now?" Fillian asked.

"I don't know. Too much." Gregory closed his eyes.

Fillian rolled over and slid his fingers along Gregory's cheek. "Stop worrying. I know what this is. And I'm not going to go running into the night because one of the kids interrupted what I hoped was going to be a little sexy time."

"But I'm sure you never expected to be cockblocked by a six-year-old," Gregory whispered.

"No, I didn't. But I also never expected to be part of a family like this. I had cousins to play with, and when I figured out I was gay, I thought I might find someone great to spend my life with, but kids were never part of the picture. Not that I don't want them or that I don't love Weston and Marnie, because they've worked their way into my heart as fast as you did. I just didn't see kids as a possibility."

"And now?" Gregory asked. "What do you see now?" He almost held his breath, waiting for the answer. It felt like this was one of those moments where an answer to a simple question could change everything. "What is it you want, when you know the full breadth of what's possible?"

"I guess I want it all," Fillian whispered. "I know I want you—all of you—to be part of my life. What that looks like, I have no idea. And I guess that I have to be patient and let things work themselves out. I know I love you, and those kids could have me wrapped around their little fingers so danged easily, it's frightening."

He stilled and let what Fillian had said sink in, warmth spreading through him. "Tell me about it." Gregory sat up. "Every time I look into Weston's eyes or when he smiles, I see Arthur so clearly. It's like he's right there under the surface. And Marnie… she is the spitting image of her mother, and yet when she's angry and her brows knit together, it's Arthur. Those kids…." He closed his eyes. "I get scared that I'm going to do something wrong. I never saw myself as a parent. Like you, I figured I'd never have kids, and then wham, Arthur and Stephanie are gone and I have two kids and a mother who resents the entire situation because she feels that she should be the one to raise them."

Fillian drew closer. "Maybe that's why you're such a good dad. You not only worry about what you might be doing wrong, but you go that extra mile, knowing your mother never could." He closed the gap between them, kissing Gregory gently and wrapping him in his arms. "You're stronger than you know."

Gregory chuckled. "Sometimes I feel like one of those girders inside a building that no one knows is rusted on the inside and completely weak and useless." He closed his eyes.

"Really? I don't agree. I'm a little shorter than you, but I'm strong. I've spent years building my muscles so I can do my job. But I see you as the strong one… because of what's inside. And I'm sort of in awe of that." He kissed him again. "Now we need to be quiet and go to sleep, or else I'm not going to keep my hands off you."

"I see," Gregory said before slipping out of the bed. He closed the door and then pushed down his boxers. "What were you saying about those hands of yours?" He hurried back to the bed and right into Fillian's arms.

CHAPTER 13

FILLIAN GOT a message about movement at Gregory's building and checked the camera feed. It was the other tenant leaving, and Fillian put his phone back in his pocket. He had watched a ton of footage over the past three days and gotten nothing. Maybe there wouldn't be any more notes, or maybe they were making too much of this because of what Lawrence had been doing. Though Carter believed that Lawrence hadn't set the fire, which meant someone else had, and what if it was this note writer?

"I see you're off this weekend," Wyatt said once Fillian pulled his cruiser into the station and checked himself in from his shift.

"Yup. I need to pick up Gregory and the kids, and then we're heading out of town." There was no game this weekend, and they had practiced already, so all he needed to do was get out of there before someone found a reason for him to stay. "I'll see you Monday." He hurried out, got in the car, and headed home.

His phone rang with a call from Gregory, and he answered it through Bluetooth. "You ready to go?"

"Just picking up the kids now. They're all packed, and we'll meet you at the house." He sounded as excited as Fillian was.

"I'm on my way there, and I'll start bringing things out." Fillian hung up and made the turn onto his street and parked around the back. Fillian hurried inside and began bringing out the gear they'd packed the night before. He loaded the cooler, packed with ice, and carried it out front just as Gregory pulled up.

"Let's load up and go," Gregory told the kids. Fillian put their gear into the bed of the truck along with the cooler, sleepings bags, and who knew what else. The kids hurried inside, and as Fillian finished loading, Gregory made sure the kids used the bathroom. Then Fillian locked the door and they all piled into the super cab and headed out of town.

"Do you guys know some camping songs?" Fillian asked once the town was behind them. The plan was to head north over the ridge, where they had reservations at a state park with a lake, a dam, and hiking trails.

The kids all called out names, and they began singing "The Wheels on the Bus."

"I'm hungry," Weston said as soon as they reached the top of the mountain.

"Really?" Gregory asked. But Fillian was ready and handed each of the kids a small bag of goldfish crackers. "Dude...."

"I'm prepared. Now, when we get there, we're going to set up, build a fire, and I have stuff to cook out. Some hot dogs, salads, and for dessert, the stuff to make s'mores." He was pulling out all the stops. "Okay?"

"Yeah," Weston said, and when Fillian turned to look, Marnie was smiling. He took all that as a yes. "Are we going swimming?"

"Tomorrow. We're also going on a hike up to the dam, and maybe we'll see some ducks and geese on the way. It's going to be lots of fun." He shared a smile with Gregory as they descended the curvy mountain road into the next valley.

"Are we almost there?" Weston asked after another ten minutes.

"Stop," Marnie snapped. "We'll get there when we get there."

Fillian grinned and said nothing, glad Gregory hadn't had to be the one to say it.

"I checked the camera, and everything has been quiet," Fillian said softly. "I saw you stopped in too."

"Just had to check," Gregory said.

They reached the bottom of the mountain and picked up speed for the ten miles to the campground.

By the time they made the turnoff, Marnie was playing a game on her tablet and Weston was asleep. Gregory pulled up to the office, and Fillian went inside, checked them in, paid for camping, and got their site information and a map. Then he directed Gregory through the campground.

"They made a mistake in the reservation," Fillian told him.

"What happened?" Gregory asked as he approached an intersection in the road. The tent sites were to the right.

"Take the left. They overbooked the tent sites, so we got one in the RV section. It has electricity and water."

"So I can charge my stuff?" Marnie said. "Sweet."

"What do we need electricity for?" Gregory asked.

"Well, now we can use the electric light instead of using up all the batteries, and we aren't going to have to walk a long way for water."

He directed Gregory to their site between two huge motor homes that looked like walls on either side. Gregory pulled in, and Fillian got out and grabbed the tent from the back.

"What do we do first?" Weston asked, jumping out.

"Let your dad and me set up the tent, and then we can all get our beds laid out. Then we'll have dinner and tell stories." Fillian rolled out the tent and went through the process of setting it up. Gregory helped, and after it fell down twice—because that's what tents did—he got it up and all the lines secured.

"Okay, get your sleeping bags," Gregory told the kids, and they hurried inside to unroll their bags right in the center. Fillian let Gregory sort that out and got the other sleeping bags, then zipped them together. Once the kids were settled, he unrolled the padding and then laid out their sleeping bags and pillows while Gregory started the fire.

"Is it dinner yet? I'm hungry," Weston declared.

Fillian unloaded the rest of the gear from the truck and got their chairs set up, then placed the cooler near the picnic table. Then he got out the things for dinner and set them on the table. After Fillian got the hot dog sticks and made one up for each of the kids, Gregory helped them cook their hot dogs so they didn't burn. Fillian sat at the table, watching them—his family. Or at least what he hoped might be his family, if he were lucky.

"Do you want one?" Weston asked Fillian. "I'll make you one."

"Okay," he said with a smile, and after a few minutes, Weston came over with a hot dog, and Fillian used the bun to get it off the stick. "Do you want to eat it? I know you're hungry." He helped Weston put on ketchup and then sat him at the table with a plate, some 7UP, and a little potato salad. "Good?"

Weston nodded, taking another bite. Fillian made up his own plate, and Gregory brought him a hot dog, lightly kissing his cheek before sitting down to his own dinner.

"Is everything good?" Fillian asked, and there were smiles all around.

"Where did you get the potato salad?" Gregory asked as he took a second helping.

"Mom made it. I asked her if she'd make up some of her special salad because everything in the stores is yucky and Mom uses bacon, and everything is better with bacon." The kids seemed to like it as well, which he would be sure to tell his mom.

"Can we have s'mores now?" Weston asked.

"You have to finish your dinner, and we'll have them a little later," Gregory said. "Finish the hot dog and the potato salad." He was gentle but firm, and Weston went back to eating.

"What are those?" Weston asked.

"Raccoons," Fillian said, catching a glimpse of the trash-can robbers. "They can see really well in the dark."

"Will they try to get into the tent?" Marnie asked.

"No," Fillian told her. "They're more scared of you than you are of them. They're just looking for food." He had put all their trash in plastic, but he hadn't put it in the can yet. He planned to take it up near the restrooms, away from their campsite.

"Eat up so we can clean this up. Then I thought we'd go for a walk and look at all the trailers," Gregory said. "There are some big ones."

The kids got excited and finished eating. "Go ahead and take them while I finish up here," Fillian told Gregory quietly. He needed a few minutes to get everything put away, and the kids were getting antsy. Gregory took them by the hand, and they headed out on their walk while Fillian tidied up. All the paper he put in the fire, and the rest went in the trash, which he took over to the bathroom cans. Then he put the rest of the food in the cooler, locked it away, then placed it in the truck. There was no sense in leaving it out.

When everything was cleaned up, he sat in one of the chairs by the fire, his gaze drifting skyward. The first stars of the night were just beginning to appear. He opened the star app on his phone and held up the screen, locating the planets and constellations.

When Gregory and the kids returned, Fillian told them stories about the planets and stars, pointing them out and letting the kids use this phone to see what else they could find.

"There's a dragon and a horse," Weston said, moving the phone around. Not all of what he saw was in the sky, but he didn't seem to mind.

"Give Fillian back his phone and let's make dessert before you both go on to bed. It's getting late, and you want to be up for all the fun stuff tomorrow."

Gregory got them marshmallows while Fillian made up the chocolate and graham cracker parts. Then they each got their roasted, and not burned, marshmallow. He smushed it inside and handed each of them their treat.

"These are good," Marnie said around small bites while Weston ate his own, getting marshmallow all over his nose.

"Yummy," Weston murmured with his mouth full. Fillian got a stick and began toasting a marshmallow of his own and one for Gregory, since he was busy with the kids.

The fire crackled as they sat around it. Fillian gently added another log. "Tell us a camp story," Weston said, still eating.

Fillian set his partial s'more on a plate. "What kind of story?"

"Not scary," Marnie said.

"With bears," Weston interjected.

Fillian made a show like he was trying to think of something. "Wow, okay. Let me see if I know any not-scary bear stories. I can try to think of one." He winked at Gregory, who sat back with his bottle of water. "Well, once up on a time… did you ever notice that the best stories start that way?" He looked at both kids. "Well, once there was this little bear, and his name was…." He waited only a second.

"Widget," Weston supplied, and they all laughed.

"Okay, Widget… and he lived in the woods with Mama and Papa bear." He went on to tell the story of the mean man who wanted to cut down the trees in their forest and how the bears banded together to scare them off, and then they had a bear party with honey and s'mores. The kids added the s'mores part. "And the bears lived happily ever after… until the loggers came back."

"They did?" Weston asked.

Fillian leaned forward. "Yes, and if you're good, I'll tell you what the bears did that time… tomorrow night."

"Okay, it's time you got ready for bed. Each of you get your wash-up kits, and I'll take you up to the bathrooms." They hurried to the tent, and Gregory settled his hands on Fillian's shoulders. "That was so good of you."

Fillian put his hand over Gregory's, and they stayed like that quietly, Fillian's heart beating rapidly and his temperature rising for something he knew they couldn't do, but his entire body longed for with each of Gregory's touches.

The kids came back out, and Gregory took them to clean up. Fillian stowed away the kids' chairs. By then they were back, and Fillian put another log on the fire, waiting while Gregory put the kids to bed.

Gregory backed out of the tent and quietly came over to sit with him. "They're so excited about tomorrow, and so tired…."

"I hope they sleep well," Fillian whispered and moved his chair next to Gregory's as the fire began to burn down. He made no move to add more to it as he looked up toward the sky. The lights from the motorhomes on either side flicked out one at a time, letting the darkness draw closer.

"I used to look up at the stars at night sometimes," Gregory said.

"I think we all did."

Gregory took his hand. "Out here you can understand why people have always looked up in wonder. Without all the light, it's easy to believe that fates and the future are written up there. Kings and queens consulted with people who could read the stars before going into battle."

"And often the results were rewritten after the battle was over to justify what actually happened." Fillian chuckled. "But think of this— what we see is into the past, not the future. The stars only show us what has happened. The light we see takes a long time to get here, and the farther away the star is, the older what we see actually is."

"Yeah?" Gregory said. "Well…." He grew quiet, and Fillian did as well. They didn't need to fill the night with endless chatter, not when there was an endless sea of….

A light shot across the sky, interrupting his thoughts and quickly burning out. "Did you make a wish?"

Fillian squeezed Gregory's hand. "Did you?" he whispered in return as another streak zipped over and then disappeared in a flash. Gregory squeezed back, and they sat watching as more meteors burned up high above them, giving him and Gregory what felt like their own private show.

GREGORY PRESSED right against him was the perfect way to wake up. The tent was quiet, and Gregory must have gotten a little cold, because he had moved closer during the night, his back against Fillian's chest. Not that he minded, and his cock was more than interested, but the kids were a few feet away. Thankfully, thinking about them made things settle down. Still, he tugged Gregory to him and closed his eyes once more, enjoying the quiet he was sure wasn't going to last.

"Daddy," an urgent young voice said, breaking into Fillian's amazing dream.

"Yeah, buddy," Gregory said softly.

"I gotta go potty."

Fillian smiled as Gregory got out of bed and pulled on his pants.

"Okay. Is Marnie awake?" Apparently she was, because all three of them got their things and left the tent, leaving Fillian alone to try to get a few more minutes of sleep. Which is exactly how much time he had before both kids piled on top of him in a fit of giggles. Fillian growled playfully and yawned before sitting up.

"Are you hungry?" Fillian asked.

"Daddy is making eggies," Weston said, still in his jammies.

"Okay. Then you get dressed and join your dad." Fillian scouted around for some clean clothes, changed quickly inside the sleeping bag, and pulled on fresh jeans and a T-shirt before climbing out and putting on socks and his shoes. He straightened the bedding and left the kids to get dressed.

Yawning, he helped Gregory build the fire before swinging the grate over the pit. "I got bacon and ham, as well as eggs," Fillian said.

"Bacon," came the chorus from the tent. Fillian pulled out the cooler and the pans to get breakfast started.

HIKING WITH the kids that afternoon was a whole new experience. They seemed fascinated by everything. "Who plants all those flowers?" Weston asked.

"Mother Nature," Fillian answered.

Weston turned back to the flowers and then looked at Fillian. "Then what does Father Nature do?" He was dead serious, and all Fillian could do was smile, lift him up, and give him an airplane ride among the trees.

"Is Mother Nature real?" Marnie asked.

Fillian let Gregory answer that one. "Well," Gregory said, "sort of. She isn't a real person, but she represents all the things that nature does on its own." Gregory took the kids off the path to a fallen tree. "See, this tree died, but look at all the small trees that are growing. That's what nature does. It replenishes itself, and new things grow when old ones die."

"Like Mom and Dad?" Marnie asked, her lower lip wavering.

"Maybe, sort of. Your mom and dad died in an accident, but they left you and Weston behind to grow up and remember them, sort of like these small trees will remember the big one that fell down and made room for them." That answer seemed to satisfy the kids, and they continued down the trail all the way out to the dam that made the lake.

The water sparkled in the sunshine as they helped the kids up so they could watch the water flow out of the lake, over the dam, and into the creek beyond. After a few minutes, they set them back down, and the kids ran off to play chase in the grass area nearby. "I used to come here as a kid with Mom and Dad."

Gregory sighed. "I don't think I've ever been here before. I've camped in other places, but not here. In the past I went with friends, but things are different now." He turned as Weston chased Marnie, both of them laughing. "I have the kids, and camping…. Well, everything is different now."

"I get that. But…?"

"Well, most everything is better now. I mean, they somehow make things better. I see things through… old eyes, I guess. To them it's all new. The flowers I would never have noticed, the trees, the lake—most of it would pass me by, but they see it all, so I see it too." He put an arm around Fillian's shoulders as Fillian's phone vibrated in his pocket. The campground had minimal service, but there must have been some here. He ignored it and stood with Gregory, watching the water and the kids playing. When his phone vibrated again, he pulled it out. The camera had caught movement at Gregory's apartment. Fillian flipped over to the live feed, but the hallway showed nothing.

"What is it?" Gregory asked as he put his phone away.

"Nothing that can't wait until we get home." He smiled and put it out of his mind. After all, he had much better things to think about.

CHAPTER 14

CAMPING WAS amazing, and the weather was great until they went to pack up. By late Sunday morning, clouds had rolled in, and thunder sounded in the distance. Gregory and Fillian took down the tent and got the gear into the truck with the cover over the bed just before the skies opened up. With everyone inside the truck, Gregory drove back toward town in the rain, being extra careful at the top of the mountain, when the truck was encased in clouds.

"Is it going to be okay?" Weston asked.

"It's fine." Gregory slowed down, reached the summit, and started down the other side. Rain pounded the windshield, and he took the curves slowly as visibility was limited.

On the way down, the fog around the truck slowly lessened, and suddenly the rest of the valley could be seen. Suddenly he slammed on the brakes, stopping just in time to avoid a panel truck on its side, crossing most of the lanes of traffic.

"Pull over." Fillian got out of the truck, then raced to the cab. "Call 911. Get ambulances and the fire department," he called. "And turn the truck around and get farther away. Now." He kicked in the shattered windshield of the truck as Gregory made a three-point-turn and pulled away before calling for help.

"There's an accident on thirty-four on the south side of the summit to the north of town. There are people inside, and we need fire and ambulance. Trooper Fillian O'Connell is already on the scene. We found the accident on our way home. He is trying to get the people out." Gregory wanted to help, but the kids were freaking out, and he needed to stay with them.

As the rain picked up, he saw Fillian pull someone through the hole where the windshield had been. He hefted them over his shoulder and hurried toward Gregory's truck. "Get farther away," he directed, and Gregory pulled farther uphill.

"Kids, climb up here in the front seat. Fillian, get him in back. Help is on the way." He helped the kids into the front and pulled out the car seats, then stowed them under the back cover.

Fillian set the man inside as gently as he could once the kids were sharing the passenger seat. "He's breathing," Fillian said, climbing in after him. "Are you still on?"

Gregory handed him the phone, and Fillian spoke to the operator. "Have the ambulance come from the north side of the mountain. They aren't going to make it from the south. The road is blocked."

Gregory turned back as the cab of the truck burst into flames.

"The truck is on fire. The driver is out, and there were no other passengers." Fillian kept relaying information as Gregory got back in the truck and pulled away from the flames, which soon engulfed the rear of the panel truck as well.

"Keep going. I don't know what's back there."

Gregory pulled back into the clouds and drove to the top of the mountain, where there was a small pull-off. He parked out of potential traffic.

"What do we do? Is that man dead?" Marnie asked, looking over the seat.

"No. He's alive, but he hit his head hard. That's why I'm holding it." Fillian kept his voice level. "Ask them how far out the ambulance is," he said, handing Gregory the phone.

Gregory repeated the message.

"We've related the message to the ambulance, but I'm not sure," the dispatcher told him. "They should be there soon."

Fillian held out his hand, and Gregory handed the phone to him. He identified himself and started issuing orders. "Tell them that we need a medevac chopper. We can get him to the north side of the ridge, and they can land on the road at the base of the mountain. This man needs attention now." His voice held a commanding edge that Gregory had only heard a few times. The kids settled in their seat, sitting close, holding each other.

"Is Fillian mad?" Weston whispered, and Marnie nodded.

"No," Gregory answered softly.

"Gregory, take us over and down the north side. I know this is tough, but we need to get to help as fast as we can, and that may mean meeting them."

Gregory put the truck in gear, kept all his lights on, made sure the kids were secured in their seats, and carefully drove down the other side of the mountain until they emerged from the cloud. He continued with his lights on until he reached the bottom of the mountain, where lights approached from in front of them.

"We're right in front of the ambulance," Fillian told the operator. "Flash your lights, and don't stop until they begin to slow."

Gregory did, pulling off, and finally the ambulance pulled to a stop next to them. Gregory lowered the windows.

"We're the people you're looking for," Fillian said as more vehicles approached.

They let the EMTs get to work. Fillian directed the fire vehicles up the mountain as he finished the call and handed the phone back. "I'm afraid this is going to take a while. They are going to need to get the fire out and what's left of the truck off the road before we can go anywhere."

"Then it's a good thing we have the cooler and stuff." Gregory turned to the kids. "We get to have a truck adventure. Weston and Marnie, it's your job to look out for the fire truck." He got out and managed to get the cooler out of the back without lifting the cover. He slipped it in the center of the back seat before reinstalling the booster seats.

Fillian was still with the EMTs and on his own phone talking, getting wetter by the second.

"Get inside before you're soaked," Gregory told him, and Fillian got in the passenger seat. "What's going on?"

"They have the truck fire out, and they're working to get one of the lanes open. Once they do, we should be able to get home."

"What about the man they took away in the ambulance?"

Fillian sighed. "No word yet. They were taking him to a school a few miles away, and they'll airlift him from there."

Gregory got some snacks out of the cooler for the kids and made sure they were settled. After another twenty minutes, they got word that part of the road was open, and Gregory carefully drove them all home.

"THAT WAS so cool," Weston said as Gregory pulled into town. "The way the truck caught on fire." Gregory figured that Weston was going to have plenty to tell his friends in day camp.

"It was scary," Marnie scolded him. "The man could have died right in the back seat." She huffed and rode the rest of the way in silence.

Gregory had been torn about whether he and the kids should just go back to the apartment. Things had been quiet, and there were cameras in the staircase. He pulled up and parked out front. "Do you want to take your gear up or…?" Fillian asked.

"What I want is for the kids to be able to stay in their own rooms." It was what was best for them. But the past week had been pretty special. He liked what it felt like to sleep next to Fillian and wake up with someone he could trust.

"How about we get the things we need to upstairs and put away. Then you and I can talk. Okay?" Fillian asked, and Gregory knew that was probably the smart thing to do.

The rain had let up, so Gregory got out and unloaded the kids' gear, then hauled it inside and upstairs. When he reached the top, he stopped at the door, chairs and sleeping bags falling to the floor.

"Fillian," he called down. "You better come up here." He waited as Fillian approached from behind him.

"Okay. Don't touch it." He set down what he was carrying. "What the hell?"

A straw doll hung in a noose from above the door with pins sticking in the belly. "Is this really a voodoo doll?" Gregory asked. "And what kind of sick person would do this? How did they evade the cameras?"

"I got an alert yesterday, and there was no one here when I checked. But damn, they must have been in and out before I could look." Fillian took the keys from Gregory and unlocked the apartment. He checked inside before he allowed them to come in. Fillian got gloves and took pictures of the doll before taking it down and placing it in a plastic bag.

The kids barreled up and inside and went down to their rooms. "Are we staying here?"

"No. I think you can stay at my house and camp out one more night. Okay?" Fillian asked.

The kids seemed okay with it. Gregory was unsettled as hell, but he didn't want to show it.

"Let's get your things brought in, and then we can go to my house."

Gregory helped Weston and Marnie put away their things. He also got the laundry together and checked the refrigerator for anything that would go bad. The entire time, he kept looking over his shoulder as if someone might be looking at him. And once they were done, thankfully, they left, and the jittery feeling, like something was about to go completely wrong, slipped away and finally abated once they reached Fillian's house.

"I DIDN'T want to ask in front of the kids, but what did you find out? And what are we going to do?" Once Gregory had put the exhausted kids to bed, he and Fillian sat on the sofa in the living room. Thankfully Weston and Marnie were out like lights after a weekend in the fresh air and all the excitement on the way home.

"Well, Carter is checking the footage, and he said he'd send it over once he had something. He got the alerts too, checked, and saw nothing. But he's going through everything. As for what we're going to do...." Fillian slid closer. "You can stay here as long as you need to. Hell, I need you here and to know that you're all safe. Carter is going to stop by to pick up the doll, but it appears to be just something bought at one of the country stores. What worries us is what was done to it and how it was treated, and the threat behind it."

"I get that. But I keep wondering... someone put it there, so how come they aren't showing on the camera?"

"We have to go through the video files, and while that sounds like an easy task, it isn't. The camera creates a file that gets sent periodically to clear its memory. Carter is getting those files and will go through them. We have an idea of the time this was placed because of the alerts we received. At least that's what we're assuming."

"Can't you just go to those times?" Gregory asked.

Fillian sighed. "He did—or he thought he did—but he saw nothing. But it could be a timing difference, so we're looking through everything to see what we can find." He seemed as frustrated as Gregory felt. Gregory had really hoped that the camera would get images of who was behind all this and bring it to an end. "It's going to take a little time. It doesn't appear that the camera was tampered with or moved, so we just need to wait."

"And it is Sunday...."

Fillian nodded. "I know it's difficult and you just want some answers. I do too."

Gregory rested his head against Fillian's shoulder. "I want this to be over. I want to know that the kids are okay." He turned to Fillian. "I saw that damned doll, and my first reaction was... it's another one. Not that I was scared or worried, but okay, here's one more thing. That is frightening to me. I'm just becoming desensitized."

Fillian lightly touched his chin. "That's what happens. It's a way for us to cope with things like this. When something first happens, it's new, but after a while, we learn to process things. That's why this one was easier. And you also know that you have backup. You aren't in this alone."

"I know that. But I want the kids to be able to sleep in their own beds. They like it here because they like you and you make this fun for them. But that can't last forever. They need stability and—"

"They have it because they have you," Fillian told him, those amazing eyes looking deep into Gregory's. "You are what they need. It isn't a house or an apartment that they need, it's you. The rest is just real estate." He hugged him, and Gregory returned it, holding Fillian tightly. "And we will find who is doing this and why."

"How do you know?" Gregory asked.

"Because it's personal. Because I'm not going to allow the people I love to be hurt this way. If Carter can't help us, then I will bring in more resources. I'm not going to rest until all this is gone."

"Do you know what the worst thing is? I keep going over everyone I know—my friends, the guys on the team, everyone—trying to figure out who could do this to me. I keep coming up empty, but I hate that I keep thinking about it. These guys are my friends, and yet I keep wondering who could hate me. It's unsettling. Not knowing if you can trust people, even your friends—the ones you want to trust." Gregory swallowed hard and tried to stop the rising worry.

"I know it is, and you have to stop. Carter and I will get to the bottom of this." He sounded less confident than he had a few days ago, and Gregory figured he was worried too. Notes, a fire, and now a veiled death threat would affect anyone, even a seasoned police officer.

Fillian's phone chimed, and he pulled it out of his pocket. "It's Carter. He says he found something, but he isn't sure how helpful it's going to be. He's working to isolate the images from the camera and he can be here in half an hour."

"Please tell him to come." Any news was helpful at this point.

Fillian relayed the message and put his phone away. "You're safe here." Fillian hugged him tightly.

"I know. Sometimes I think I'm over it. This has been going on long enough… and it's one more thing. At least whoever is doing this didn't try to set the building on fire this time. They just sent me a message that they want me dead."

Fillian shook his head. "Nope. What they want is to scare you. I'm not sure why, and I don't know what they think this is going to get them, but I get the feeling that we'll find out soon. The notes, the fire, the doll, all of it seems designed to keep you off balance."

He shifted on the sofa, deep eyes meeting his. There was so much strength in Fillian's gaze that it felt like a warm blanket wrapping around him. Gregory breathed deeply, a sense that he could do this filling him.

"They're doing a really good job of it. Just when I think this is over, something else happens." He closed his eyes and let his attention travel to Fillian's touch, gentle and yet strong enough to take away some of the fear. "I keep wondering, what if they do something to the kids?"

"But this isn't directed at them," Fillian said. "It's directed right at you. It could be some sort of retaliation for something. I'd like to say that the simplest explanation is best."

"But who have I hurt?" Gregory asked.

"Okay, let's look at this. Lawrence stalked you after he got out… well, because you turned him down and didn't accept his advances. He wasn't balanced before, and that whole incident fixated him on you. Thankfully he's now back in jail and can't do anything more." Fillian leaned closer. "But there could be things we thought he was doing that this second person was behind. That muddies the water a little. But as of now, he's out of the picture." Fillian's gaze grew harder.

"It feels like we keep doing this and just spinning our wheels."

A soft knock cut him off. Gregory got up and checked to see who was out front before opening the door and letting Carter inside.

"I'm sorry about all this. How was the camping trip?" Carter asked.

"It was really good," Gregory told him as he led Carter into the living room. Fillian stood, and they shook hands.

"Let's go to the dining room," Fillian offered, and Carter went right through, opening the laptop he'd brought in with him.

"I suppose we should get right to it. Like I said on the phone, I'm not quite sure what we have, but I'm hoping the three of us can figure it out." He sat down and brought up the video. Gregory and Fillian brought chairs around so they could see.

"The time in the camera is off by an hour for whatever reason. It doesn't matter, except it took longer to find what I wanted. I cut out the section of footage that we wanted, and we're about two minutes from any action." He started the video, and it showed an empty hallway. "We got a lot of footage just like this. There were a number of instances of your neighbor coming and going, but other than that nothing—up until right here. And this is what I think caused the first alarm we received."

The door opened, the edge of it just hitting the picture frame. Someone in a big dark blobby sweatshirt with the hood on went up the stairs, stopped at the top, and then returned after maybe a minute, head down so their face wasn't visible.

"Who the hell is that?" Gregory asked, tilting his head to the side. "You said there were two alarms. Did they set off both, coming and going?"

"No. The system would send this as one alert. This is the first one," Carter reported. He skipped ahead, the empty hallway footage slipping forward quickly. "This is ten minutes later." He stopped, and the door opened once more. A figure entered the picture, but then the image went wonky, like an old-time TV screen when the signal wasn't strong enough. "There's some interference. I noticed it in other parts of the footage as well. I think it's something in the building. It goes away just as they turn the corner toward your door, and everything is fine until they make an appearance again, then it goes wonky again. You can see movement coming closer, and then, just as they are about to leave, the image clears again. At first I wondered if they were trying to interfere with the camera, but the same type of pattern repeats other times when no one is there. So I think it's a sucky coincidence."

"Great," Gregory groused.

"Okay. So we have little to work with. But let's start with the first guy," Fillian said. "That's the easier one." Carter returned to that spot and ran it through. "First thing, they weren't carrying anything, so unless the doll is in a pocket...," Fillian mused.

"How long were they out of sight?" Gregory asked. "Back up the video and time it," he suggested. Carter did, looking up when he finished.

"Eighteen seconds.... What are you thinking?" Fillian asked.

"That if they had the doll in a pocket, they would need to fish it out, get it prepared, and then tack it up before leaving, all in that short a time. And look at the way they climb the stairs. They aren't in a hurry, and there's no indication that they know they are being filmed. It's a slow gait. I don't think this is our doll planter."

"Can you zero in on the face area on the way down?" Fillian asked, sliding an arm around Gregory's shoulder. "We'll figure this out," he added softly. Gregory had hoped that the cameras would be a slam dunk and easily highlight the person responsible.

"It's too dark, and the angle of the head makes it impossible."

"What's that?" Gregory asked, pointing to a lighter blotch on the sweatshirt. "It looks like a logo of some kind."

Carter zoomed in a little. "Good catch. I thought that was a bit of pixelation, but you're right."

Fillian leaned closer and smiled. "That's the logo for Grant Communications. That's where Stevie works. Shit, yeah. I recognize him now. But what is he doing here?"

Gregory felt a chill run down his spine. "I hate the thought that one of the guys on the team...."

"Don't jump to conclusions. Like you said, he didn't stay long, and he didn't look like he was in a hurry. So maybe it wasn't him. Fillian and I will pay him an official visit and see what he has to say." Carter turned to Gregory. "I'm more interested in this second visitor. They stayed out of sight longer, so they had more opportunity." He returned to that part of the video and ran through it again.

"It definitely isn't much," Fillian said.

"Is there a way to clear away the static?"

"I tried but didn't get much, because this is the way the video was stored. So these images are distorted." Carter sounded as frustrated as Gregory felt.

"Maybe try clipping out the good parts. Let's get rid of the static and piece together the images of what we have. Then we can go frame by frame," Fillian suggested. "Maybe there will be something then."

Carter turned away from the computer and looked at each of them before shrugging. "I can try, but I don't know if we'll get anything from it." He turned back to the computer as Gregory found himself nodding. He agreed with Carter and was discouraged as hell, but they had to try, even if it was a futile effort.

CHAPTER 15

GREGORY ASKED Fillian about making some coffee. "Sure," Fillian agreed. "I have some good decaf."

"Perfect, thank you," Carter said without looking up from his laptop. "This shouldn't take too long. I just need to cut out the sections we don't want." He continued typing while Fillian worked in the kitchen.

"I'll get a few munchies too," Fillian offered, and once the coffee was done, he and Gregory brought everything into the dining room. Gregory poured mugs while Carter finished up.

"There isn't a lot, and I divided the sections up with a few seconds between them. But the whole thing is twelve seconds long." He played the video and then did it again.

Fillian got nothing from it because it was too choppy. "Can we slow it down?"

Carter did, and Gregory leaned over his shoulder as it played. "There isn't a lot of detail."

"No. But I want you to try to zero in on the shoes if you can. We have only a few seconds at the top of the stairs."

"What are you hoping to see?" Fillian asked.

"I don't know. Maybe if this is a man or a woman? No one pays attention to shoes, and it's the one place where people sometimes mess up." Carter shrugged, and they went frame by frame. "Look there. The shoes are dark, but those are a woman's shoes. They are flat, but... keep going to the next frame... see right there? The light coat covers most of her, but the shoes show right there."

"Yeah, but what does that get us?" Fillian turned to Gregory, who had paled as he stared at the screen.

"Go up to the head." His tone was so soft that Fillian wondered what he had just seen. Gregory swallowed as Carter reset the video and they went through it frame by frame once more. Fillian didn't know what Gregory was looking for, but after three frames, he pointed. "I know that."

"What, that smudge?" Fillian asked.

"It's not. That's a hair pin. See if you can get a better image of it," Gregory said, and Carter moved through the frames, each one getting clearer.

"I'll be...."

"Yeah. I know who has those hair pins." Gregory cleared his throat. "They were a gift from my father to my mother when they first got married. It's one of the few things my mother loves that came from him. She wears them all the time." He pulled out the chair and sat down. "The woman in that video is my mother. She wears those shoes because high heels aggravate her legs too badly."

Fillian's eyes widened. He had suggested her as a suspect, but that had been just to cover all possibilities. What the hell kind of mother did all this to her own son?

"You're sure?" Fillian asked quietly, shaking his head.

"I'm sure it's her." Gregory looked completely devastated, and Fillian couldn't blame him. He knew exactly how he'd feel if the situation were reversed.

"What in the hell. Why would your mother pull something like this?" He was angry on Gregory's behalf, along with being completely aghast. He had seen some weird things since joining the force, and he had heard of some even stranger stories, but this one took the cake.

"Yes. Isn't that a total steaming pile of crap. I'm sure—it's definitely my mother." Gregory stood quickly enough that the dining room chair tipped over backward and landed on the carpet. "What the hell am I going to do? My own damned mother." He went into the living room and began to pace. "What the hell was she thinking? Her grandchildren could have been hurt in that damned fire stunt... or worse." He began to pace back and forth across the room.

Fillian got up. "It's going to be okay."

"How?" he snapped.

Fillian had to keep calm for his sake. "Look, I know this sucks, but it really is going to be okay. You know what she is now, and once Carter and I are done, so will the police and probably the prosecutor."

Gregory turned to him with murderous fire in his eyes. "Don't tell me that we have to take this one step at a time or that we have to let the evidence guide or... I don't know. Give me anything other than bad television dialogue. I want to go over there, yank the crazy old lady out of bed, and strangle her while I look deep into her eyes as the life drains out of her." He shook hard, and Fillian didn't know what to do. "I want to hang her by the ears from the rafters of her garage."

Fillian stepped back, letting Gregory pace once more.

"It's okay," Carter said from behind him. "Let Gregory get it out. He needs to let all this hurt out, and at least he's doing so right away so it isn't all bottled up."

The stream of darkness coming out of Gregory quickly abated, and he stood in the center of the room, head down, looking lost and confused. Fillian gently guided him back to the dining room, righted the chair, and got Gregory to sit.

"Look, I know you're angry, and that's cool, but we don't know that your mother placed the doll. She could have been coming over to see about you and the kids. You hadn't talked to her in a while. Maybe she was trying to see how you were doing." Fillian had to try to offer some explanation, because as much as Gregory had jumped to a conclusion, they didn't have proof of anything yet.

"But…."

"Hey. We need to talk to both of them."

"Then I'm going with you. I want to look them both in the eye."

Carter cleared his throat. "I don't think that's a good idea."

"If you don't let me come, then I'll confront my mother on my own, and there's nothing either of you can do to stop me." He crossed his arms over his chest. "She's my mother, and I can visit her if I want to. And so help me God, I will confront her, and if she did it, I'll…." He sat and shook hard. "The hell she's put me through, the worry, the fear—she needs to feel some of that. She really does."

Carter stood, and Fillian followed him out of the room. "I can't take him to talk to her. Do you have any idea what my captain would do if he found out about this?"

Fillian could only imagine. "I know. But think about what would happen if he confronts his mother alone." He was truly frightened. "I have never seen him like this. We have to try to keep him calm and make sure he doesn't do anything all of us will regret. I mean, if he decides to leave, I can't stop him." No matter how worried he was.

"But those threats—"

"Are only angry words until something happens. You know that." Fillian was worried that in his state of mind, Gregory would act on them.

"Then we talk to Stevie tomorrow to try to eliminate him before we confront the mother." Fillian followed Carter's gaze to Gregory. "Your job is going to be to calm him down and get him to understand that it has got to be us who do this, not him."

Fillian nodded. "Thanks for bringing over the video. At least we have some answers... but the really hard work is ahead of us." Just looking at Gregory told him that this was one hell of a minefield.

Carter packed up the computer and said good night. Gregory thanked him and said little more. Fillian saw Carter to the door, and when he returned, Gregory was putting on his jacket. "I have to talk to her."

"No," Fillian said flatly. "This isn't for you to handle. Let Carter and me take the lead." He wanted to snap at him but stopped himself. "You need to be here for Weston and Marnie. Remember, they are the really important people in all this. Not you or me, but them."

"I know. But that... that... woman... she...." He sputtered, and Fillian pulled him into a hug and held him tightly.

"The kids need you. And we don't know anything for sure yet. Just try to calm down, and we'll get to the bottom of this. We know more now than we did, but we don't have all the answers. We'll get them, I'm sure of it, but you need to let us do our job."

"And what am I supposed to do?" Gregory asked. "I can't just sit here and wonder what is going on. I have to look her in the eyes. She's my mother, and I have to confront her."

Fillian understood that. "Maybe. I can see why you feel you need to, but let's make sure we have all the facts first. We don't know for sure that it was her, and if you're wrong—if *we're* wrong—then it could make trouble for us." Gregory seemed less jumpy, and Fillian hoped that meant he was calming down. "Carter and I are police officers, and we deal in facts and things we can prove. Right now, we have her at the door, but that's all. We don't know if she's behind this or not. But the good thing is that Carter and I know where to start looking, and that's a big deal."

Gregory swallowed hard and nodded slowly. "I know. And I appreciate that you're trying to help me, but sometimes it feels like there's a huge hole opening up, and I swear it's going to swallow me whole. I need some answers. The thought of my own mother... regardless of how selfish she is.... What does it say that she might have...?"

"If it's true, it says a lot about her but nothing at all about you," Fillian told him. "Remember, I spent a lot of time looking over the fence into the yard growing up. I used to watch that pool in the summer, and your mom was never around." He leaned closer. "Do you know what I just remembered?"

Gregory shook his head. "No, what?"

"That that pool looked so inviting and perfect, but you didn't get to use it all that often either. It was beautiful and sparkled in the sun, but it was just as off limits to you as it was to me." He smoothed his fingers over Gregory's cheek. "You were just as much an outsider as I was." Gregory blinked but didn't say anything more. "Come on, it's late. You have to go to work in the morning, and I'm on duty as well. I know this is going to sound callous, but we need to get on with things. Carter and I will look into what we have, and we'll talk to Stevie."

"You can't talk to my mother without me. Promise me that," Gregory said almost frantically. "You have to promise me that if you think it's her that I get to be there when you talk to her." He swallowed hard.

"I can't do that. But I will talk to Carter. That I can promise." Fillian didn't have control over all the moving parts. "Now, you and I need to clean things up down here, and then we can go upstairs. You need to rest."

Gregory rolled his eyes. "Is this where you say that things will look better in the morning?"

Fillian scoffed. "Okay, I won't say it. But whatever happens, I'm here for you, so try not to worry about it. We will find out what happened, and if your mother is behind it, then I'll be there with you to roast her on a proverbial spit. That is, if she is truly guilty."

Gregory shrugged. "I don't know whether I'm hoping it's my mother or Stevie. The thought of either one is enough to make my stomach roil. But like you said, I have to let you find out."

Fillian took Gregory's hand and squeezed it. "Why don't you go on upstairs, and I'll lock up and turn out the lights."

Gregory nodded and headed up the stairs while Fillian closed up and followed him. He ran into Gregory as he came out of the guest room. "They're both out."

"Good." It was time he helped Gregory work out his own tension so he could get to sleep… and Fillian knew just the way, and it involved warm hands and a lot of patience.

"DADDY," WESTON said as he bounded on the bed the following morning. To Fillian, it seemed like he and Gregory had just closed their eyes. "I'm hungry, and it's light out."

Fillian groaned and rolled over. The clock read just before six. He yawned and pulled the covers over his head.

"It's okay, buddy," Gregory said gently. "Go on back to your room and get dressed. I'll be right in, and we can go find you some breakfast." Weston jumped off the bed and hurried out. "I'll take care of him. You rest for a while."

"Did you sleep?" Fillian asked.

"Not much, but it's okay." He kissed him and left the room. Fillian stretched and burrowed under the covers for a little while longer, which turned out to be ten minutes before his phone rang. He would have ignored it, but the call was from Carter, so he took it and arranged to meet him at eight. Fillian called in to let the department know about his meeting before dressing and heading downstairs.

"You're up. Do you want eggs?" Gregory asked brightly.

"Daddy makes good eggies," Weston said, already shoveling some into his mouth. Marnie had a plate and seemed to be waiting on hers.

"That would be nice." He sat down and spread a napkin to make sure he didn't spill anything on his uniform. Gregory brought him coffee and eventually a plate of eggs with toast. It had been a while since Fillian had someone take care of him like this. A simple meal, but done with care.

"I have a meeting with Carter at eight," Fillian said between bites. "We'll develop a plan and go from there."

"Remember your promise," Gregory said, holding the spatula mid flip.

"I'll do what I can, but this is largely a local case, and Carter is the one who has the lead. I'm here to provide support." He finished his breakfast and took the dishes to the sink. "I need to get going." Fillian kissed Gregory, pausing close to him. "I really like this, having breakfast like a family, kissing you before I head to work."

"Me too," Gregory said softly. "I'll see you tonight."

Fillian hurried out to his car, checking the time. He called in to Dispatch to let them know where he was and that he was on duty while he drove to the Carlisle Police Station, where Carter waited with more coffee, the fuel every cop ran on.

"Do we have anything new?" Fillian asked after taking his first sip.

Carter nodded. "I still want to talk to your teammate, but I don't think he has anything to do with this." He picked up the evidence bag with the doll inside and turned it over. "The doll noose was made with green twine, the kind used by gardeners. So I made a little stop earlier this morning. Your teammate Stevie lives in that new development to the west of town. All of the yards are new, and the plants are small. There is nothing to tie up."

"You know," Fillian said softly, "the houses on the street where Mrs. Haber lives are older, and they have mature landscaping."

Carter pulled open his desk drawer and pulled out a bit of string. "I got this off one of the other shrubs at the address we have for the Habers out on Walnut. It's the same exact thing. Of course I can't use this in court, and it isn't definitive...."

Fillian sighed. "Let's talk to Stevie and see what we get."

"Agreed. But then we're going to have to talk to Mrs. Haber, and that is not going to be pretty for anyone."

Fillian called his teammate, who was working from home. He arranged to meet Fillian in fifteen minutes. "Let's go." Solving a case was usually a high... but this one only seemed like a looming pit.

"HEY, FILLIAN." Stevie was smiling until he saw Carter too, both of them in uniform. "What's going on?" He stepped back. "Do you want to come in?"

"We have a few questions we need to ask you. This shouldn't take up too much of your time." Carter got right down to it. Stevie gestured, and they went inside the spotless new home.

"What's this about?" Stevie asked. "How can I help you?" He looked right at Fillian.

"You visited Gregory's place over the weekend."

Stevie nodded. "Yeah. He wasn't home. I wanted to talk to him about some things...." Stevie looked toward the back of the house, and then his gaze traveled back to Fillian. "They're personal, and since I was downtown, I stopped in to see if he had a minute. But once I knocked, I remembered that you and Gregory were gone for the weekend, so I came back home." Color rose in his cheeks, and he lowered his gaze.

Fillian turned to Carter, who excused himself and went outside.

"We're asking for a reason."

"Yeah. I know some shit's been happening with Gregory, but I needed to talk to him about something." The color was back, and so was the looking around. "Look, this is hard... but I needed some advice about sex, and he's the one I knew I could talk to. But he wasn't home, and

I figured I could talk to him later." His voice was soft, even though he seemed to be the only one home.

"Okay. I don't need to know what you were going to ask. You can talk to Gregory about that, okay? But answer this—when you got to the door, was there anything unusual?"

Stevie looked at him like he had grown another head. "No. It was just a door with a number two on it. Brown...." He truly seemed confused, and Fillian believed him.

"Okay. Thanks, Stevie." Fillian put out his hand and smiled.

"Aren't you going to tell me what you're looking for?" Stevie asked.

"Not unless you want to tell me the sex question you have for Gregory." Fillian grinned at Stevie's discomfort. "Then I'll be going. And thank you for your help. We appreciate it." He left the house and joined Carter on the sidewalk. "There was nothing on the door, and what he told me jibes completely with what we saw on camera."

"So it seems." Carter trailed off. "I wouldn't want to be in your shoes. Having to question your boyfriend's mother."

Fillian chuckled. "We do what we have to do. Besides, we don't have direct proof that points to her with the notes or the fire, and the evidence is circumstantial with the doll. We may need that to move forward, but Gregory doesn't. And if he decides that he needs to have it out with his mother, then we need to let him. She's a real piece of work."

"So what are you suggesting?" Carter asked.

Fillian decided that he needed to tell Carter everything. "I question her and let Gregory be there to look her in the eye. I'm thinking that maybe Gregory would like to be the one to confront her, but...." From a police perspective, they might get a lot more out of her. But from the boyfriend point of view, he was worried that it was a lot to ask of Gregory, and he hoped it wouldn't be too much. "I don't want him to get hurt, but I...."

"You can't see a way around it," Carter supplied, completing his thought.

He nodded slowly. "I know it isn't what Gregory wants, but we could talk to her anyway. It would save him the pain of having to confront his mother about why she would do these things to him."

Carter shook his head. "You can't shelter him from something like this. He'll have to deal with it. I suggest we find him, see what he wants to do, and go from there. Believe me, I understand wanting to protect the ones I love. I would do anything to make sure Donald and Alex don't see anything that isn't bright and happy, but that's impossible. Donald has a gut-wrenching job that he's amazing at. I don't think I could do what he does for those children he works with in a million years."

"I know. But…."

"If Gregory is willing to help us put an attempted arsonist behind bars, then so be it." Carter's gaze grew hard. "Whoever set that fire in the hallway knew what they were doing. It wasn't an accident, and it wasn't designed to smolder and create lots of smoke. We believe that it was meant to go up in a rush, but some of the papers inside were wet, and they didn't burn as quickly and created the smoke. Basically, you were all very lucky."

"Okay." Fillian so wanted to spare Gregory all of this. "Let me call him." Fillian called Gregory's cell. "I'm here with Carter."

"Was it my mother?" Gregory asked, flatly and without any preamble; even his voice got quieter.

"We believe so, though we don't know why. Stevie came to ask you a question, and he said that the doll was not on the door at that time, and I believe him. But we have little to go on."

"Doesn't matter. I'm going to kill her." The anger coming through the phone nearly knocked Fillian over.

"No. Do nothing," he retorted firmly. "We need you to help us. Carter and I will meet you at the house after work. Promise me that you won't do anything. What we need is a confession. Then the local police can take over and she can be charged." Fillian was scared of what Gregory might do. "You doing something rash isn't worth the hurt it could do the kids. They need you, and I need you." His voice broke. "So please just do your work, and we'll devise a plan when you get home. I promise. This isn't going anywhere." Fillian turned to Carter. "We could have patrols check Gregory's building and my house on a regular basis as a precaution."

Carter nodded and got on the phone.

"Promise me," Fillian said to Gregory. "I need that. Just stay away from her and don't do anything. We need to tie this up so we can make a strong case."

"But she…," Gregory sputtered and then grew quiet. "Okay, I promise I won't do anything, but if you think I'm going to be able to concentrate…. I don't want to hurt the kids." Fillian didn't say anything, but if Gregory confronted his mother on his own and it didn't go well, she could use that against him to try to get custody. This had to be done right.

"I understand. But don't do anything. I love you, and I'll see you at home right after my shift." He ended the call and slid his phone into his pocket.

Carter arranged for the patrols, and then they agreed to meet Gregory at Fillian's once their shifts were over before parting to go on with the rest of their day. Fillian had no doubt that the clock was going to tick forward very slowly.

GREGORY JUMPED up from the sofa as soon as Fillian came into the house. The kids were playing some mixture of Lego and Barbies on the floor. "What's the plan?" Judging by the mug on the coffee table, Gregory must have downed half a pot of coffee.

"My mother is going to come over to sit with the kids. She'll be here in half an hour." Fillian hung up his hat and took Gregory into the entrance hall. "We need to speak to your mother, you know that."

"And you want me to sit back while you or Carter talk to her." A knock interrupted the conversation. Fillian went to let Carter inside and closed the ornate Second Empire style etched glass door behind him.

"No. The plan is for you to speak to her. You can confront her any way you see fit."

"And you want me to wear a wire?" Gregory asked.

"No. Just get her to confess. I went by the house. It's a lovely evening, and she has every window open to catch the breeze. So we're just going to listen. All you need to do is get her talking," Carter said. "We aren't going to prep you or tell you what to say. Just let her have it. You're angry, and you know she's the one who sent the notes and who set the fire. Bluff if you have to, but just let her see your anger and hurt. If we're there, she'll just clam up."

"But you think that because I'm her son she might feel some sort of guilt?" Gregory grinned, but without a hint of happiness. "My mother doesn't feel guilt or remorse. Never has. She only thinks of what she wants and goes for it."

Fillian drew close enough that he could see the violet flecks in Gregory's eyes. "Then use that. Call her on it. You know her better than anyone else."

Gregory sighed. "Of course I'll do it. I want to give her a piece of my mind." Fillian could already tell that Gregory's mind was flying ahead. "And I know exactly how to get to her." He took a deep breath. "I take it you want to do this right away."

"Tonight if possible."

"Let me call my mother and find out if she's home." Gregory went into another room and made the call while he and Carter waited. "They're having dinner, but I told her I'd stop by to see her at seven thirty."

"Maybe we should have something to eat," Fillian offered, hoping that Gregory would have a chance to calm down a little.

"After I talk to her. I don't think I can keep anything down right now. I'm too…."

Carter put his hand on Gregory's shoulder. "You need to be calm and keep your wits about you." The way Gregory's hand shook, Fillian wasn't sure it was possible.

CHAPTER 16

GREGORY TOOK a deep breath as Fillian pulled to a stop in front of his mother and stepfather's large house in the Old Mooreland section of town. "I don't know if I can do this." He turned toward the house with all the lights on. It looked warm and inviting, but Gregory knew it was just the opposite.

"I know you can," Fillian told him. "You'll do it for the kids." His eyes were so confident. Fillian radiated strength and self-assurance.

"Okay." He closed his eyes, pulling up images of those damned notes, that stupid doll, and most importantly, the fear the kids radiated when they were leaving the apartment, heading down the back fire escape. "I got this." He opened the door and got out, then marched up the walk to ring the bell.

His stepfather answered the door. "Charles," Gregory said, determined to hold on to his anger. "I'm here to speak to my mother."

He nodded. "She told me, but I just got home to surprise her."

Gregory stepped closer. "I appreciate that. But she and I have to talk, and she can either talk to me, or I'll make a phone call and she can spend the evening at the police station. Either way, I'm afraid your reunion is about to crash and burn."

Charles stepped aside, his eyes widening. "What the hell has been going on?"

"I'm sure Mother will tell you her version of events in good time. But right now, she and I need to talk. Where is she?"

Charles rolled his eyes like Gregory was being overly dramatic. "In the Florida room."

Gregory strode through the living room to the screened-in room filled with freshly painted white wicker furniture with bright floral cushions. Palms stood in the corners. If Gregory didn't know better, this room could have passed for a piece of the tropics.

"Gregory," his mother said, then paused to sip from her glass. "With Charles returning, I forgot you were coming. Can we talk another time?"

"No." He closed the door and took two steps to stand over her. "It seems you've been busy, Mother. So have I, and the police." He leaned over the chair. "I got each of your little missives. Too bad you weren't careful enough not to leave traces. And your latest little gift. Do you think we don't have you on camera?" He stood up straight and crossed his arms over his chest, letting some of his anger out but keeping the rest in check. "I got you in full, living color. And my next step is to go to the court to get a restraining order. Those kids will be eighteen before you ever see them again."

His mother set her glass aside, the first cracks showing in her well-practiced façade. "Gregory, I…."

"What did you hope to accomplish by all this? The notes, the fearmongering." He wasn't going to let her off the hook.

"Your brother and that woman he married should have left guardianship of those kids to me. I'm his mother, and I raised both of you. I know how to be a parent. What do you know? What the hell does a man like *you* know about children? You'll never have any of your own." She picked up her glass like she hadn't just said some of the most hurtful things possible.

"So you decided to do what? Prove that I wasn't capable?" Gregory asked.

"I don't need to do that. All I need to do is drive you hard enough that you crack and realize that you can't do this. You should have seen yourself after that first note. You could never take pressure, and all I needed to do was keep piling it on. That incident with that man attacking you… he was perfect. He started all of it, and all I needed to do was make sure it continued." She sat back like she was fucking satisfied with herself.

"So you didn't know that he's been in custody? That we know the notes weren't from him, just like we know he didn't set the fire in my building?" He had to keep the pressure on her. "The longer she talked, the more likely he'd get the confession for the big stuff. "Was your plan to burn down the building? Then what? Hope we all came to you for help? Then you'd step in and take the kids…?" Shit, that was it.

She went silent, her lips pursed.

"Was that it, Mother?" he snapped. "Is that what you fucking thought?"

She jumped to her feet. "You never should have been given those kids. They are all I have left of Arthur, and he and that bitch decided that you should raise them. How do you think that made me feel?"

"So you did set the fire?" He wasn't going to let up. He was too damned close.

"Of course I set the fire, and you were supposed to burn up with the building." Her eyes were wild, and she shook enough to spill tea all over the floor.

Gregory took a deep breath. "Did you hear all of that?" he asked loudly.

"All the way to the sidewalk, clear as a bell," Carter answered.

"It's over, Mother. That is Carter, a Carlisle police officer. I'm afraid Arthur's children will never be coming to live with you." He looked around.

Her eyes widened as the full scope of what she'd said barreled into her. "Charles…," she cried, hurrying to open the door. "Charles…." She stepped into the living room in time to see Carter and Fillian, followed by her husband, waiting for her. "Charles, you need to make all of these people leave. I…."

Gregory shook his head before taking a step back. "You need to go with these men, Mother. They're going to take you down to the station. They have questions for you." Gregory walked past her, Fillian, and Carter, heading outside for some fresh air. He needed to breathe and try to clear his head.

His own mother had tried to set his place on fire. She hated him enough that she wanted him to die.

Gregory stepped off the sidewalk as Carter and Fillian guided his mother in handcuffs to Carter's police car. Once she was secured in the back, Carter got in and drove her away. Gregory tried to feel something for her, but at the moment, he was blank.

"What is happening here? What did you do to her?" Charles asked, hurrying out of the house.

"I didn't do anything. I'm sure you heard what she said. I'm sure the *neighborhood* did." Gregory lifted his gaze. "If you want to help her, then I suggest you get a good attorney."

"You're filing charges? Against your own mother?" he asked.

"My mother set fire to the building I live in. She confessed to it not ten minutes ago. She damaged my landlord's property. She harassed me and the kids for weeks. I'm sorry, but any charges that she has coming were brought on by herself. She did all of it. It's my job to protect my niece and nephew, and I will. Part of that is now to keep them away from her." He shrugged.

"Yeah," Fillian said gently.

"Is *he* responsible for all this?" Charles asked.

"Your wife is," Fillian said. "We have her confessing to it, and there are multiple witnesses. This is as open and shut as anything I have ever seen." Fillian put an arm around Gregory's shoulders. "Come on. It's time to go. Nothing good can come from any of this." He squeezed Gregory gently, holding him in strong arms. "But Gregory is right. Get her a good lawyer and an even better doctor. She's going to need both of them." Fillian guided Gregory back to the car.

"What more can I do?" Gregory asked. "And what do I tell the kids?" He climbed inside and closed the car door, staring out the front window down the residential street.

"Nothing. At least not now. Wait until they ask, and then tell them a version of the truth. That Grandma did something bad and that she needs help. Because your mother definitely does. From there, you see what happens and how things play out."

"But my own mother…," he said softly. "She wanted to drive me into giving up the kids… and I actually wondered if I was doing the right thing. I let her really get to me and…."

"Yeah. But those kids love you, and you were worried for their safety, the way the best parents would be. You didn't do anything wrong." Fillian started the car, and Gregory rode back to the house in silence, sinking into his own thoughts.

THE KIDS were excited to see him, crowding around for hugs, and Gregory put on a mask of happiness for their sakes, then thanked Fillian's mother for watching them. The kids went to play, and he sat at the dining room table and stared at the wall, his eyes tracing a crack in the plaster.

"I take it things were difficult," Verona said as she sat down. "Being a parent isn't an easy job."

Gregory lifted his gaze, wondering if she was going to try to defend his mother. At the moment, Gregory didn't think he could take that. He

needed to be angry and indignant, to hold on to it, or he was likely to
back down.

"I'm aware," he said flatly. "It's the hardest job there is."

"And yet anyone can be a parent. All you have to do is have a
kid. There are no training classes or certifications. Consequently, some
kids get great parents who give all the love and attention possible. They
get the ones who spend time with their kids and help them grow into
responsible adults. These parents give of themselves and love their kids,
putting them first." She rested her hands on the table. "Your mother is
not one of those, and she never will be. But you are. I know you feel
bad about what happened, but you didn't have anything to do with that.
Your mother brought it on herself, and not merely because she was a
bad mother. She took her behavior and made it criminal." She patted
his hand. "You did what you had to for the kids because you are a good
parent."

"Really? I feel selfish and...." He didn't even have the words.
Maybe *roadkill* was a better description.

"Gregory, those two adore you, and you feel the same about them.
You put them first, which is how it should be." Fillian rested his hands
on his shoulders. "Now stop beating yourself up for things that are out of
your control and remember what's truly important."

Weston came over, and Gregory slid back in his chair. Weston
climbed onto his lap and leaned against his chest. Fillian gently kneaded
Gregory's shoulders, and Gregory closed his eyes as he sat with Marnie
next to him, doing his best to let the shadows and worry slip away.

Verona pushed her chair away from the table and stood. "Thank
you," Gregory whispered.

"Oh, you're welcome, honey." She checked the time. "I think I
need to get home, and you need to get these two munchkins to bed." She
smiled, lightly patting Fillian on the cheek before leaving the house.

"I know your mother is right," Gregory said quietly.

"Do we have to go to bed?" Weston asked, sounding half asleep
already.

"Yes. Now go clean up your toys and go upstairs to wash up and
put on your pajamas. I'll be up to tuck you in, and tomorrow we'll go
back home."

"Why?" Weston asked. "I like it here. Grammy took us out back to play. I like it, and if we stay, then we could get a dog because there's a place for it to go poop."

Gregory turned to Fillian, and they both broke into smiles. "I see. You think you have that all figured out." Gregory tickled Weston before putting him down. "Go and get ready for bed."

Weston raced up the stairs. "Marnie, we're going to get a puppy."

"I didn't say that," Gregory called, but it was clear that no one was listening to him. "God," he groaned.

"You know," Fillian said softly, "you could get the kids a dog if you all moved in here. We could rework the rooms upstairs so they each had their own space, and yeah, we could get a dog." Fillian slipped his hands around Gregory's waist and rested his head against the back of Gregory's shoulder.

"Isn't it too soon?"

Fillian humphed. "We've known each other since we were kids. But it isn't something you have to decide today or tomorrow. It's just something to think about. The kids would have more room, and there's the yard." He tightened his hold a little.

Gregory agreed as he slowly turned in Fillian's embrace. "Do you have any idea how tempted I am to say yes? To take the chance and get to sleep next to you every night and wake up next to you each morning? That's so enticing."

"I know exactly how you feel," Fillian said. "So is that a yes?"

"Let's take things one step at a time." Right now, at this moment, that was the very best Gregory could offer. There had been so much upheaval in all their lives that he needed a little distance, and it was hard to think of anything else when he was this close to Fillian.

He drew even closer, Fillian's breath ghosting over his lips. "As long as those steps lead me to having you, I'm all for it."

EPILOGUE

FILLIAN CLIMBED the stairs to Gregory's apartment and strode inside to scoop the final box up off the living room floor. "Is that the last of it?" God, he hoped so. He had gone up and down those stairs at least a hundred times.

"Yeah. The place is empty, and I've swept everything out." Gregory looked around the room before taking the dustpan, broom, and garbage bag. Fillian left the apartment with Gregory behind him, then locked up and placed the key in the mailbox the way the landlord had requested. Fillian set the box in the back of the truck, and Gregory added the trash and cleaning stuff. The wind picked up, blowing a few street tree leaves around his feet.

"Let's get going. The weather said to expect snow, and we should get this unloaded before that happens." Fillian got into the truck, and they headed for the house and unloaded the last of the stuff.

The kids had already been moved and each of their rooms set up. They seemed happy. Fillian's mother opened the door as he began carrying in the last of the kitchen boxes. For now, these things had been earmarked for storage, so Fillian climbed the stairs to the third floor and placed them in organized areas. Up and down he went until he swore his legs weren't going to take another step, passing Gregory as he made his own trips.

Finally it was over. All their things were in the house, and the furniture, an amalgamation of what both of them had, filled the rooms. Old things they didn't need had been donated, and the house had a warmth it had never had before.

"I should get home," Fillian's mother said once they were done and able to put their feet up for five minutes. "The kids are playing outside." She kissed each of them on the cheek and put her coat on before grabbing her purse. "I'll see all of you for Sunday dinner." She waved and was off. Verona had taken to having all of them over every Sunday for a family dinner.

"You know we have one more thing to do," Gregory said.

Fillian sighed. "I know. Look. You take the truck and get what you need. I really want to finish getting the last things put away. That way we can all get settled without these boxes getting in the way."

"If you're sure," Gregory said before getting up and going through to the back door. He called the kids, and they all trooped back through, faces red from the cold. Gregory shepherded them out the front and into the truck, the heavy front door closing behind them, leaving Fillian alone in the quiet house.

So much had changed, and most of it for the good. It had taken until the end of summer for him to convince Gregory to make the final decision to move in. By then, he had cleared out his office and made it ready for Weston. He'd also gotten the guest room cleared so it could be Marnie's room. Mostly that consisted of going through things he'd carried with him for too long and finally making the decision to let them go. His shifts at work had also changed for a while, and he worked third shift for a month to cover someone who was out, but he was back on days and grateful for it. And their rugby team ended the fall season undefeated, which was a surprise to everyone.

The biggest change was in Gregory. He smiled more, and his heart seemed lighter. Prosecutors had worked out a deal to get his mother the help she needed, and if she complied with the orders, she'd stay out of jail.

Fillian wandered from room to room, emptying the last boxes and breaking them down. He unpacked the last of the kitchen things, then took the flattened boxes and the final items to be sold back to the garage, where an entire wall was lined with things to be unloaded in a huge spring garage sale.

Flakes of snow fell as he closed up the back and went through to the house to get out the things for hot chocolate and cookies for when the rest of them got home. His life was a lot noisier than when he was single, but it was filled with warmth and love.

"Papa Filly," Weston called as soon as they were back. He ran through to where Fillian was putting milk in the microwave to heat. Where they had come up with that name, he had no idea, but it had stuck, and he was now Papa Filly to both kids. He really hoped that name changed. "Look what we got."

A reddish brown and white dog raced up to him. "Well, look at you," he said, kneeling down to scratch behind her ears. She was about twenty pounds, fluffy, and maybe a little pudgy. He continued petting her, looking up at Gregory. "What happened to Dixie?" They had looked online and had settled on the gray mutt with expressive eyes.

"He was adopted yesterday. But this girl here looked at us like she was family."

"Yeah, Papa Filly," Marnie said. "Her name is Lulu."

She pressed right to Fillian, looking up at him with those huge eyes. He had to admit she was gorgeous. "And she's going to have puppies."

Marnie began to dance, and Fillian widened his eyes and looked at Gregory like he was crazy.

"She needed a home. Mitchell rescued her from a breeder outside Newville. When he got her, she was in bad shape. He didn't know she was pregnant at the time. She needed a place where she could have her puppies in safety and where she wouldn't be abused. Mitchell told me that she's five years old and that he believes that this is her sixth litter of puppies. We'll have her spayed once she's given birth. She's mostly Cavalier King Charles Spaniel." He knelt as well.

"I think she's beautiful." Fillian stood up while Lulu began to explore the kitchen. "I have the things for cocoa, so all of you hang up your coats." The kids hurried out while Fillian got the bowls and mat they had already purchased in anticipation of getting the dog and placed them in the corner. Gregory put a little food in the bowl. Lulu ate, drank some water, and then continued her explorations.

"Can we watch a movie with Lulu?" Marnie asked, hurrying back into the room while Fillian finished making the cocoa.

"Sure. It's your daddy's turn to pick the movie." He brought everything into the living room and set the mugs on the coffee table. Gregory chose *Migration* because none of them had seen it yet. He and Gregory sat together on the sofa with Marnie and Weston at the table with their drinks. Lulu hopped up between them and settled right down.

Gregory held his mug, smiling before leaning over. "Love you," he whispered softly.

"Love you too," Fillian said gently. They shared a kiss before he turned to look at the kids, at his family. Sometimes life's road was curved, but somehow he'd still managed to get everything he wanted.

Keep reading for an excerpt from
Pulling Strings
by Andrew Grey

DEVON DONALDSON stood outside the Four Seasons in downtown Philadelphia, glancing up at the imposing edifice.

"What are you waiting for?" Karen asked as she got out of the taxi, straightening the hem of her ankle-length royal blue gown. "Come on. We're supposed to be here." She took Devon's arm and led him inside. "You look very nice in your tuxedo."

"It's a rental," he blurted out, then instantly wished he hadn't. No one needed to know that. He should learn to keep his mouth shut.

"I won't tell anyone." She patted his arm, and they continued their way inside, crossing the imposing lobby, with its large crystal chandeliers and polished marble floors, following the discreet signage to the ballroom, where music wafted out into the hall. Devon fished his invitation out of his pocket and handed it to the attendant. Karen did the same.

"Have a good time," said the tall man, who probably also served as security, motioning them inside.

The ballroom was already filling with people, all dressed to the nines. Devon still wasn't able to figure out how he had ended up with an invitation. Coopers, Littman, and Mauer sponsored the event to benefit the National Multiple Sclerosis Society each year, and tickets were expensive. Devon certainly didn't have that kind of money lying around.

"There's the rest of the team." Karen waved and let go of Devon's arm to walk over to the others.

Devon followed her and took a place at the table in the center of the room. At least he knew his fellow team members: Mark Calvinson, Susan Malton, and Lee Kwan. He greeted each of them with a handshake, while Karen hugged them, and then they both sat down.

"You aren't going to end up dancing on a table like last year, are you, Mark?" Karen asked.

"I did not," he replied indignantly. "I merely ended up sitting on the edge of one."

"You nearly toppled the entire thing over," Susan clarified, and everyone chuckled. "Maybe that's why we have these drink tickets instead of the open bar like last year." She shot Mark a glare that didn't last very long.

Devon settled in his seat, reached for a glass, and filled it from the crystal pitcher of water on the table, wondering how long he could just sit here without having to say anything. Not too long, apparently.

"Guys, this is Devon's first foray into the world of rubber chicken and schmoozing for dollars." Karen grinned at him.

"Just wait until the auction." Lee leaned over. "That's when the big boys all pull out their wallets and fight over who can buy the biggest… equipment." He winked, and everyone else groaned.

The recorded music up until then had been largely background. As a small live orchestra began playing, a few couples shifted out of their seats to dance, while at the same time a line formed at the bar. Devon turned slightly so he could watch the musicians and listen to the music while the others talked. It was mostly gossip about who was doing whom, and Devon wasn't really interested.

"Yeah, apparently the designs were copies and…"

Devon turned, suddenly tuned in to what Susan was saying.

"…they are still tracing how it could have happened."

"I hear she's interested in you," Lee told Mark, who stood right away and sauntered over to Gloria from marketing, the subject of their interest, only to be shot down faster than he could say "supply chain integration." Mark returned to the table, smacked Lee on the back of the head, and vowed to get even with him.

"Do any of you dance?" Karen asked. The other guys all shook their heads, but Devon nodded slowly. Karen got to her feet, grabbing his arm once again. "Then why don't you show me the floor?"

Devon stood and properly took her arm to lead her through the tables to the floor. "I haven't danced in a while."

"I'm sure you remember how," Karen said with amusement.

Devon cocked his lips slightly, whirled her into his arms, and spun her into a waltz in elegant style. "Of course. Four years of lessons with my mother, because Dad refused to go and she was determined." He glided Karen through the steps, making her smile, until the number ended.

She stepped away, clapping politely along with the others. "Who is that?" she whispered, and Devon followed her gaze to a stunning, darkly intense man who half frowned as he watched the dance floor, his arms crossed over his chest. "Man… he's got the whole 'tall, dark, and broody' thing going on."

"If you like that sort of thing," Devon said, swallowing hard, because while he wasn't into the brooding thing, he wouldn't kick him out of bed if he got the chance. His tuxedo was cut beautifully—that was no rental. Even in the jacket, his wide shoulders and trim waist were evident. That was a man who knew how to take care of himself, even if he seemed about two seconds from shouting orders at everyone in the room.

"Oh, me likey," she whispered.

The music started again, and Devon pulled his attention away from the sight against the wall. The tempo changed, and Devon broke into the fox-trot, taking Karen right along with him.

"Damn, son, you weren't kidding. Your mother must be so proud."

"She was, yes." That was all the acknowledgment he gave, but Karen missed a step. Devon picked it up, guiding her through until the number ended. Then he applauded and escorted her properly from the floor. "I think I'm going to have a drink. Would you like anything?" he asked.

"No thanks. I'll see you back at the table." She glided off across the room.

Devon made his way through the increasing crowd to the bar. He got in line and slowly moved forward, glancing at where Tall, Dark, and Broody seemed to be watching him in return. Devon turned away and paid attention to what was in front of him.

As he neared the bar, the hair on the back of his neck stood up, and he knew Tall, Dark, and Broody was right behind him. He didn't dare look around even as sweat broke out under his shirt collar. Granted, he had no reason to be nervous—he hadn't done anything wrong—but the man's presence sent his pulse racing.

"Can I help you?" the bartender in a white shirt and black vest asked.

"Whiskey and soda," Devon ordered, handing over the ticket. A few moments later, he took the drink, thanked the bartender, and purposefully walked back to the table. Only once he sat down did he chance to look back. Tall, Dark, and Broody was nowhere to be seen, and Devon silently chastised himself for being so stupid.

"You looked great, Devon," Susan said. "Maybe we could dance later."

"Did you grow a right foot?" Mark chirped, and turned to Devon. "Last year she wheedled me onto the dance floor, and I ended up with two broken toes and enough bruises that it hurt to walk for a week. Don't do it, my friend. It's not worth the agony." He dashed away as Susan lunged for him.

"Are you all having a good time?" the supervisor, Judy Spalding, asked from next to Mark. "No table dancing this year." She looked right down at Mark. "Remember, everyone is here, including all of the partners. This is definitely a time to impress. Don't just sit here and talk to each other. Get up, mingle, meet people. This is the one night of the year that most of the hierarchy barriers are down. So it's a chance to make an impression."

"Thanks, Judy," Devon said, then finished his drink for courage and pushed back his chair. Before he'd left the house, he had determined that he needed to meet and talk with at least ten people he didn't know tonight. Devon was usually quiet—his dad said he was shy. He knew it was something he needed to work on if he was to get noticed and have the chance to go anywhere in the company.

Girding himself, he walked up to a group of people he had never met before, all standing in a circle, and took the only empty place, next to a woman in a cream-colored gown that glittered with sequins. "Your dress is stunning," he told her as the others talked.

She turned to him, a smile lighting her face. "Thank you, young man."

"You're very welcome. It really is beautiful, and you are gorgeous in it."

She smiled again.

"I'm Devon Donaldson." He extended his hand, and she took it, shaking it gently.

"Marie Mauer. It's very nice to meet you. Is this your first one of these?"

"Yes, ma'am. I'm new at the firm, just six months ago, and I'm sort of learning my way. It's a wonderful evening."

"I saw you on the dance floor. Was that your wife you were dancing with?"

"No. She's a coworker." Now Devon thought maybe he should have gotten another drink, but no. The last thing he wanted to do was dull his wits, even as his belly roiled in fear.

"Lionel," Marie said. "I'd like to introduce you to Devon Donaldson." And just like that, Devon shook hands with her husband, one of the three founders of the firm.

"It's good to meet you, sir," Devon said, meeting the man's steely gaze. His dad always told him to meet strength with strength.

"Likewise." Lionel released Devon's hand, and another man who Devon didn't know put his hand on Lionel's shoulder and drew him away from the group.

Marie sighed and shook her head. Her smile slipped away for a few seconds and then returned. Devon was about to excuse himself when the music changed and Marie turned to him. "Would you mind?" She motioned to the dance floor.

Devon nodded, guiding her out and politely taking her hand. He gently put his other hand to her waist, and they stepped into the dance.

"It's always work," she whispered, her attention half on her husband.

"You dance beautifully," Devon said.

"Don't kid a kidder, young man. You are the one making me look good." She smiled nonetheless as Devon glided her in a wide circle around the floor. Tall, Dark, and Broody stood just off the floor, and Devon felt Marie shiver in his arms. "I hate that man and told Lionel not to hire him for any reason, but he doesn't listen to me about anything." She scowled as the man moved away from the crowd. Once he was out of sight, her movements became fluid again, and Devon put the incident out of his head, intent on showing Marie off to everyone in the room.

"Where did you learn to dance like this?" Marie asked. "Young people only seem to know that bump-and-grind stuff." There was no heat in her voice, just a statement of fact as she saw it.

"I took lessons with my mother. She and I used to enter dance competitions, and we won a few times. Mom was so pleased, and she used to hand me off to all the daughters of her friends whenever she got the chance. Mom thought that dancing would be a way for me to meet girls and eventually find a girlfriend and wife." Devon smiled and leaned into the movement. "Didn't work, though." He smirked slightly, not fully at ease with her. She was one of the founders' wives, after all.

"Whyever not?" She truly didn't seem to understand his little joke.

"Because I'm attracted to the boys," Devon answered, and Marie smiled and chuckled right along with him. "And guys are much more interested in bump-and-grind than they are the waltz, quickstep, or fox-trot." He smiled and led Marie into a flourish as the music ended.

He released her and applauded lightly, sharing a smile as her husband approached and guided her away.

Devon melted back into the crowd of people and returned to the table, where only Lee waited now. "The others went to get drinks," he explained.

Tall, Dark, and Broody passed near them, sending his own particular dark shadow over them. Lee sat up straighter, and Devon slipped his hands under the table, fidgeting nervously like he was a third grader who had just been naughty and was worried about being caught.

"What's his deal?" Lee asked as he moved away. "This is supposed to be a party, but he's casting a pall over everything he looks at." Lee sipped his drink.

Devon didn't dare turn to look at the man, though he was well aware of his continued presence. The others returned and the mood lightened, even as Tall, Dark, and Broody continued standing nearby.

"Ladies and gentlemen...." A man in a bright tuxedo stood onstage with a microphone. "I'm Gary Phillips from marketing. Welcome. Our live auction is about to begin for the really good items. Don't forget the silent auction tables off to my right. They close in an hour. All proceeds go to charity, so bid early and bid often." He continued warming up the crowd and then brought up the first item, a fifty-five-inch television.

Devon didn't pay much attention, since none of these items were anything he could hope to afford. The hairs on the back of his neck prickled once again, and Devon stood, getting a little tired of whatever game the man was playing. Without turning around, even knowing he was there, Devon approached the bar, got another drink, and returned to the table.

Applause broke out as an item was sold and another put up for bid. Devon sat and sipped his drink before figuring that was doing nothing but making him more nervous. Picking up his drink, he walked right past Tall, Dark, and Broody, girding himself as he joined another circle of people. Thankfully, this one didn't include the firm's founders, and he recognized James Abramson, the head of one of the other development teams.

"Are you having a good time?" James asked. "This is your first year, isn't it?"

"Yes. I joined the firm this year," Devon explained, his nerves rising once again. "It's a good place to work, and everyone has been very welcoming."

"I'm glad," James said absently as his attention was drawn elsewhere. Another item was brought up for auction, and James bid but dropped out rather quickly as the price escalated.

Devon turned to watch the auction along with the others. He caught Tall, Dark, and Broody watching him, and Devon met his gaze, meeting those almost-black eyes for nearly a full minute before he looked away under their intensity.

Most of the group drifted away as the auction continued, and Devon returned to the table once more. He'd joined two conversation groups, actually talked to people he didn't know, and hadn't made a fool of himself. He'd count that as a successful evening. Devon took his seat at the table and spent the next hour talking to his coworkers. They shared gossip, and Karen even leaned over the table, wildly speculating that Tall, Dark, and Broody was some sort of secret agent.

"Maybe there's something going on, and he's here to foil whatever's happening."

Lee rolled his eyes. "You have way too much imagination for a computer programmer," he teased.

"Please," Karen said. "I swear he could take me as one of his Bond girls any time he wanted." She fanned herself, and Susan did the same. Clearly the ladies had a thing for guys like that. Not that Devon could blame them. The guy was gorgeous, in a "come to the dark side" kind of way.

He drew closer to their table. Devon wondered what he wanted. He was standing right next to Devon, near enough that he could smell the muskiness that rolled off him in heart-lightening ways. He didn't dare move, focusing on his drink. It was like this ominous, yet hot presence loomed over him. Devon wished he could simply stand and extricate himself from the situation, but if he stood, the entire table would get one hell of a show. So he sat still, like an embarrassed teenager, concentrating on his drink, willing the guy to move on.

"Are you warm?" Karen leaned to him and asked. "You look flushed." She poured him a glass of water, and Devon drank most of it.

"Thanks." He breathed evenly through his mouth, in and out, purposely keeping his control. A panic attack niggled at the edge of his consciousness, and he knew that was the worst idea on earth. He had to keep it together. He didn't need to make a spectacle of himself. This guy wasn't interested in him, and whatever was going on had nothing to do with him. The most handsome man he had ever seen in his life was just standing nearby, watching. It had nothing to do with him—Devon kept repeating that to himself. The tightness in his chest loosened, and his head throbbed less. He drank some more water to give himself something to do. Finally, he felt the tension wane, and his vision became less tunneled.

He turned to find the man farther away. Devon inhaled deeply, then released his breath once more. He poured himself another glass, drank it, and glanced around to see if he was the center of attention. Thankfully, no one seemed to have noticed. But Devon had had enough for one evening. He checked his watch and used the excuse that he was going to look over the silent auction items to get away from the table and give himself something to do until he could leave.

THE TALK in the office all day Monday was about everything that happened at the gala, which included the fact that Judy had bid on one of the vacation packages in the auction but didn't win, as well as that James had won an item in the silent auction that one of the partners had had his eye on. James, it seemed, was faster. Gossip ran rampant through the office.

Devon did his best to keep his head down, getting his work done and trying not to listen to any of it, even when the subject turned to him dancing with Marie. He poked his head over the half-wall partition to where Karen sat, shooting her a nasty look, and she grew quiet and suddenly had work to do herself.

People would talk, and he had better things to do, Devon reminded himself as he packed his messenger bag to go home and said good night to the others. He used the bathroom and then returned to grab his bag and head toward the door. He was tired and wanted nothing more than to go home for some peace and quiet.

He left the building, walked through the heat to the subway station, and descended into the stale air. He scanned his pass and went through the turnstile, joining the flow of human traffic toward the subway platform. He held his bag close and continued the familiar trek, waiting in the line until the train whooshed to a stop and the doors opened. Unlike others, Devon let people exit the train before getting on. It was full to the gills, so he stood, placing his bag between his feet and holding one of the handholds as the doors shut once again.

The ride was so familiar, Devon didn't need to pay much attention to the stops. His internal body clock told him where he was as they rode south. People jostled in and out along the way, and Devon made sure he had a good grip on his bag with his feet, holding on as the train started and stopped so he didn't end up on the muddy section of the floor.

At the stop before his, a large group of people got off, pressing all around him. A seat opened up, and Devon let go of the handhold as people hurried forward. He nearly fell and only managed to grab his bag and plop into the seat to prevent himself from falling. He sighed and set his bag on his lap as the train zipped on to his stop.

Devon was grateful to get off the train and climb the steps out of the station, up into the fresh air. He inhaled and took a second to breathe before striding through the relatively quiet sidewalks of the residential neighborhood to his home above a drugstore.

His apartment wasn't large, but it was plenty big enough for him, with a small bedroom off a decent-sized living room. He had a tiny kitchen, but it worked for his life. Most of the furniture he got at secondhand stores and the Salvation Army, carrying it back piece by piece. It made for an eclectic mix of things, but it was all his and this was home. He loved it… mostly because no one was going to take it away from him. No one would come in from work and tell him that tomorrow they were moving to yet another town, and that he'd have to attend another school with another group of kids that he was just going to start to get to know before he had to move again. This was stable; this was his.

Devon set his bag on the coffee table and went right to his refrigerator. After pulling out a bottle of cold water, he drank half of it and placed the remainder back inside to keep cold, before wandering into the bedroom to change out of his work clothes.

He put his shirt in the dirty clothes and hung up his pants and suit coat, along with the tie. He hoped he could get one more wear out of them before he had to have them dry-cleaned. Instead of hanging them in the closet, he put them in the bathroom near the open window, where a steady breeze could air them out for him. He tried to get a second wear out of his clothes in order to save some expenses, but it wasn't always possible.

A pounding at his door made him jump. Devon hurried to pull on a pair of shorts and a T-shirt, rushed to the front door, and peered through the peephole. Tall, Dark, and Broody stood in his hallway, glaring back at him. "What do you want?" He wished he'd grabbed his cell phone off the dresser before coming out.

"I need to talk to you," he said, pounding on the door once more. "You need to talk to me, or else you'll talk to the police."

Devon undid the latch, keeping the chain on, and cracked the door open. "I'm the one who's going to call the police if you don't go away." He closed the door once again, glaring through the peephole. "Go away."

"You need to talk to me, Devon," he said, more softly but with the same urgency. "It's important."

"How do you know my name? Are you following me? You a stalker or something?" Devon leaned against the door, his leg shaking. Damn, he'd been looking forward to a quiet night. "Just go away." He sounded whiny even to his own ears.

"We need to talk," he repeated.

Devon pulled the door open slightly. "Why?" He peered out into the hall, wishing his neighbor was home, but she was away on vacation for the week visiting her kids. Mrs. Lowenski always knew what was going on and could be counted on to be nosy enough to call the police for him. As it was, he was on his own.

"I'm not a stalker, and I know you saw me at the gala. You are probably aware that Mrs. Mauer knows who I am."

"She doesn't like you," Devon said.

He shrugged. "A lot of people don't like me."

"Let me see some identification," Devon said, and the man pulled out a card and handed it to him. "Powers McPherson. Private security and investigations." He turned the card over, but there was nothing else on the back. "This is really helpful." Devon rolled his eyes. "Anyone can have business cards made up that say anything. Go away and leave me alone."

"I've been hired by your company, and as I said, we need to talk. Now, we can do it like this in the hallway, or you can let me in." He wore a suit that probably cost as much as Devon made in a week, and his shoes shone brightly. Powers didn't look like the kind of guy who would mug someone, but Devon still wasn't sure. Still, from what Marie had said, Powers worked for Mr. Mauer, and he didn't want to get in trouble.

Reluctantly, he stepped back and slipped the chain off the lock. Then he opened the door and allowed Powers to enter. Devon closed the door and moved back out of his reach. "What do you want? And what kind of name is Powers anyway?"

"It's a family name." Powers stepped around him to the sofa and sat down. "I guess manners weren't part of your upbringing."

Devon went into the bedroom, grabbed his phone, and held it for easy availability, then returned to the living room, where he found Powers going through his bag. "Just as I thought." He pulled a manila envelope out of the bag, holding it up.

"That isn't mine," Devon stammered. He'd never seen it in his life. "I didn't put that in there. It's not mine." Shit, he'd seen enough television shows to know he was in trouble.

"Then what is it doing in your bag?" Powers asked as he opened it to pull out two sheets of paper and a small portable computer drive.

"I don't know." Devon clutched his phone even as he saw his stable, quiet life flying right out the window before his eyes. "I don't know what it is because I never put it in my bag. Maybe you put it in there to try to trap me or something. Is this a test of some sort? Maybe an initiation to check my loyalty to the firm?"

"No. It certainly isn't, and I didn't put it in there." Powers sat back, going through the documents.

"What is that?" Devon asked.

Powers leaned forward. "You need to sit down, and you and I have to have a very serious talk."

Devon's knees felt weak, and he slumped into his chair, the comfortable one he usually watched television in, but it now felt like one of those stiff wooden chairs that people get interrogated in, in the movies.

"What I want to know is who gave you this and who were you supposed to deliver it to?" Powers leaned forward, his dark eyes as serious as a heart attack.

"I don't know. It was never given to me. I don't know what you're talking about… delivering it. I don't know what it is, and I…." Damn, Devon's hand shook and he thought he was going to be sick. "I've never seen that before. Honestly." His hand shook more, and his vision began to tunnel. His heart pounded in his chest, and he breathed deeply. "I don't know what that is. I never saw it before in my life."

"It was in your bag," Powers said.

"But I didn't put it there!" Devon placed his hand over his chest, sucking in air, his head starting to spin. "I told you, I didn't take it and I didn't put it in my bag. I don't know who did, and I have no idea what this is all about." He managed to get a deep breath of air, gripping the arms of the chair as tightly as he could. "I don't know anything about whatever this is." His feet began to tingle, and Devon knew he had to get hold of himself or he was going to end up in the hospital like the last time, and then he wouldn't have a chance to try to explain and he'd be out of work and….

Devon took a deep breath and then another. He took the bottle of water that Powers offered him, sucked it down, and forced air into his lungs. "You have to believe me." Devon blinked and continued his breathing exercises as the tingling subsided and his vision slowly returned to normal.

"Then how did this get in your bag?" Powers waved the envelope in the air.

"I don't know." Devon finished the water and set the bottle on the coffee table. "I packed my bag the way I usually do when I leave the office." He reached for it and emptied the contents on the table. "These are my pens and my reminder book." There was also a roll of cherry Life Savers and some paper clips. "I brought home these papers to try to work through this tonight because everyone kept talking about the gala all day and I couldn't concentrate. The rest of this is mine, but I didn't put that in the bag." He half pleaded because he needed Powers to believe him.

"Let's say that's true. Then how did this get in your bag?"

"I don't know. I left the office and rode home on the subway like I always do. The cars were crowded and all, but…." He paused. "Hey, how did you know that I might have this stuff? Were you following me? Did you put it in there and now want it back?" He was grasping at straws.

"No. I didn't put it in there, but I was on that subway train. I had intelligence that a pass-off was to happen on the train, and then I recognized you from the gala and figured I was onto something. So I followed you and… look what I found."

"So, you didn't see anyone put this in my bag either?" Devon had to question it. Whoever had done it was good, because he hadn't seen anyone. "It must have been during the crush. I was nearly bowled over when the car started and a lot of others pressed against me." At least he had an idea of how the envelope could have gotten into his bag, but why it had been put there was beyond him.

"No. Because I don't think it was. I think you either copied the information yourself or had someone give it to you."

Devon swallowed hard. This was getting to be a circular exercise. "Then call the police. Have them check out the envelope. If I put it in there, then I must have handled it and my prints and DNA would be all over it. They aren't, because I've never seen that before and I never handled it. Why someone slipped it into my bag, I have no idea, but the person you're after isn't me." He glared at Powers and then held out his phone. "Go ahead, call them." He was getting tired of this little game and just wanted it to end. "How do I know you aren't the one after this information for yourself and this isn't all a ruse? Marie certainly didn't like you, so maybe you're trying to get even somehow."

For the first time, the confidence in Powers's eyes wavered slightly. "You really want me to do this?"

"Yes. Go ahead. Call the police. Tell them what you found in my bag, and I'll ask them to fingerprint the envelope. Of course, I'll also make sure they ask you all about your business and what you're doing here. I'm sure the Philly PD will be most grateful for civilian help." Devon's smirk lasted a few moments, and then he sat back when Powers didn't take his phone.

"Let's say I believe you," Powers said. "I'm not saying I do. But let's just say. Why would someone drop this into your bag?"

Devon leaned forward slightly. "I don't know. Maybe they made a mistake, or maybe they saw you and panicked. Or maybe whoever it is knows me from work and thought I was the courier, when there was someone else they were supposed to give it to. I'm in the dark just as much as you are." He was calming down, and his mind clicked into gear. "What I don't understand is why anyone would do this to me. What did I do?" He leaned close, trying to get a glance at the papers. "What are those?"

Powers hesitated and then slid the papers across the table. "Specifications."

Devon didn't touch the pages but looked them over. "They're the cover pages for two program specs. That's all." He leaned closer. "I'm not familiar with this system, but that's all they are. There are no details or any information that could be used by anyone. I presume the meat of whatever this is, is on the drive there." He pointed but didn't touch it either.

"Yes."

Devon stood.

"Where are you going?" Powers snapped.

He glared and waved his hand toward the door. "To the bathroom. You can come with me if you want, but we're on the second floor. I don't think I'm going to shimmy out the window." He was stuck until he could somehow convince Powers that he wasn't involved in whatever was going on. Devon used the bathroom, then returned and sat back down.

"I'm still not buying that you aren't involved in this," Powers said flatly, without the vehemence he'd had before.

"Have you checked the files at work? I don't have access to any of these programs, so I can't get them. The system controls what I can see. It isn't like I can check out any program I want. I can't even get to the program specifications for programs I'm not authorized to access." Devon leaned forward.

"What if you were just supposed to deliver them?" Powers pressed.

"To who? I don't know anyone outside my own team at the firm. You saw me at the gala, I know you did."

"Yeah, quite the social butterfly."

Devon chuckled nervously. "I talked to Marie and was so nervous that I nearly wet myself. I danced with her when she asked, and then afterward Mr. Mauer led her away. I didn't know what to do, so I went back to my table." He swallowed hard. "I actually had to set a quota for myself of the number of people I'd speak to that I didn't already know before I could leave. I'm no butterfly—more like a wallflower. So regardless of what you think, I have no reason to take anything from work or to deliver papers or whatever else is on that drive to anyone." He closed his eyes, trying to keep his nerves at bay.

"Okay," Powers said. "Let's say you're telling the truth." He slid the papers and drive back into the envelope.

"Good, then you can go now, and I can make myself some macaroni and cheese and a salad, and go to bed. I have to be at the office before seven tomorrow, and I still have some things I need to get done." Devon picked up his bag and went to the door. Powers didn't move. "What now? I didn't take anything, and I wasn't going to deliver whatever is in that envelope. And if you get me fired...." The thought sent a ripple of fear running through him.

"I'm not going to get you fired. But there's something you haven't thought of." He paused, probably for effect, and it worked, with Devon's nerves spiking. "If this was slipped into your bag, and it wasn't meant for you, then someone is going to want it back. And it isn't going to take a great deal of effort for them to realize that it was given to the wrong person, and then they're going to come looking for it." Powers sat straighter, and Devon groaned.

"Then you handle it however you see fit and leave me out of the whole thing." He waved his hand. At least Powers was beginning to believe him. "I didn't do anything to get involved in this. I just want it to go away." He went to the kitchen area and pulled out the things he needed to make his dinner. He didn't have a great deal. Old Mother Hubbard and Devon had a lot in common right now. Devon did find the blue box of mac and cheese, and there were just enough fixings for a salad. He needed to go to the store.

"Do you think that whoever is behind this is just going to walk up to you and ask nicely for the information that was incorrectly slipped into your bag?" Powers asked. "This is part of a huge theft. Someone is after proprietary secrets from your firm, and these are worth a great deal of money... millions. Enough that people will kill to get what they want."

Devon turned quickly enough that he knocked the box of mac and cheese on the floor. The pasta spilled everywhere, and Devon groaned before trying to scoop the wayward pieces back inside. "That's just great. So now what? Keep the door locked and hope that someone doesn't try to kill me in my sleep? Maybe I could turn what you found over to Mr. Mauer and tell him what happened." Yeah, that was a good idea. He didn't know Devon at all and would probably fire him on the spot. He felt the panic attack starting up again and plopped himself on the floor, picking up single pieces of his dinner. "What am I supposed to do now?"

Powers came over and helped Devon to his feet. "You are the first real lead I've had in this case. I honestly don't think you're involved in this." He might just have been saying that—Devon could hear the uncertainty in his voice. Powers was probably just trying to soothe him and calm him down. "But right now, you're all I have. And I was serious. Someone is going to try to get that information back. Until they do, I'm going to stick to you like glue." He released Devon's hand.

"What does that mean?" Devon swallowed hard, trying to discern the implications.

"It means that it looks like I'm staying here tonight. I'll sleep on the sofa and won't bother you." Powers stared deeply into Devon's eyes, sending a jolt of fear and heat to Devon's core.

"Here?" he croaked. "You're going to stay here with me?" Devon took a step back. "How do I know you aren't the person sent to retrieve the information and aren't going to kill me in my sleep?" Maybe he was being a little dramatic, but this was the weirdest situation he could ever have possibly imagined.

"Yes. I'm starting to believe you, but I'm not letting you out of my sight. Those papers and drive are the only link I have to whoever is behind this, and I have to follow the lead to make sure this stops as soon as possible." Powers took a single step back. "Do you like Chinese?" he asked, staring at the bits of macaroni on the floor, slowly shaking his head. "As a show of good faith, I'll order us some delivery. There's a good restaurant a few blocks away."

"Okay." Devon was too shaken and surprised to say anything else. What the hell had just happened to him? All he wanted was his orderly, quiet life back, and every way he looked, it seemed to get farther away by the second.

Scan QR code below to order

FIRE AND SAND

ANDREW GREY

Carlisle Troopers: Book One

Can a single dad with a criminal past find love with the cop who pulled him over?

When single dad Quinton Jackson gets stopped for speeding, he thinks he's lost both his freedom and his infant son, who's in the car he's been chasing down the highway. Amazingly, State Trooper Wyatt Nelson not only believes him, he radios for help and reunites Quinton with baby Callum.

Wyatt should ticket Quinton, but something makes him look past Quinton's record. Watching him with his child proves he made the right decision. Quinton is a loving, devoted father—and he's handsome. Wyatt can't help but take a personal interest.

For Quinton, getting temporary custody is a dream come true... or it would be, if working full-time and caring for an infant left time to sleep. As if that weren't enough, Callum's mother will do anything to get him back, including ruining Quinton's life. Fortunately, Quinton has Wyatt for help, support, and as much romance as a single parent can schedule.

But when Wyatt's duties as a cop conflict with Quinton's quest for permanent custody, their situation becomes precarious. Can they trust each other, and the courts, to deliver justice and a happy ever after?

Scan QR code below to order

FIRE AND GLASS

ANDREW GREY

CARLISLE TROOPERS 2

Carlisle Troopers: Book Two

State Trooper Casey Bombaro works too hard to have time for a love life, never mind a family. But when a missing persons case leads him to three scared kids and eventually their uncle—an old friend from Casey's college days—all that changes.

Bertie Riley hasn't seen his troubled sister, Jen, or his niece and nephews in years. Now suddenly Jen is gone and Bertie is all the kids have. Worried sick about Jen and overwhelmed by his new responsibilties, Bertie doesn't know how he's going to cope. He doesn't expect Caey to step in and lend a hand, but his attraction to his old friend doesn't surprise him. Years may have passed, but those feelings have never gone away.

For the first time in his life, Casey wants something to come home to. Bertie and the kids fit into his life like they are meant to be there. He struggles to balance a budding romance and reassuring the kids with investigating a rash of robberies and tracking down Jen. But when evidence suggests Jen might not only be missing but complicit in a numbe of crimes, will Bertie and the kids forgive Casey for doing his job?

Scan QR code below to order

FIRE AND ERMINE

ANDREW GREY

CARLISLE
TROOPERS
3

Carlisle Troopers: Book Three

When Prince Reynard escapes his gilded cage, he runs as fast as he can in search of a taste of freedom. Predictably, he gets pulled over.

State Trooper Fisher Bronson doesn't know the handsome stranger in the rental car, but he does know the guy was driving way too fast. Still, Fisher takes *to protect and serve* seriously, so he helps Reynard find a hotel for the night.

Then the hotel catches fire.

Apparently Reynard hasn't covered his tracks as well as he thought. But is it paparazzi on his tail, or someone much more deadly? Either way, when Fisher offers him a room for the night, he's grateful for the refuge.

Reynard is generous and kind, but Fisher knows he's hiding something. Finally Reynard confesses the truth: as prince of Veronia, his life is structured and ordered for him, but as Reynard, in Carlisle with Fisher, he has the freedom to become a person he actually likes. To Reynard's surprise, Fisher likes him back—not for his title, but for the man he is. But duty, family expectations, and whoever is after Reynard could spell the end of their relationship before they get past *once upon a traffic stop*.

Scan QR code below to order

STEAL MY

Heart

ANDREW GREY

Hilliard Bauman's life and his law practice are in Ohio, so when he inherits a home in California, his first instinct is to sell. Then again, his law partner is also his ex-partner, so maybe starting over wouldn't be so bad. Either way, he needs someone to fix up the house first. That's where Brian Mayer comes in.

Brian Mayer will do whatever work he can get, whether that means dog walking or painting fences. But in a small town where everyone knows everything about everyone, finding jobs can be difficult— especially if you've been wrongly convicted of theft. When Hilliard hires him to fix up his great-aunt's place, it's a relief on Brian's strained bank account... but tests Brian's heart to its limits.

As Hilliard digs into Brian's case and the botched investigation of the original crime, things really start heating up—both between him and Brian and in what should've been a cold case. This time when cops try to lay the blame at Brian's feet, he has Hilliard in his corner. Can they solve the mystery, put Brian's past to rest, and find a new beginning together?

Scan QR code below to order

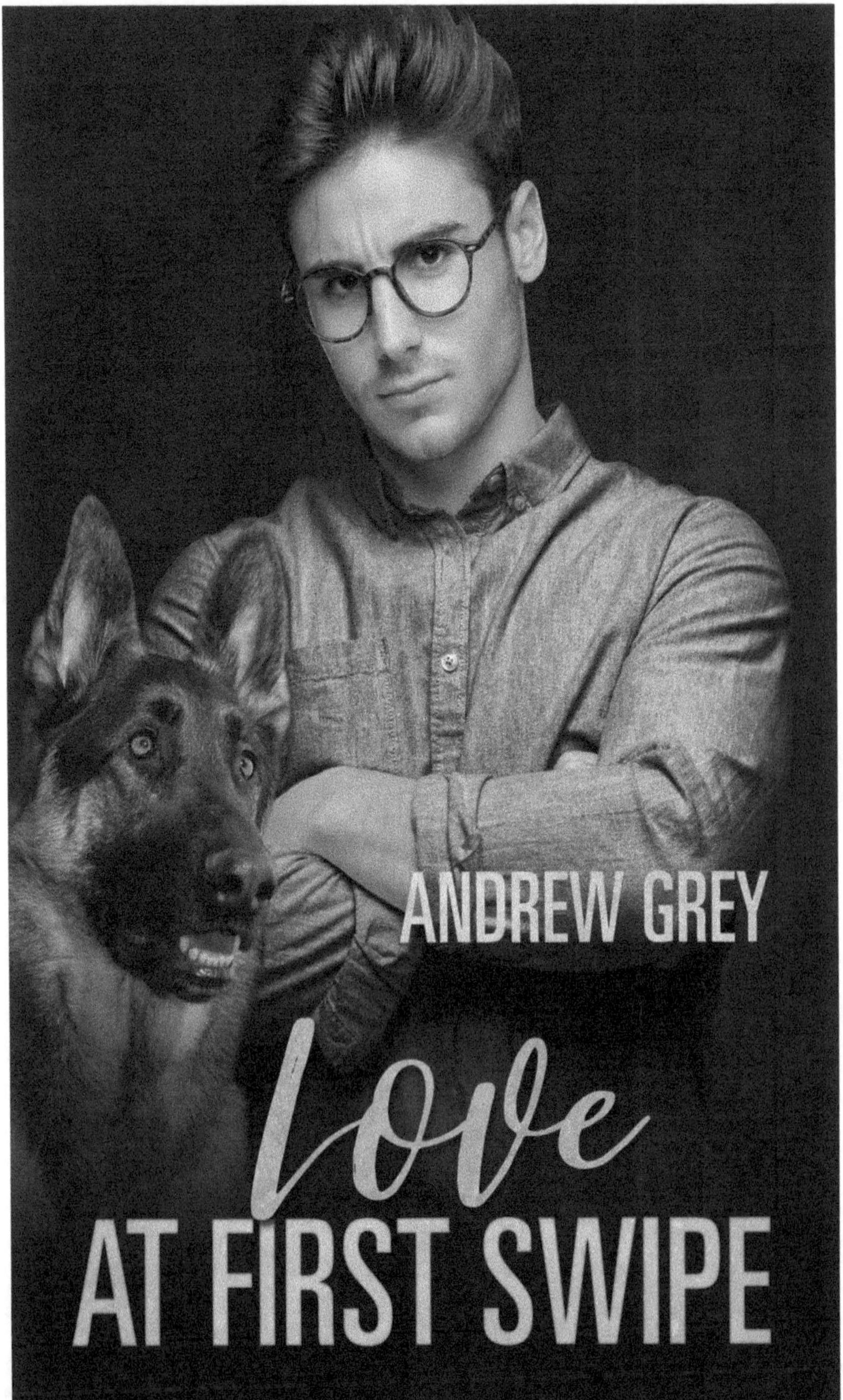
ANDREW GREY
Love
AT FIRST SWIPE

Darby Wright has fought for his independence ever since he lost his sight as a child. But even now that he has his own home and a good job, his overprotective mother doesn't believe he can handle himself. Darby's determined to prove her wrong, but there are some things—like finding his guide dog's potty accident—where an extra set of eyes would come in handy.

Enter See For Me, an app that connects blind clients with sighted volunteers. See For Me is designed for just this sort of emergency, and it's through this app that Darby meets Reynaldo. Lust at first voice turns to more when Darby and Reynaldo run into each other at a local sandwich shop, where Renaldo seems as nice in person as he was in app.

With Reynaldo, Darby can feel his world expanding. Reynaldo doesn't just support him but understands him and sees Darby as more than his disability. But will being with Reynaldo mean giving up Darby's hard-fought independence, or will it mean gaining something more than he ever dreamed?

Scan QR code below to order